The dragon under the hill

By

Paul R. Price

First Print 2019

ISBN: 9781796853551

Imprint: Independently published

Copies available via Amazon books

The dragon under the hill

This book is dedicated to the memory of my grandparents,

Frederick and Elsie May Price who I never got to meet,

Lily James whose goodbye was too long but too soon and John 'Jack' James, who I still miss. Mamo and Dado.

Special thanks to

Stephen (Jonesy) Jones

Cristyn Jones

The dragon under the hill

Also available by the author

Mupply & the Dog Library

The dragon under the hill

Prologue

It is said that Wales has one hundred and thirty-seven mountains and hundreds upon hundreds of majestic rolling hills, which is a lot for such a small country. From the staggering heights of the Snowdonia range in the north to the forthright beauty of Pen Y Fan and the Brecon Beacons in the south. Mighty rises claim and command the landscape from Mynydd Moel, Tryfan and Cadair Idris to The Black Mountain, Bera Mawr and Great Rhos; Cadair Bronwen, Cyfrwy and The Drum to Fan Nedd, Yr Aran and so many more. These dramatic peaks have shaped a nation, a people and a culture. Silent monoliths, bold and proud in a way it's people are not. They are the source of life giving rivers, home to the hardiest creatures, goading the breathing weather, characters in every story in a country's long history and the cradle of so many legends. Legends of giants, wizards, bards and knights; mighty kings, princes, fairy-folk and druids; lake maidens, shape-shifters, giant birds and water horses; wolves, heroic dogs, witches and monsters.

Some legends live there still.

It's one of those long held traditions, dogs chase cats, cats chase mice, mice like cheese and husbands make fun of their mother-in-law. In certain areas of Wales there is heard a tongue-in-cheek, playfully naughty but affectionate nickname for mother-in-laws, the 'Grawen'. Which in the Welsh language can mean 'crust' or 'rind' but in this tradition, is taken to mean 'Dragon' (although 'ddraig' is the actual Welsh word for dragon).

This provides plentiful amusement for the husband, as the word can be pronounced in a tasty deep growl, rolling the 'r', for extra effect and he can double his fun if he can get his kids to call her it too.

But once, the odd mother-in-law wasn't the only dragon terrifying the locals in the mountains and hills of Wales.

5

The dragon under the hill

Before there were cities or towns, tarmac roads and concrete buildings, cars, trains, planes and bicycles, electric lights, gas cookers, radio and television; pylons, windfarms and communication masts; before there were cathedrals and churches, governments, hospitals or supermarkets, police, soldiers or doctors; before there were schools and teachers and exams; before the Romans, Anglo Saxons and Normans; before viaducts and canals, sewers and industry; before stainless steel, rubber or plastic; before there was medicine, science and even English; there was the greatest legend of them all, dragons.

Once, Wales was the land of Dragons.

The dragon under the hill

Chapter 1

I never knew either of my paternal grandparents.

One of the defining moments of my father's life happened at the meagre age of only eight, when his own father, then only in his forties himself, suddenly died of a heart attack. There were children from a previous marriage, already adults by that time with lives of their own but it was a devastating and shattering blow to Fred's young second family. Sadly, due to their circumstances, mainly poverty, my father's large family, consisting of his mum and three younger brothers had to leave their small-holding and be split up. There weren't the systems of care or support we have today for those in need, once the bread winner was gone, it was really a definitive and cruel end to your way of life.

The youngest child, a mere babe in arms was probably the most fortunate, taken with his mother to live with her relatives in Cardiff. The two middle brothers bore the brunt of the misfortune and went into care. While the oldest boy, my father, went to a local foster family who lived on a small farm. Whilst there he was treated more like hired help for the most part and never really felt an accepted part of his new family. He left as soon as he was able. Sent to work down Tower Colliery coal mine over the next valley at the age of fourteen, he grew up strong and learned to be self-sufficient and struck out on his own after an argument about money, while still in his teens. Ever since those days he has lived life on his own terms and no one else's. A deep respect for his foster father did still remain but, alas, another father figure was taken away from him too young. Sadly, his beloved mother died in her forties, shortly before I was born.

In contrast, my mother's family couldn't have been more expansive, with great-grandparents, great aunts and great uncles, alongside aunts and an uncle, as well as my other grandparents. They lived in an older part of the same estate and just around the

The dragon under the hill

corner from my junior school which meant they were a large part of my life growing up.

Neither Lil or Jack James sprang much over 5 feet tall, if at all and both sported dark black hair. It wasn't until many years later that I came to learn that my grandmother always dyed her curls and my grandfather never washed his, just added another layer of Brill cream to slick it back with. I always called them Mamo and Dado.

I would usually see them a couple of times during the week and their home was the bustling centre of family events and a joyous focal point at Christmas, where the extended clan would gather together. They lived in the same residence all the years I knew them, 97 Oak Road. A simple, nondescript mid terraced house among streets and streets of identical homes with their attached dark brick coal 'cwtches' and plain front lawns. Its layout is still very clear in my mind with its interconnected rooms where a wilful child could do laps, a round circuit, going through every room on the ground floor until snagged to an abrupt halt.

On entering through the front door, with its central slender pane of frosted glass, you could either go straight up the stairs, turn left and enter the front room which was always kept for 'best' or turn right and enter the most useless, characterless and impractical excuse for a room I have ever seen in any home anywhere. It didn't even warrant a name and only served as access to the living room or a dumping ground for shoes and coats. The small living room was certainly the hub of the home, where most time was spent. From there was accessed the back door into the ramshackle garden with its brambles, unkempt grass and in the wilderness down the bottom, my grandfather's blue work-shed. The living room also had the door to the small kitchen, which seemed old and outdated even to my young mind. From there, the front room could be entered and exited at the opposite end and the circle was complete.

The dragon under the hill

The area they lived in had a noticeable sleepiness to it and is still quiet even today, despite the vast increase in the number of cars.

In a rare prompt of loneliness and with time to kill I drove passed their old house recently, a momentary detour of nostalgia. The doors and windows had changed and from what I could glimpse the new occupants had knocked through some internal walls. I'm not sure what I expected to find but it was clear there was nothing there for me – maybe it was just enough to keep the pilot light burning under all those old memories.

Their street backed on to a huge local park and it was easy for my young frame to squeeze through the stand-alone garages to gain entry, even if the gate was locked, for hours of unrestricted play.

In all the years from the first stumbling moments in the infant's school to the last goodbye at junior school, Monday was always the day when that jangling bell prompted the short walk to go there for lunch (or dinner as we called it). Alphabet soup, beans on toast or hot dogs with buttered rolls were the usual fare and always accompanied by a glass of pop, while being quizzed about school and lessons or the toe curling "are you courting yet?". Which was usually met with an embarrassed "aw leave off Dado".

Standing on its metal legs, the old TV was continually on in the background, a game show or maybe a western would play, pawing at you for attention, like a lame dog. It had the oddest mechanism for changing channels I've ever come across - stuck on the windowsill of all places, was a large white dial that you turned and clicked into place. In order to change channel, you had to get up (usually the youngest person in the room was nominated), walk around and behind the old wood-grain plastic TV set, pull back the curtain and click the dial to the required number.

I always had one eye on that ticking clock though. Not just because the break from school seemed so short, those precious

9

moments of freedom being eaten in huge chunks each time I looked away but because when lunch time was nearly over, just before being allowed take the short walk back to school for the afternoon, there would have to be endured one of the most dreaded experiences of my little life. Inspiring terror in my young soul, Mamo would announce those hated words, "Time to scrub your faces before you go back to school". There was no way you were getting out that front door without it and it was probably fair enough as I imagine I wore the remnants of my dinner on my cheeks and chin but my Nana didn't ever trust you to wash your own face, no, because then it wouldn't be 'done properly'. What you got instead was a deceptively strong woman, forcefully holding the back of your head with one hand, while ramming a soap filled wet flannel she had just rinsed under the kitchen sink tap into your tensed, defenceless face with the other. No amount of wriggling, squirming or evasion did you any good. The woman had a grip of iron. Your face was smushed, rubbed and scrubbed, your ears invaded and your eyes stung, until your nose was so full of foaming soapy water that, spluttering, you had to sneeze it out to breathe. Then and only then was the ordeal over and you were finally free, although you were still sneezing residual soap suds all the way back to school. I imagined that my face must have shone like Moses on the mount, with the amount of forceful scrubbing it received. Eventually, I taught myself to sneeze on command and this at least shortened the experience, which was a small victory.

That's not to say she was ever cruel or hurtful to me, (although I am told she had the capacity) far from it – it is just a funny, quirky memory of a strong woman that all my family can relate to.

I had the blessed good fortune and advantage of being the first born of many grandchildren (and great grandchildren) to come from their four daughters and one son. My position as first to the table was very much to my benefit, I was doted on and privileged. Although my grandmother did not approve of my name,

The dragon under the hill

thinking it too common, warning my mother that when she called my name 'half the children in the street would come running'. Due to childhood hearing difficulties, I would speak very softly, for which she gave me the moniker 'The Phantom Mumbler', I was still never made to feel anything other than special and loved.

In recent years I have learned they were the strictest of parents. Their style harsh and unyielding, stifling children's natural urges to play and make noise. Punishments were server and often violent, the oldest two children receiving the more extreme of the consequences, my nan being the most ardent perpetrator.

She was always kind and loving towards me, always tried to feed me up and gave me money for sweets, always took an interest in my life and always told me I was handsome and when I was older 'all the girls would be after me'. In later years, she would always make an effort to stay up late, to be the first person to call and wish us a Happy New Year after the chimes of Big Ben had stopped.

Mamo, my nan, Lil to her friends, always wore flowery dresses, clip on earrings and always smelled of foundation, which she thickly applied. Life for her was plagued with crippling arthritis and ill health, looking back she wasn't someone who laughter and frivolity came easily to and her discomfort was probably why. Especially in her last decade or so and it meant for a number of those years the lucid conversations grew fewer and further apart. When she sadly passed there was mercy there because the person I knew had slipped away and I had said goodbye to her in my heart years before. Christmas or the family itself have never been the same without the strong woman I loved dearly and cherish, a matriarch indeed.

I was named after my grandfather, well partly, we share middle names. My grandfather's name changed depending on who was speaking to him and where he was being spoken to. Some people called him John, others Richard, apparently his mum called him 'Shuni', most people called him Jack but I always knew him as Dado. I am happy and honoured that I grew so much closer to my grandfather in the following years after Mamo went and we got to know each so much better, not just as two relatives in their allotted roles but as two individual men, in different stages of life, enjoying each other's company. Due in part to my being grown up and able to relate to him on another level but mostly by making more of an effort to visit with him and simply spend time. I have so many fond memories of that bonus time and I still miss him.

I never experienced any of the intolerance, sternness or bouts of ill-temper I am told he was prone to in his younger years; age and experience had mellowed whatever cursed him. He had a playful, 'wicked' sense of humour and would take special pleasure in winding up the medical staff who cared for him at his home or during one of his hated stays in hospital, even once convincing one poor nurse that she was hearing ghosts.

I remember his hair was continually slicked back and he always wore a white vest under a shirt and one of those 'old man' cardigans, both often blue. He loved to hear the great Nat King Cole, watch classic movies and read odd little western themed novels you don't see anymore. He always drank loose leaf tea because he upheld he could 'taste the linen' when it was made with a teabag. His retirement days were spent studying 'form' for his little bets on the horse racing and he cherished his little terrier dog and the companionship they shared. While his health allowed, he indulged his little vices with a trip to the local betting shop or a catch up with friends in the adjacent social club. In latter days, health did not allow. The old burgundy settee that had served for decades, gave way to a single bed and the little living room, apart from the odd occasion, became the boundary to his world.

When he came to the realisation that even driving short trips was no longer safe for him, he handed in his licence and kindly offered me his little car. Despite my dad's advice, who being

12

very mechanically astute had checked it over and told me not to go near it, I happy accepted the offer. Tax and insurance was soon organised and on the allotted day, I filled up the old faithful navy blue Volkswagen Golf and drove away. I managed less than 30 miles before its engine dramatically and very publicly blew up in clouds of pungent, acrid blue-grey smoke on the motorway. The rescue tow home allowed my dad ample time for a multitude of grumpy 'I told you so' and 'you wouldn't listen to me'. When I told my grandfather, he could only see the funny side and just laughed and laughed.

While other family members laughed and drank in festive celebration in the front room at Christmas, we would sit together watching Casablanca and chatting. He would tell jokes and laugh wildly at the punchline, even though he'd told them before and laugh even more when you'd complain. "Ow, Dado you've told me that one loads of times". Often this peaceful fellowship would be interrupted by a relative late to the proceedings popping in to say hello or an errant child running through the room waving some newly acquired toy or a family member giving my grandfather his gifts and him faking joy and surprise on receiving the umpteenth pair of socks or set of hankies. As they watched him opening these trinkets they would always add the obligatory complaint "I didn't know what else to get you, you're so hard to buy for". When they left he would mercilessly mock their unimaginative gift and its usefulness to him.

Sometimes, I find myself idly singing in that Bing Crosby baritone scat style when I am doing something around the house in an absent-minded fashion and remember Dado did that all the time, while he pottered about. He was great at just pottering about but could also craft marvellous things if he had a mind to. One of the best gifts of my childhood was a black wooden castle that he made for me; complete with great corner turrets, a solid wooden base and proper tiny green tiles adorning the floor. It was the scene of many battles, sieges, conquests and sometimes car

13

crashes, alien invasions and even the odd dinosaur rampage, for many beloved years.

A plasterer by trade and particularly skilled at rendering, I spent a short couple of weeks labouring for him when I was about eighteen. I witnessed him to be an accurate and meticulous workman – favouring wise planning and having everything correct before starting. Never in a hurry, he seemed to accomplish a great deal with minimum effort. Although, my abiding memories of that time are mostly of carrying heavy buckets of freshly mixed cement up ladders to the top of the scaffolding to keep his 'hawk' continually supplied. The mix and consistency of the cement had to be just right, otherwise it would be refused and I would have to alter the mix in that clanging, tumbling mixer. Ten pounds per day and calf muscles I could hardly get my trousers over being my rewards.

Of all these wonderful memories, most of all, I remember his stories.

He loved to tell stories from all parts of his life as men do as they get older, to shine a momentary light on days, people and places gone dim. From him playing in the Salvation Army band as a child, to his latest prank on the Doctor who had visited him at home for a check-up. Some tales were short with a punchline and some still make me laugh when I think of them today but it was only in later years that he shared some of his experiences of being a very young man in the Merchant Navy during the second World War, sporting the customary tattoos as proof. I still have his service medals.

It was smoking that got him in the end, as it invariably will. The last chapter of his last story taking place in hospital after a short illness. Although I lived away at the time it is a source of profound and deep regret for me, that on a brief trip home I skipped my customary visit. Not wanting to see him uncomfortable in hospital and in truth, considering my own discomfort with visiting

The dragon under the hill

those in hospital. Promising myself to catch up with him next time in our usual spot but it was a vow I would never keep. I've no doubt Dado understood at the time and could be in no doubt of his importance to me, then and now.

Even though he would often repeat certain stories and tell me ones I'd heard many times before, I wouldn't stop him. I often thought I should have recorded them somehow and certainly dearly wish I had. Especially now, as most of his stories are only alive in my vague recollection and as time passes their details fade, like sun-bleached colour and come to mind less and less.

All except one. One story he only mentioned once in 70 years and it was told to me and me alone. Before that too fades from my mind, like ancient ink on parchment, I will tell it here. Only once and to you and you alone.

Chapter 2

There is something truly special about the opalescent hills of Wales. There lies magic.

Each one broods and seems to cogitate on the history and dreams it is filled with. Each one a bridled oasis of myth and madness. Each one bountiful in its own legends, fairy tales and folklore. Each one still ringing with ancient songs and bardic poems, lovers stolen moments, the prayers of the saints, the footsteps of pilgrims, the cries of woad painted warriors, the chants of the Chartists and the blood of martyrs.

The hills of Wales are beautiful and like nowhere else, a cherished, well-watered prize. All countries have their lands and climbs, hills and mountains but these, these are unique. Wave upon wave of cresting land, broiling and battling sea-like in breathless strength. Wild without being a wilderness, enticing and foreboding in equal measure. Flowing curves, like the sultry shape of a giant goddess who once laid down on her side to rest and was covered in blanket of trees and grass, where nature soothed her to a never-ending sleep.

There is no colour green like the hills of Wales. Pearl like depth and pitching life; no sight as dramatic as a bucking behemoth storm clawing over the horizon, roaring in moods and thunder and nothing as comforting and secure as living in a valley surrounded by such hills on every side, like the strong, protecting walls of a verdant castle.

To leave them is to leave Mother's arms, to leave your slot in the jigsaw. To leave them is to lose sight of the generations of footprints and force the great song silent with distance. To leave them is to know the 'Hiraeth', to feel it mine to the core. More than homesickness, far more indeed. It is to be a bird no longer able to fly, a fish out of the sea or to be truly and profoundly lost. It is a

The dragon under the hill

yearning and an unquenchable longing, a physical pull on the soul and a continually echoing call to come home.

For generations, hardy hill farmers have tended the land, coaxed and wielded the untameable landscape, cared for the roaming sheep and Welsh cobs. From their eagle high view, they have rooted and watched. Part seer, part sage, and part enchanter they have been custodians of its stories and keepers of its soul. Each one up and down the land knows each hill and field they care for like a part of themselves and crave no riches beyond its borders or know no wealth beyond its freedom. Every dingle, ditch, dell and stony cairn is read like braille and they receive all its blessings and curses equally with wisdom and stoic strength, that has also been handed down from generation to generation. The rich soil mingling with their bones from birth. They know their part in the breathing of creation, they no more own the land they walk on than a flea owns the dog on which it fleetingly lives. They belong.

Evan James was the fifth generation of his family that he knew of to live and work at Bryn Y Ddraig farm but regrettably he knew, he and his wife would be the last. Neither of them as young and strong as they remembered, each step now just the slightest bit slower than the one before, each day clearly drawn on their faces with deeper lines. Although she did not quite share his deep love of the farm, his wife was his backbone and unwavering anchor since the day they were married. Maggie, who everyone knew as 'Maggie Ducks' for some reason now long forgotten (although a rumour was once whispered that her father had webbed toes), was not overly warm and quite serious but together they shared one simple truth, they knew being where the other was in the world was exactly where they should be and were fully content in this knowledge. And there's a lot to be said for that.

They had children (and now grandchildren) but although well raised with vibrant childhoods and a deep affection for their parents and the upbringing they'd been afforded, neither of them

17

had the necessary love for the land and had sought their futures elsewhere, as soon as age allowed.

Their first born, their son David, had inherited so many of his parent's good qualities and since a child had never been one to waste words but could communicate as much with his wide smile and as a written saga. His childhood had been one of raising found fox cubs or abandoned chicks; learning to imitate the bird calls he heard; drawing squirrels, hedgehogs, stoats and rabbits and watching quietly as badger cubs emerged from their sett for the first time, to take their awkward first steps into the moonlight. He was mesmerised by the prevalent plants, trees and animals and his privileged proximity to them, his unrestricted access and how is life interwove and flowed with what he could see out of his own bedroom window but the harsh realities of running a farm was too much for him and too hard to reconcile. David understood all too well that certain animals needed to die to put food on the table and that it was right and proper but he knew from his youth that he could never make some of the hard choices a farmer needs to make from time to time and knew this life was not one he could lead. He would only be doing it out of a sense of duty to his father, which would have been reason enough had his father asked but it would have been an existence totally without joy or conviction. After his nineteenth lambing season, he left and moved to Merthyr Tydfil for work and there found love. He met and married the lovely Bronwyn; who was his true North and who his parents loved and cherished as their own.

Their daughter Cerys seemed to have spent her entire youth with barely a foot touching the land, whether lost in some daydream or fantasy she was continually running. Running away from her brother chasing her with muddy palms, running to the barn to see the new foal or chick, running with one of the sheep dogs tripping one another, running to the sound of a passing horse driven cart in electric curiosity and running home to tell of her findings. Often, she was running on some adventure that only

The dragon under the hill

existed in her 'world', that only see could see. She talked with breathless excitement as if against the ticking clock and was only vaguely aware of a working farm around her as she sped from one joyous imaginary tale to another and she was the princess in all of them. Before her parents knew it, she had been whisked away by a wealthy land owner's son when she was only just of age and from that day on there were few whispered fairy-tales or sound of joyous fleet foot running on the farm. The besotted young man, had seen her observing his journey passing the farm one day and stole their jewel from its sceptre. They now lived her real life fairy tale, as part of 'society' in England, which may as well be the other side of the world.

Evan and Maggie understood their children's choices and although disappointed, could not apportion any blame. They knew well the burden and commitment the farm would ask – for some, the weight of the land is too heavy.

Evan was deeply respected by all who knew him and his wife well honoured. Fellow farmers and residents of the nearby village of Rhywle would seek him out for advice or just the reassurances of his opinion, a select few words of guidance or if the vet was unavailable, to save a lamb, pup or foal.

By just smelling the air, he could tell you when it would rain or by watching the sheep, divine that a storm was coming. He knew the type of bird from only a few notes of its song or the smallest discarded feather, spy its perch or nest through a myriad of leaves and branches. The smallest clump of fur snagged on fencing wire was a book to him, interpreted with lightning speed and confidence. He could tell where a rabbit was hiding in a field despite it hunkering down and being invisible to others, where the barn owl nested or where a badger had walked the night before. He knew each animal by its track, footprint and dropping and where to stand to best see the spectacle of roosting starlings at dusk. He knew where the truly luscious grass would grow, what flowers would bloom almost to the day, where to pick goosegogs,

19

The dragon under the hill

blackberries, sloes, apples and nuts, sorrel and elderflowers for making drinks; wild garlic, parsley and mint, rowan buds, rosehip and honeysuckle for flavourings and which mushrooms are safe to eat.

Although able to read nature like an open book, Evan would often have to ask his wife what day of the week it was, as she kept a calendar by the fire for noting special dates, although she mostly liked it for the pretty pictures of water colour paintings representing each month of the year. Sometimes, in his busy moments, he even needed reminding of the year; he thought it was either 1936 or 7, most of the time that was close enough. His heart beat to a more ancient theme and some everyday worries and concerns just could not reach him.

Knowing this very well, the local Reverend would make the journey to visit Evan and Maggie regularly, instead of the other way around.

A small stocky man with wild black curly hair thick as midnight, the Reverend Rhodri Thomas had an aura of charismatic authority and peaceful dignity. His parish was spread out over a large area pinwheeled around one small chapel. Yet, he knew every single family in the locality with an accepted intimacy. Knew their names, birthdays and the voice of every man, woman and child without looking. He loved and cared for them like the best of sheep dogs, singlehandedly keeping the devil away from his flock with tears in his prayers and fire in his sermons and dogged devotion in his steps. His clear tenor voice carried hymns to the very heavens, each note held to the edges of his lungs, each word alive with belief. He loved to sing, whether others were enjoying hearing it as much as him or not was not really pertinent but that is every Welshman in a nutshell.

He considered himself an avid student of antiquity, an expert on folklore and passionate local historian. Keeper of the land's ancient tales and genealogies gone by. Holding tight not

The dragon under the hill

only his love for the land and its people but the reason why. Why each hill and its farms, each river with their crossings and bridges, each copse, wood and wall with their hidden secrets, held the name it did and where it came by it. He could recount each tale in vivid colour and authority. He believed that part of his role was to pass this knowledge on, hating the thought of these beautiful stepping stones in time being lost in the too fast flowing waters of modernity.

He was his congregation's own personal saint and prophet. He was a leader, father, comforter, teacher, counsellor, conscience, scholar, elder and moral plumb-line to all but to a few he was the dearest of loyal friends.

It was his oldest and dearest of friends that had brought him out this evening, the journey to their home from his, a well-worn path indeed.

While Maggie bustled around making tea, clattering the best plates and cups, Reverend Thomas - although here he was only Rhodri or Rhodri Bach; ('bach' being Welsh for 'small') would sit in a chair one side of the glowing fire and Evan in his chair on the other side and the old friends would act out the same playful pantomime. Evan poked the fire into beautiful warmth with a fencer's adept thrusts, radiating a snug embrace around the room, the flame from the kerosene lamps flickering and adding a lucid homely glow and the ancient cedar wood clock thudding each tick, it began.

"Missed you both in chapel on Sunday", Reverend Thomas would open with.

Evan would squint and think hard, "O, is it?" Then motion to his wife, "Maggie, when was Sunday?"

Without looking up or skipping a beat, she could always answer with the events of any day asked. "Sunday was the day

21

The dragon under the hill

Heini chased a fox down that rabbit warren and you spent the afternoon digging her out. Silly ol' girl."

On hearing her name, the farm's sheep dog looked up expectantly from her usual cosy position laying in front of the fire and scanned the room and its inhabitants. Once she had decided whatever was happening was nothing to do with her, her head flopped back down and she closed her eyes. 'Heini' means 'spritely' in Welsh; she was a beautiful liver and white springer spaniel with soulful brown eyes, from a pedigree of exemplary working dogs going back generations. Though age had robbed her of most of the exuberance she showed as a pup that had gained the young dog her name. She was still the best sheep dog in the hills.

Evan would then gesture the Reverend to refer to his wife's answer, as if that settled the entire question, before repeating the mantra he said every time. "Anyway, if you really want to meet with God, there is no better place than these hills. Nearer see?"

"No doubt", the Reverend would respond "but will you try and come next week?"

"O Rhodri…", Evan would plead, as innocent as a choir boy "I always try", and the old friends would laugh together, the play having reached its satisfactory conclusion.

By then Maggie would have served them and joined them by the fire, scooting the wooden stool next to her husband's chair.

After that, it was down to the real business. Over tea and a slice of Maggie's fruit loaf, would be discussed all the happenings of the farm; what the weather had in store, and especially local events, spiced with the odd morsel of gossip or burning questioning from Mrs James. How was baby Rhiannon down the way? Had old Nana Price recovered from her chest? Was Iestyn's oldest courting? Were Mrs Barrow and Mrs Bennett

22

still not speaking after what was said? Sometimes Maggie would respond with her customary "Oo never!" in feigned shock to some news or an answer she got to one of her questions or in mock offence when Rhodri would refuse to answer as he was told in confidence and pretended to chastise her for being a gossip.

Reverend Thomas had already shared a lifetime with them and knew these precious folk down their marrow and veins. He could anticipate every gesture and response, he knew they would give to others in need even if it meant they themselves were left with nothing; would give aide without question or thought of their own needs and had a love for people in the area they talked about that rivalled his own and prayed for them all by name day and night.

There was added excitement to the news this time, as they had received a letter from their Bron. In its carefully written pages, confirmation that, as planned, next week their grandson would coming to stay and spend the summer on the farm.

The evening would continue in this fashion until the Reverend Thomas, who could read people like Evan read the land, would knowingly pick the right time to call the evening's fellowship to a close and the second script of the evening would be performed perfectly. His hosts remonstrated at his leaving announcement – it was too early, one last tea for the road, surely there was time for cocoa, didn't he want more cake, maybe he should stay the night as it was dark and a long walk home, he must take some fruit loaf home with him and there'll be no argument...all met with a good natured decline. Finally, Rhodri would creak out of his chair and Maggie and Evan would ease out of theirs, only Heini remained where she was. Embracing both his old friends in turn, in quiet tones he would ask the Lord's blessing on them and their home before bidding them goodnight. Arm in arm the loving couple would stand at the farm door to wish him a safe journey home and watch him stroll down the path and disappear into the night's shadow. There they would linger

23

The dragon under the hill

together, looking at the stars, momentarily lost in their own reflections and hearing different echoes, before sharing a brief kiss.

Closing the door and getting ready for bed, Maggie would tidy away the crockery and Evan would compact the burning embers of the dying fire, look down at his dog and teasingly rebuke her while giving her a goodnight pat. "Some guard dog you are girl, you didn't even bite him".

The dragon under the hill

Chapter 3

"Shuni, get back in this house now this minute!" A mother's yelling voice caused a lively street football match to suddenly fall silent, freeze in time and in horror. Each lad's heart stopping mid beat, until that moment of sweet relief when they realised that the poor boy in trouble, isn't them.

"Aw, Mam! If I go in, there won't be even sides", came the distraught reply as the guilty party scanned his playmates looking for any assistance. All the other participants looked everywhere, except at the troubled lad, he was beyond their help. As if manufactured from some great organic mould there was little to distinguish one of the playing boys from the other, each similarly adorned and with their dark hair slicked back. They sympathised with their fallen comrade but were itching for the awkwardness to be over and the game to restart. Unremarkable in appearance, Jack was smaller and slighter than most and quieter and more considered in temperament but was one among the group like a cobble in the road.

"John Richard James…", she added, her staccato voice even higher. Jack knew this was serious, it had escalated from 'Shuni' to his proper full name now being used, she need say no more.

"I gotto go boys, see you again." Were the resigned words of goodbye, as Jack picked up his tank top from the road where it had been masquerading as a goalpost, dragged it over his head and stomped back to his house. The sound of the restarted game mocking him from behind as he mounted the single step. As he squeezed passed his mother through the narrow front doorway, a sly but forceful smack on his backside spurred him forward.

"As soon as my back was turned…", was the last thing heard before the door slammed shut.

The dragon under the hill

Their little Dowlais home was a simple two up and two down with little windows, shingles on the roof and an outside 'privy'. Made of corrugated iron and wood, and justifiably cold and damp, found by following a handful of mismatched paving stones set randomly amongst the unkempt foliage down the bottom of the garden. The pattern-book grey small terraced house was identical to hundreds of others in the area and thousands across the town. Streets upon streets of them, seemed to tumble down the hillsides like frozen waterfalls. All built in the eighteen-hundreds by the then Lords of the land, the Iron masters. A profunctor ill woven blanket to house the myriad of down-trodden, oft-scarred workers from their scorching, brewing and belching Iron-works. The mighty volcanic monoliths of Cyfathfa and Dowlais once dominated all around, as they roared and seethed day and night, so brightly the sun need not rise. They were demonic Northern Lights making the town continually burn and glow from afar, like the eternal fires of Hades.

"Sneaking out and kicking a ball in the street with your best clothes on and you know you are going to your grandparents later!" Through gritted teeth she reprimanded the now forlorn figure, who sat on the arm of the settee, hands rammed in his pockets in defiance.

Dressed in his best stiff, white cotton, short-sleeved shirt with a blue stripe; knitted woollen cabled, grey tank top; belted, black short trousers; knee high, black socks and sturdy, studded brown leather boots. Boots so strong and robust he could kick a hole in a stone wall and not feel a thing. They were as solid as a house brick and just as comfortable to wear. By the time they were worn in and supple enough to be bearable, they were grown out of or the soles were worn through, needing repair. Repairs would occur many times in the boot's lifetime but they were never the same afterwards. His hair still damp and sweet smelling from his recent preparatory bath.

The dragon under the hill

A grumble escaped from his frustration, "I don't see why I have to go, can't I just play out with my mates?" To a young lad's mind, there are few things more important than playing with your mates, even fewer things important enough to be dragged away from them when a footie game has broken out.

"No boyo", came the succinct response, his mum refusing to rise to the bait.

"But Mam", Jack pursued the point, "It's the summer holiday. I don' wanna go when all the boys are having fun. I'm left out mun." The summer break from school was a sacred time for every youngster. Six long, heavenly weeks where their only jobs were to get from under their mother's feet and to come when called. The rest of the time was to do with as they saw fit, the wind taking them where it may, the freedom of unfettered youth. To have this time stolen was incomprehensible.

"Stop your moaning. You like your grandparents and you'll have a great time on the farm." Consoled his mother.

Jack played his final card, badly "I don' wanna go and you can't make me!"

Although expected, this move easily lit the touch-paper and a few short minutes later poor sniffing Jack was confined to the room he shared with his brothers Idris and Desmond, sitting on his bed feeling roundly scolded, his little leather suitcase his mother had packed earlier, next to him. The back of his legs still red from his mum's reproaching hand and ears still rebounding the words of his clipped telling off. Possibly worse was to come. It was one thing to push his mother's buttons and get a reaction but dad was due home shortly to see him off and he was the proper authority. Although with a much longer fuse, pushing dad's buttons could really get you in trouble.

He sat and listened to each crawling second.

The dragon under the hill

Jack's heart jumped as he heard the front door opening and worry rose as he could hear his parents talking but was unable to make out the details or tone. Panic kindled as his father's unmistakable footsteps made their way quickly upstairs. What had mam said? Was he in for another scolding? Was he in serious hot water? Thankfully, when his father gently opened the heavy white door to his sons' room, entered and sat next to him on the bed, he seemed unruffled.

"Your mam says you don't want to go and stay with your Nana and Grampa?" his dad queried calmly.

Jack could feel his father's expectant stare but just shook his head.

'Why, son?" came the gentle question.

The boy's response was mostly the inaudible mumbling of a typical child struggling to articulate their feelings and really not wanting to engage but his father knew his offspring well.

"Shuni bach, I know you'd rather be out playing with your mates but let's be honest son, we can't always do what we want. Life's not like that. Don't you think I'd rather be playing football or spending time with you than going to work every day in that smelly ol' tannery?" He waited for a response, it came in the shape of a minute nod from his son, then continued "And I know it doesn't feel like it now but it'll be great, don't forget it's where I grew up".

A slightly appeased Jack looked at his father as he resumed "You might see foxes or badgers, red kites or a kestrel and that noisy old barn owl if he's still there, all sorts. Your mates will still be here when you get back and where will they have been? Nowhere. And what will they have seen? Nothing."

Jack's spirits lifted, his curiosity engaged.

28

The dragon under the hill

"Anyway, my folks are getting old these days, so they could do with a bit of help. Can you do that for me boyo?"

Jack nodded. His father smiled, patted his lad on the shoulder and got up to leave. As he reached the door and put his hand on the doorknob, he paused.

"Cheeked your mam, did you?" he asked.

"Yes dad. Sorry dad", the boy blurted with contrition.

"And how did that go for you?" his father asked, this time a smile he could no suppress growing on his face.

"Not good, dad" Jack began smiling in return.

"Aye, I bet", laughing.

"Come on then".

Jack jumped of his perch, heaved his suitcase with both hands and followed his father out of the room.

The dragon under the hill

Chapter 4

In the brown paper bag containing the journey's provisions his mother had given him, Jack had already discovered and eaten the doorstep thick cheese sandwich that had been wrapped in brown grease proof paper and the hardboiled egg. Only the shiny green apple remained. Jack had a funny thing where apples were concerned; he didn't mind the taste but the thought of the sensation of his teeth touching and breaking through the tough apple peel made him squirm and it was like electricity going through his teeth and brain. His parents always dismissed it as silliness, only his big brother Idris sympathised and would always peel or slice apples for him with his penknife. He could do with Idris now.

He still had half his sweet cloudy lemonade left in the hinged top pop bottle but the best part of his fare was the little paper bag his dad had slipped into his coat pocket containing a quarter of mixed sweets; bullseyes, aniseed balls, humbugs, lemon sherbet, pear drops, winter nips, jelly babies and white mice. Each one was relished as a different side of heaven in Jack's mouth, each suck, chew and lick was savoured as the rare treat it was. A wiser lad than him would have tried to save a portion of the sweets for another day but the journey was long and dull and it wasn't long before another tasty morsel was calling out irresistibly to the little boy.

According to Jack's best estimations, the main section of the journey was over and having successfully navigated the changing of buses at Builth Wells and at Beulah, he would soon be at his destination. The trip was a major undertaking for Jack, the fact that he was doing it alone made him prone to worry, growing more concerned as the day of travel neared and had for some while been harbouring nagging questions that increased now he was undertaking the journey. 'What if there was no one to

30

meet him?' 'What if his grandparents hadn't got the letter or had forgotten he was coming?' They could have got the wrong day or wrong time. 'What would he do?' As these nagging bees buzzed around in his mind, their noise building, the small bus trundled over an old humpback stone bridge that spanned the river and started climbing the small hill. The village square and its pub came into view. There, standing outside, leaning on his crook, with a spaniel dog sitting next to him, was the unmistakable figure of his grandfather. From the flat cap he always wore, his well-worn dark green Barbour wax jacket, thick wool jumper to his black rubber boots, he was the archetypal man of the hills.

The welcome sight of his grandfather triggered Jack's memory of those final few minutes with his parents before he left and his father's parting words. After he had said sorry to his mother for his disgruntled episode, she had taken his hand and his father had taken the other and all three walked jovially together to the bus station. His mum waited with him until the bus came and helped Jack on with his suitcase, speaking briefly with the bus driver but Jack didn't hear what was said. She handed him his coat with the bus changes written on a piece of paper pinned to his coat lapel and a brown paper bag containing his packed lunch. She hugged and kissed him trying her utmost not to let the tears flow until he left as not to upset the boy and made him promise to concentrate so he didn't get the bus changes mixed up and that he would write as soon as he got there. After instructing the driver again to 'look after her little boy' she remained until it left, exuberantly waving as the bus pulled off. Only after the bus was out of sight did she give in fully to the tears, how they flowed.

His father couldn't wait with them as his lunch break was nearly over and had to go back to his work. He hugged his boy, slipped a small white paper bag into Jack's coat pocket with a wink and almost as an afterthought, with a serious air, spoke to his son.

"One last thing Jack, your grandparents are the best of people but your grandfather is set in his ways and has certain

The dragon under the hill

rules, he'll tell you when he meets you, promise me you'll do what he says?

Jack's nod in reply earned him a 'That's my boy' from his parting father.

Stepping off the stationary bus, his journey complete, the curiosity that the memory had sparked within him quickly disappeared as he was met by an affectionate spaniel, wagging her tail in excitement. Jack stooped down and giggled as the exuberant animal nearly pushed him over through the petting and pats.

"Her name is Heini. She doesn't usually fuss over anyone. She must like you." Rumbled a clear voice, it was deep, assured and full of calm.

Jack looked up to see the wiry but solid man he knew to be his grandfather. He recognised his craggy worn features under the flat cap from when he saw him a couple of years ago when he and his grandmother had visited them in Merthyr.

"Duw, there's grown you have boy, since I saw you last. How old are you now then?" Evan queried.

"Twelve, Grampa", Jack replied. Warming to the situation, he forged on "Idris is nearly seventeen and wants to join the army and little Des is only a tot."

"O, is it?" came the response, then with little wait. "Anyway, no use us standing here talking all day. Your gran is waiting at the house, bursting to see you. Come on Heini". The dog spun on its heels and trotted alongside her master as he began striding off. It took Jack a few moments to recognise that was the signal that they all were leaving and he was meant to follow the man and dog. It took him longer still to realise he could not spot his little suitcase nearby because his grandfather had scooped it up and was carrying it for him. He quickly scuttled to their side, heavy boots clopping on the ground.

Jack rounded a corner just in time to see Heini leap onto the back of a small horse-drawn cart and sit down, next to the suitcase. His grandfather undid the leather reigns from the post they had been tied to, mounted the cart and waited.

Over his time visiting his grandparents Jack would learn many things about his grandfather; his kindness, wisdom and sense of humour but also the annoying way he expected those around him to read his mind because the next step was obvious, wasn't it? This being one of those occasions, eventually Jack joined his grandfather, clambering up onto the front of the cart before the muscular little horse was geed on.

After a few miles of silence, Jack could not contain his curiosity anymore and blurted out the question he'd been nursing all day, "Dad said there were rules."

"O, did he now?" responded Evan, looking at his grandson.

Jack nodded.

"And, what do you think they could possibly be then, boyo?", he added with an amused pause.

The boy thought for a while and tentatively ventured, "No cheeking Nana or getting your clothes dirty?"

"Well", said Evan slowly, "A good boy like you shouldn't need a rule to know not to go cheeking his Nana, now should he? And let me warn you now, if you did decide to give cheeking your Nana a try, you would only ever do it the once." He looked down at the boy wide eyed, as if to communicate something really scary. "As for getting your clothes dirty," he carried on in a normal tone, "I'd like to see anyone spend an hour on a working farm and not get his clothes dirty. That's not saying Maggie won't chase you out

33

The dragon under the hill

of the house with her broom shouting, if you tried to track mud in on your boots on to her nice clean floor though."

Evan decided to put the boy out of his misery and reinforce the importance of the rules that he had told to his own son, not twenty years ago and his own father told to him many years before.

"There are three rules you must always obey, otherwise I shall have to send you straight home – now count them out with me on your fingers so as you'll remember them better". Ordered Evan.

"Number one", both he and the boy held up their thumb in representation. "You must never pee anywhere near the farm's stream. It's the only source of clean fresh water on the hill. Not only do the animals drink from that water but we do as well."

Jack felt the end of the sentence elicited a clear nod of understanding.

"Number two", they added their index finger for a two. "I keep a shotgun in the house for shooting foxes and the odd rabbit. You must never, ever touch it when I am not with you. I will show it to you, let you hold it and even shoot it if you want but only when I am with you. Is that clear?"

Again, the boy nodded, half of him glad that these rules seemed easy so far and the other half excited that he'd been promised he could shoot a real gun. Now that would certainly be something to tell his mates back home and make them jealous.

"Number three", together they both held up three fingers. "At the very top of the hill, at the very edge of our land is a small field with a stony cairn in it. You must never go to the field or explore the cairn."

This time instead of a stiff nod of agreement Evan was met with a quizzical frown from the boy's face and slightly defiant "Why not?"

Jack quickly regretted the aggression of his speedy question as he saw his grandfather's thougher darken and become stern.

"Listen now boy, it is enough for you to obey the rules as I see fit to lay them out, I shouldn't have to explain myself to you."

For many minutes, they rode further on in silence. The only sound the steady plodding of the horse's hooves, the odd call of a bird startled from its place in the hedgerow and the creaking of the suspension springs responding to the bumps in the track, which seemed all the louder as man and boy were left with their own thoughts. Evan realised that it had been a very long time since he had needed to explain something to a child and noted that he was out of practice and even worse, his famed patience was not what it used to be. He regretted his harshness and knew he would have to relearn tolerance of these things this summer. He spoke as gently as he could, reaching out.

"Some will fill your head with legends and old fairy stories about that cairn. The truth is we have always stayed away because it is unsafe. There are potholes everywhere and you could easily break a leg and ancient caves long overgrown with grass so you could fall in and we'd never find you. A dangerous place see."

"O, righto", Jack responded, a question formed in his mouth but before he could ask it, his grandfather continued.

"Oh, I mustn't forget. It marks the boundary between our land and Old Man Roberts's land. Now, Old Man Roberts is not a bad soul when you get past the grumpiness and stinking temper and general dislike of people but he's got the meanest, nastiest, wildest dog I've ever known and old Cymro ('Cymro' means

The dragon under the hill

'Welshman' and for some reason has been an incredibly popular dog's name in Wales for centuries) is allowed to roam free and a dog doesn't know one farm from another. I've had to shoot a warning shot at the black beast on more than one occasion – just knowing he's around puts me on edge with my sheep, especially during lambing. Believe me boy, you never want to run into that rabid old thing at night." Said Evan with drama, shaking his head.

Jack nodded in satisfaction at the received explanations and the relationship was restored.

"But Grampa" Jack piped up, "what legends?"

Jack could not tell if his grandfather did not hear his question or if he chose to ignore it, he suspected the latter. He was about to chase up the issue when his grandfather announced.

"Here we are. Home sweet Home."

The spindly wooden cart with its flaking racing green paint and squeaking rust laden suspension springs, rounded the turn into the farm and after a short climb, the high hedgerow gave way to the part-paved courtyard and the white farmhouse. It was a small two story thick stone building, whitewashed from top to bottom, with solid wooden doors and small windows. It's steep slanting heavy slate roof, specifically shaped against the often blustery weather, had low deep eaves that gave the whole structure a look of hunkering down and holding onto the side of the hill like a limpet on a rock. For centuries it had clung to the landscape, not even Evan knew how long it had stood.

Before the cart stopped Heini leapt off and disappeared. Evan steered the pony level to the farmhouse's front door where Maggie appeared smiling, drying her hands in her pale blue apron.

"Here are my boys", she said as the cart drew to a stop. "Come here John, let me look at you".

The dragon under the hill

Jack clambered down and stiffly stood in front of his grandmother for inspection. Crouching down she placed her hands on the boy's shoulders, looking him up and down with thoughtful intensity.

"Well there's skinny you are. Following your mother's side no doubt but you've got your father's looks, that's for sure."

Jack was sizing her up in return, he noted how her clear blue eyes seemed to dissect him like an ice-cold scalpel, his very viscera exposed. Her narrow face was angular and her greying hair pinned and intertwined into a tight bun, solid as iron. Her smile was not easy and she had the air of a matron or headmistress and smelled strongly of carbolic soap. In that moment, he understood completely his grandfather's warning about the consequences of tangling wills with this woman. A route he certainly decided he would avoid going down.

Ushered inside, passed the rough doormat, Jack found himself near the large table the kitchen revolved around. The other half of the room was the living space semi-circled around the large stone fire place, which as was customary, had a tin bath hung over it. Floored in nothing but well worn flag-stones with one old patterned tasselled rug in front of the fire.

Following instructions, he sat on a worn wooden bench on one side of the table, glass smooth through years of use. Adorned with a white linen table cloth, it had been set with blue and white crockery, a cosy covered tea pot in the centre, a small jug of cream, one plate with fruit loaf cake, another dish containing a homemade blackberry tart with lattice pastry top, one with stacked uniform Welsh cakes, a plate of freshly baked bread sawn into thick slices and surrounded by butter, cheese, pickles, preserves and marmalade; and finally, much to Jack's consternation, a large bowl piled high with rough skinned, mottled red apples.

The dragon under the hill

"You must be half starved after that long journey all on your own. Now, what would you like? Help yourself to the bread and spreads and I'll pour you some tea."

Jack stared at what would normally represent months' worth of sweet treats at home. Eating with his eyes, wanting to taste every morsel and experience everything. Not wanting to miss out, he just couldn't decide and totally overwhelmed, only managed a mealy shrug.

"Why don't I give you a little bit of everything and see how you get on" his grandmother quickly decided.

"Oh, thank you", not realising that was ever an option, Jack drooled as his empty plate was perfectly piled, receiving a Welsh cake, a thin slice of blackberry tart, a half slice of fruit loaf, a chunk of cheese, a couple of pickled onions and accompanied by a cup of freshly brewed tea. He quickly spread butter over his slice of fruit loaf and was just about to take his first tantalising bite when he felt a cool firm hand on his.

"We'll just wait for your grandfather to join us John" his grandmother said, in that flat way she had of speaking. It wasn't unkind but it was direct and especially for a child was incredibly difficult to read.

Seeing an opportunity to break formalities, he smiled at her and said, "O, you can call me Jack. Everyone calls me Jack...except mam, who calls me Shuni."

This did not get the response he hoped for or expected, "I certainly will not! Your parents chose to name you John and that is what you will be known as in this house." Sternly stated his grandmother. Taken aback, this added to the boy's general unease.

The few minutes it took for Evan to join them at the table seemed a lifetime to the salivating young lad in this newly frosted

38

atmosphere. His inviting plateful of food crying out to be eaten, his Nana silently, serenely waiting, the loud clock mocking with each tick and 'What on earth is he doing?' whirlwinding around his mind. It was torture.

After an age his grandfather finally appeared and made himself comfortable. With great relief Jack aimed the loaf to his open mouth, again feeling a hindering cool hand on his. As she did Evan launched into saying Grace, not a single word of which actually registered with the waiting youngster, a chorus of "Amen," it was finally time to tuck in.

Jack leapt in and ate like a lean dog, missing the happy smiles that his grandparents exchanged. Each mouthful a delicious joy as he ploughed through his plateful. Crumbling rich pastry delighting him. Even a simple slice of bread was raised to heights of gleeful flavour by each preserve tried in turn and by the time he was pouring the thick cream watching it envelope and embrace his tart like snow on a mountain top, he felt at ease and a little more at home. The power of a good meal shared. His answers to his nan's questions less one word answers and more descriptive, fulfilling her need for detail. He carried on munching long after the others had finished.

While the boy ate and drank, Evan and Maggie discussed the errands he had run earlier in the village, who he had seen and the news he'd heard, the timing of the bus, the journey home and what they had talked about on the way. Jack's mind tuned in and out to their conversation while revelling in the taste indulgences. Until the conversation moved to a topic which did grab his full attention.

"Oh, that unpleasant little man from the Ministry called around again. What's his name...Mr Deacon?" Maggie stated in her usual matter-of-fact tone.

The dragon under the hill

"Is it?" replied Evan in a gruff tone, his ardour rising. "Not again?" He puffed hard and then asked his wife "and what did you tell him this time?"

"O, he started off with his big words 'explaining' it all to me again speaking to me as if I was a child and as if we haven't heard it all from him before. So, I stopped him in his tracks and told him we would never give up our farm while there was any breath in our bodies and offered him the kitchen knife to kill me dead there and then, (you know the big one) as 'that was the only way I was leaving, dead in a coffin', I shouted." She recounted resolutely.

This made Evan splutter into his tea, "A bit dramatic like Mags, in it?"

This only got a perfunctory self-satisfied shrug from his unrepentant wife.

This amused her husband even more, Jack was enthralled, "And what did he say to that?" her husband asked.

"He turned a funny shade, said how 'that wouldn't be necessary', 'he didn't want to stab me' and 'could I please be reasonable and put the knife away'. I can't remember what else I shouted but he left very quickly after that, with one of the geese honking after him." She ended with an innocent smile.

Evan roared with laughter and Jack joined in, both imagining the scene, "That's my girl." Evan stated when he had breath enough. "And that will be Elenore I suspect, that goose thinks she's a guard dog half the time." This statement was aimed at Jack and rekindled the mirth.

Evan could sense Jack needed some context and thought back to his earlier experience in the cart and knew an explanation was due.

40

The dragon under the hill

"You see lad," he said, easing into the subject, "that man has been sniffing around this valley for weeks now, visiting each farm again and again, either offering to buy it or exchange it for some other land elsewhere. Originally, we all thought it was some private land owner or something. It took us a good while to get to the bottom of things the way he tried to bamboozle folk with his clever words and fancy clothes. Turns out he's from the government, some Ministry, the War Office or some other and they are looking to clear us all out of our beloved valley so that they can use it and blow it up. They want to move their army in, train soldiers, shoot real bullets and I don't know what else."

This triggered a passionate rant from Maggie, who had always taken great personal exception to the historical exploitation of Welsh resources, land and people by their Anglian neighbours. "Why they have to come here to do it and can't find space in England, I can't understand", she voiced. "It's just like that poor little village up North that they kicked everyone out of their family homes they'd lived in for years and flooded the whole thing, just to make a reservoir for the English to have water to drink."

"As long as the local farmers stick together" Evan continued, nodding to his wife, "and keep saying 'no' we'll be alright but he's a persistent toad, I'll give him that and he keeps coming back, even when Old Man Roberts tried to shoot him."

"He's just lucky that horrid dog Cymro wasn't nearby at the time, else he'd be 'that man from the Ministry missing a leg'." Maggie added "Anyway, nothing for you to worry about John, finish eating while I clean up."

The only downside of the feast was that his grandmother had insisted he take an apple from the bowl, despite his protestations about being full and not being a fan of apples. He left the table wonderfully satisfied but with another unwanted apple in his possession.

The dragon under the hill

The first order of business after lunch was being shown around the farmhouse, including the small room he would be staying in, and then the rest of the farm. The outbuildings, barn, pig pen, chicken coup, goose house and finally the outside toilet. Then came helping with various daily chores. Drawing water from the well fed from the mountain stream and other underground sources, feeding the animals and making sure the feed is secure stored away in the barn and covered to discourage mice, fetching wood for the fire and then as the sun started setting, how to build and light the fire in the stone hearth beneath the hulking chimney breast.

The short evening passed tranquilly. Sitting on the floor sharing the fire side rug with Heini in front of the crackling flames and cradling a mug of cocoa, Jack listened as his grandfather imparted a little of the history of Bryn Y Ddraig farm, his family and the valley. Periodically his grandmother would produce a cherished photograph for Jack's consideration from the hardback grey family album she had brought out and was fondly flicking through, its pages discoloured with age and use. It's ordered black and white images an honoured chronicle of days gone by, a languid pool of memories to dive into and float.

'This is your father and Cerys when they were babies', 'This is your dad around about your age', 'This is your parents on the day of their wedding, your mother looked so beautiful'. All of which the boy pleasantly soaked up with amusement until the fire started to dry his eyes and his yawns became more pronounced.

"Off to bed with you now", ordered Maggie, as it became clear Jack was giving in to fatigue. "You'll be up on the hill with the sheep tomorrow, so you'll need a good sleep. Come on." She grabbed a candle holder with a stubby candle in it, pulled a match from the box on the mantle and striking it quickly, carefully watched the ignited flame blossom before using it to light the candle. She threw the spent match into the fire and made for the stairs.

42

"Sleep well lad", said Evan, picking up his large black leather-bound family bible to read where he'd left of the night before adding, "Nos da" (which is Welsh for 'Goodnight').

"Goodnight, Grampa", yawned Jack, following his grandmother.

Jack's allotted room was small and simply furnished and smelled of old wood, fresh linen and white vinegar. The bare wooden uneven floor slightly gave way under foot and pitched noticeably to one side. The only decoration, a framed hand stitched ornate motif in red thread against a white background that read 'Bless this house' hanging above the bed. Against one wall was pressed a single bed with multicoloured linen sheets and knitted woollen blankets, all covered with a patchwork quilt. Opposite, stood a dark wood double dresser with a jug of water and large plain bowl for washing and a single candle, which his grandmother lit from the candle she had brought.

"You should be warm enough but there are some extra blankets in the dresser if you need them." She paused to look out of the small window, "Full moon tonight, there's bright it is." thinking out loud.

"As soon as you're washed up, changed and in bed, blow out the candle, no use wasting it", she said leaving.

"Goodnight, Nana", Jack called behind her but to no response. It's little things like that which cause children to wonder if they are liked by the adults in their lives. There are many ways people give and receive love and from what he had already experienced would be hard pressed to argue he had not been shown love since he had come into the home but it is another thing entirely to feel that you are liked for the person you are.

He was dog tired but sleep eluded Jack. Whether it was the events of the long day he'd been replaying in his head, being in a strange bed in a strange house and all the odd noises an

The dragon under the hill

individual house makes, especially an old one like this surrounded by animals but really, he missed the company of his brothers. He missed Desmond's heavy breathing and odd mumbling and he missed Idris's low rasping snore and pinging mattress spring when he shifted his weight in the bed opposite his. Eventually he tired of tossing and turning and his vain attempts to drop off, sitting up he grabbed the top blanket and cocooned himself in it and kneeling on the bed he stared out of the window into the night, onto the hill. The old window frame had seen better days and tracing the back of his hand across the edges of each of the four small panes, Jack could feel the wind finding its way through the least secure portions.

The moon was indeed bright, like a signal light and created a clear silhouette of the rising land. From where he sat, Jack could make out the top of the hill and at it's very peak what had to be the stony cairn his grandfather had talked about earlier. It looked old and mysterious, a dominant master of the whole hill. Jack wondered who had built it and why and what were the legends his grandfather mentioned but wouldn't tell. He stared and stared at the rugged crest, as if in staring the answers would appear written in the sky, until the cold drove him back into bed and to eventual sleep.

If only Jack had kept watching a few moments longer he would have witnessed the hill's crown move, the cairn momentarily coming alive, something stirred, flickering with an odd momentary glint, then the shape was gone

Chapter 5

"John, time to get up," accompanied a loud knock at the door that woke Jack from his fitful sleep. "you hear me?" continued the violator of his slumber.

"Uh?...Yes Nana...coming Nana" came the hazy reply, the boy struggling to regain his senses. Even in his half-awake state Jack knew better than to argue or complain.

He slowly dressed and still drowsy, made his way downstairs. His Nana was in the kitchen area with her back to him cooking with a heavy frying pan on the range wood-burning cooker.

"What time is it?" Jack enquired, rubbing his eyes.

"Nearly six." Came the curt response, followed up with "your grandfather will be in for his breakfast in a moment."

"Six?!" Jack repeated incredulous, he was finding things quite confusing but did not dare verbalise his next thought 'What on earth did you wake me up at this unearthly hour for woman?'

"Sit down," she ordered, "what would you like for breakfast?"

Jack usually did not eat at breakfast time, often waking up feeling bilious with a pronounced gag reflex. The shock of being woken up at this hour certainly didn't help his appetite. His mother would be constantly nagging, writing the behaviour off as an attempt to gain attention from a middle child but even then, first thing in the morning he could usually only manage some tea, if anything. He may have been able to explain this to his grandmother given the chance but instinctively he knew it would not be heard or received in this instance. He decided to pick the least offensive item he could think of to his weak waking stomach.

The dragon under the hill

"Could I have toast please Nana?" he managed.

"Fine." Replied his Nana without turning around, "there is plenty already on the table. Would you like some eggs or bacon or mushrooms, anything to go on top?"

"No thank you, toast is fine". Jack reluctantly took the top piece from a pile of toast, opened a jar of blackcurrant jam and spread a thin layer. He had taken a few nibbles when his grandfather and his shadow, Heini, came in.

"Lovely day!" He announced to no one in particular as he entered the room. Placing his crook behind the door, resting it against the wall and placing his cap on another hook. Removing, then hanging up his coat, while simultaneously slipping out of his rubber boots, he joined his grandson at the table.

"Bore da, lad" (which translates as 'good morning') Evan said as he sat, "did you enjoy your nice lie-in?"

Jack looked up at him with a jolt, was this a joke? "Lie-in?" he echoed back.

Placing a plate on the table in front of Evan, it was Maggie who responded in a way that conveyed her grandson's sleep was somehow of personal offence to her. "Your grandfather has already been working on the farm for 2 hours this morning. He wouldn't let me wake you until breakfast, you'd 'had a hard day' and 'a long journey', he said". She couldn't help but slightly sneer in her last sentence.

"Now Mags," Evan reprimanded.

Last night while in bed, they had a long conversation as Evan shared his realisation that he was out of practice dealing with children and it would require a lot of effort, patience and tolerance to relearn and treat their grandson properly during his stay. Evan recognised that this 'rustiness' would also be true for Maggie,

The dragon under the hill

double so probably, as she had to work hard at the simplest of human interactions anyway. They agreed to be as gentle with the boy as they could, without 'sparing the rod'.

Jack was immediately taken aback by the contents of his grandfather's breakfast, aghast that someone could tackle such an amount, so vigorously, this early in the morning. There were thick slices of streaky bacon with a good amount of fat still left on, two poached eggs, a large pile of fried mushrooms, fried diced potatoes and two slices of reheated black pudding. If he had not felt queasy before, Jack certainly did now witnessing his grandfather dowse it in salt then demolish the greasy fare. By way of fanfare, using some buttered bread, he wiped the plate clean to finish.

Evan was definitely a morning person. Without the need for a clock, call or alarm, he always rose unbidden before dawn at his most refreshed, energised and oddly talkative. He loved to be outside, at some lofty vantage point to see the world awaken around him. To see the sunrise over the prized valley. Changing from a dim haze of light at the edge of his vision to bright daybreak's waters flooding over the hills like molten gold. How the colours changed from their sullen greyscale shades to vibrant living hues, like each instrument in an orchestra coming to life one by one. Each note in the chorus getting louder and warmer moment to moment. Even before the old rooster would crow his alarm, the starlings were already leaving their roost, a jackdaw's crass voice would puncture the song of the linnet, stonechat, hedge sparrow and finch, all annoying the dew laden breaking of the day.

Then Evan would break his own silence with a soft "Good morning Lord", as if he was addressing an old friend, before quietly praying and thanking God for all He had made.

By the time he had checked on the animals, drawn more water and performed his usual morning duties, he was ravenously

The dragon under the hill

hungry and in fine mood. He looked down at his ever-present dog, addressing her. "Heini ol' girl, time for breakfast, I think", adding with a smile "let's rescue that boy from his grandmother, shall we?"

While finishing up the dregs of his tea he leaned towards Jack. "Right then my boy, ready to meet the sheep and see the rest of the farm?"

"Er, I think so?" came the unsure reply.

The boy watched his grandfather intently as he donned his rubber boots, Barbour coat and hat and retrieved his crook, ready to respond to any cue, however subtle but before Jack could follow him out the door his grandfather inspected him from top to toe, "Wait a minute lad, you can't come with me up the fields like that."

The boy stood bewildered, looking himself up and down "Why? What's the matter Grampa?"

"Well, it's those lovely boots of yours, I can't be letting you get them all muddy – your mother would have my guts."

"They're the only shoes I got" came the disconsolate reply.

"Oh, stop teasing the boy" came Maggie's exasperated voice from behind him, which prompted sniggers from Evan. She appeared next to them with a pair of small thick black rubber boots.

"Here John", she continued "these should fit you nicely, although you may need some thicker socks." Placing the footwear down at his feet and helping him off with his boots. "These used to be your father's when he was young and are yours for the time you are here".

The dragon under the hill

"Aw, thank you, Nana," came the happy response as he quickly swapped boots and trotted out the door to catch his still sniggering grandfather.

Over the next few hours Jack would have many occasions to be extremely thankful for his new footwear. While trying to follow his grandfather, listen to what he was being told and take in all the sights and sounds of the land – the boy often found his foot slip from under him unexpectedly, sink into a boggy piece of ground he did not notice or make squelching noises traversing ankle deep mud. A couple of times Heini nearly caused him to trip up as she would appear from nowhere and want to be next to her master, if that meant cutting across the boy's path, then so be it.

Together they walked the whole boundary of the farm. It seemed to cover the whole flank of the valley, from the highest peak to the winding track running down the centre that followed the river. With his vivid description and detailed knowledge Evan painted layer upon layer of life and meaning on the land as he explained to his young ward how the weather had stirred the landscape into shape, how the waters collected and flowed wearing and sculpting; and how hundreds of years of farming footprints had whittled each field and track. It seemed to Jack that is grandfather could talk for hours on the smallest blade of grass or drop of dew, if it was on his farm.

After one of these many tutorials, Evan break his thoughtful silence, almost startling the lad.

"Right, time you met some of the animals, eh?"

First, Jack was introduced to the four brown Welsh cobs that roamed the hillside. Like most mountain horses they were semi-feral and no creatures were hardier or more suited for mountain life. Although smaller than the average horse, they are stocky and muscular, with thick legs giving them sure footing, their thick hair and mane defence against the chilling wind. Throughout

49

The dragon under the hill

their history these Welsh breeds have had many uses, including cavalry horse and pit pony, as well as a working animal on farms.

These mountain ponies allowed themselves to be used on the farm by Evan more by mutual agreement than actual ownership. A symbiotic relationship, they received care, additional feed and shelter during the cruellest of winter in exchange for the occasional discomfort of the halter being buckled and the reins attached, to be led or saddled to be ridden or the full harness added with its bit, collar, girth and trace for pulling the little cart, which was the James's only transport.

The four horses came and greeted Evan, recognising him as soon as he had walked into their line of vision and after a short visit with him, some soft words and scratches, they sauntered back to their grazing. He then propped himself against the dry-stone wall leaning on his crook, his dog sitting near his feet. Once comfortable the farmer gestured towards to the horses.

"The big old fella'" Evan said pointing, "that's Merlin. He's as strong as a pair of oxen and does most of the work. The darker one is Hazel and the two younger ones with her are called Gwen and Doris. They'll all come when their name is called, if they've a mind to, that is", he said

Jack had no experience with horses and hadn't realised how big these creatures were until he was up close, their bearing and strength made him quite wary.

His grandfather instinctively picked up on the boy's hesitancy and concern.

"Listen to me carefully and by the end of the day, I'll teach you how to deal with any horse you aren't familiar with."

A happier Jack looked up and nodded.

"First thing to remember is that you always approach any horse quietly from its left-hand side – don't surprise him thought, make sure he sees you coming. Now, if you have to walk to where a horse is standing, don't go stomping right at it. Make an arc when you walk, eventually coming around to the animal's left shoulder. Never approach a horse from behind, that's a fast way to spook the animal or even worst get yourself kicked into next Wednesday."

He began the reminisce, "I remember trying to teach Mr Bennett's youngest Gethin but there's a wilful boy if ever I met one. Never listened. Anyway, even after I'd explained to him, all tidy mind, he came charging up behind the horse, the exact opposite of what I'd just told him and spooked the beast. Well that horse caught him a beauty right on his chin, took off he did, flew through the air in a beautiful arc. He was out cold before he landed. Didn't do him any lasting damage, but even he won't do that again, still got the scar."

Jack shuddered at the thought of being kicked with those powerful hooves. As his grandfather continued the boy tried hard to remember accurately all he was told.

"Always be talking to the horse, softly like, in a low voice and it's best to have a treat, slice of apple maybe. Now, when offering anything to a horse, you must always do it with your palm and fingers flat. We want to keep all our fingers if we can." Evan wiggled his fingers comically at his grandson. Jack vowed not to forget, he wanted to keep all his fingers right where they were.

"If the horse turns away, starts shifting his body away from you, then that's a sign he's not interested, otherwise you can start to scratch and pet him on his neck and flanks. See how that goes before moving higher or touching their head."

Evan made two mock ears with his hands on his head for demonstration. "Now, the pony will subtly tell you if he's not happy with you. The ears are your guides see. If they are up and forward,

51

The dragon under the hill

that's a good sign. It means he's listening to you, he's OK with you there" he made the shape with his hands. "But if he whinnies or his ears are flat against his head" again making the shape, "then that's a horse to step away from."

"Getting the trust of a horse is something that takes time. Just be calm and clear what you are trying to do and you'll be fine. Now, quietly now, go up to old Merlin there and make friends." He pointed to the largest male of the four, "Go on when you're ready, he won't harm you. I'll be here."

Jack walked slowly and cautiously away, trying to remember all his grandfather had taught him. Following the instructions as he remembered them in order, tentatively at first, he soon ended up next to the big animal, happily stroking and scratching the muscly horse, who nuzzled him in return. Jack was elated, not only to feel that connection with this animal he'd been so intimidated by earlier but to have successfully completed his task, learning skills from his grandfather. He spoke in a low voice, telling Merlin that they were now 'mates' and not to forget while stroking and scratching him further, turning to see the old man smiling, the merry lad quickly returned to his waiting grandfather.

"Did you see Grampa? I did as you said. He likes me", said Jack urgently.

"Good lad, good lad", said Evan smiling knowingly. He knew that Merlin's temperament was such that you could fall on him from the sky and the gentle giant would still let you pet him but he was pleased the boy had listened so well.

Following a thoughtful pause, Evan announced "Dinner boyo".

Their welcome lunch consisted of thick sandwiches of fresh sliced egg with pickled beetroot and onions on the side, Welsh cakes and more tea (and the now expected imposed apple). Jack wolfed down his share, while between each tearing

52

mouthful, explaining in great detail to his grandmother this morning's adventures, the things he had learned and his conquest of the cobs, his grandfather nodding jovially in agreement.

The afternoon found them following the flock of sheep to where they were foraging high up the hill a mile or so up the valley from the farmhouse. Jack listened as his tutor explained how to tell if the sheep were healthy and strong from an initial inspection of the flock as a whole. Then, with a speed that surprised jack, the farmer closed the distance between himself and the flock and snared a fleeing ewe with his outstretched crook. Expertly manhandling the struggling sheep, it was immediately subdued and held between his knees resting on its buttocks. Jack was shown how to physically check the wellbeing of the sheep, to check its teeth, legs and hooves for decay. To check the fleece and skin for scab, mange or ticks before the sheep was released, recognising it was no longer held tight the ewe flicked her back legs in derision and quickly joined the flock.

From where they stood, the lesson moved on. How the flock moved up and down the valley looking for the sweetest fresh new grass growth and when they reached an obstacle like a ditch or narrow gap, how the group would manoeuvre, circle and broil around it until just one brave ewe jumped and the rest would effortlessly follow.

Evan knew each ewe by name from birth, remembered how they'd lambed in Spring and which of them would be coming to the end of their time on the farm. Knowing each and every quirk but tending kindly for them all the same. Even he had to admit they were stupid animals, thick headed at times and that blind compulsion to follow the leader was so deeply ingrained and forceful, it was sometimes dangerous. Once, in his youth he saw two sheep walking a cliff edge in single file. The first sheep misjudged the ground and fell over the rocky precipice and despite the fact the second sheep must have seen this happen, it still followed the first and died the same death. Sometimes, he thought

53

that half of Heini's job as a sheep dog was to save the sheep from themselves.

In his simple, immature manner Jack continued to process this relationship these custodians had with their animals. "You seem to really like you animals grampa, do you cry when they have to go to be made into food then?"

"Cry?" Evan replied, "no, I don't cry. I'd be lying if I said when I was a youngster the death of a dog that has been with you since a pup or an old horse didn't pluck at the old heart strings but things are different now. So much has happened and I've seen so much coming and going – it's all part and parcel of what we do see."

Evan related the annual cycle of the life of a sheep farmer to his grandson. Picturing the lean and the plenty, the times when sheep looked after themselves and the perilous times where every waking hour was spent caring for their livelihood. The period they were in now was mostly about keeping an eye on the flock, taking care of the upkeep of the farm and gleaning from the land. The winter months was the real battle ground, a fight against the testing pitiless elements, a back breaking effort to barley keep his animals alive. There was the great winter of 1927, the worst in living memory. Where they were like moles tunnelling through the feet of snow fall to find their animals before they yielded to the horrific temperatures. Some farms never recovered after losing everything in those mighty blizzards. Then came spring and with it lambing, the 'make or break' time for any farm. A disaster in that period could spell the end for even the most established holding. He repeated the old farmer's saying to his grandson, with solemn reflection.

"The old farmers used to say about their flock, 'January thins them, February skins them and March decides who lives or dies'. It can be cruel on these hills at times."

The dragon under the hill

To lighten the mood, he also gave Jack a lesson in the various whistles and shouts that farmers through the centuries had used to communicate their will to their dogs. 'Come by', the signal for 'wheel to the left', 'lay down', 'go behind' and the changes in the whistle pitch for urgent attention. Jack's attempts were shambolic and his toneless whistles just made them both laugh loudly and Heini stand motionless, head to one side, looking very confused indeed.

"Let's sit for a spell before we head home." Evan said pointing with his crook to some large boulders further up the field. As a younger man Evan could run up and down these hills all day, carrying a fully-grown sheep if need be and not tire but as the days wore on he found the increasing need for a rest and the subtle art of pacing himself. He longed for a portion of that youthful vigour and effortless strength back but in deeper thought would not swap it for any of the wonderful days he had spent with his beloved wife on his beloved land.

They sat facing down the hill, with an amazing view up and down the valley and across to the opposite mountain. Jack thought how much the chequered mosaic of farm fields made the whole valley look like a beautiful patchwork quilt, pacifying, soothing and enfolding. He didn't realise there were so many shades of green and browns, how each hue changed as the sun moved across the landscape and as it lowered and the light yellowed, each colour shone with a tint of gold. The cool wind ruffled his hair and feeling calm and peaceful, Jack broke the silence and asked his grandfather something that had been weighing heavy on him.

"Grampa?" plucking up his courage.

"Yes lad?"

There was another pause as Jack ordered the words in his head.

"Why doesn't Nana like me?" He revealed sadly.

Hardly able to hide his surprise, Evan responded, "what on earth would make you think that lad?"

Initially Jack shrugged, Evan just waited patiently. It's not easy for a lot of adults to show enough emotional maturity to put things they have felt into words that another might understand. It is a lot harder again for children and those in adolescence doubly so.

"She's 'hard' in her words and...and didn't like me being asleep, when you were working" said Jack trying to explain. His grandfather waited but that was all the boy could put into words.

"O, boy bach, you couldn't be more wrong, let me tell you now", his grandfather said ever so softly.

"Did you know your Nana spent two entire days baking, cooking and making jam and pickles, all so you would have plenty of lovely things to eat when you got here? She gave the whole house a spring clean and scrubbed every inch of your bedroom on her hands and knees for your arrival. For weeks after she got you mam's letter, she's been telling everyone in the village how her grandson is coming to visit and how pleased she is. Now does that sound like someone who doesn't like you?" Evan asked.

"No" was all Jack could say, now a bit overwhelmed.

"I do know how you could get confused. How my Maggie comes across a lot of the time, doesn't always show her true heart but that's just the way she is. She's never going to be all cwtches and kisses like your mam but believe me, that woman would fight a bear for you (and she'd win). A more loyal and faithful woman, you'll never find lad".

"O right" contemplated the boy, understanding a little bit more.

56

"See those ewes over there?" Evan gestured with his crook. "Their lambs follow them around stumbling about and exploring the field and for the most part the ewe just lets the lamb get on with it, learn for itself like – it might seem a bit hard on the lamb but when he needs her she'll come running, even put herself in harm's way, there is nothing a mother won't do to protect it's young".

"I have to learn Nan's ways – how she's different to mam, is what you are saying" said Jack trying to verbalise his grasp of the patient explanation he was getting.

"Aye, lad, give a little thought to what is behind what she says." Evan looked around him for another example. All those years of teaching his own children about life and people, through the patterns of nature was a real skill that was coming back to him now.

Pointing to a bird soaring through the valley, Evan asked "Do you know what kind of bird that is?"

Jack squinted into the sky, he thought it was some kind of bird of prey but he wasn't certain. "Dad said I might see a red kite or kestrel while I am here."

"As it happens it is a kestrel, you can tell just by the way it hovers." He relayed.

"Oh, is it?", replied the impressed boy.

"Now come breeding time, she'll have 4-6 eggs and she'll sit on those eggs and won't move a muscle for weeks, very devoted, until they hatch. Then she'll join her partner in spending most of the daylight finding food for the noisy open-mouthed chicks, who are always hungry and crying out for more. Due to one thing or another usually only one or two will make it and by and by, well, there'll come a time when these chicks are ready to fly off but the nest is nice and cosy see, very comfortable, so the

The dragon under the hill

chicks don't want to leave - no motivation for them to fly off lad. So, do you know what the mother bird does?" queried Evan.

"No, Grampa" came the quick response.

"She pushes those chicks out of that nest, forcing them out one by one, whether they want to go or no. They have to fly then. Their mum knows they will and they always do. It might seem cruel at the time to the fledgling bird but it's the best for it in the long run." Evan made his final point "so, never forget your Nana and I love you very much and are happy to see you here, however it might feel at the time."

Jack nodded. The message was now drummed home, the subject exhausted by both parties the boy decided to re-visit another topic.

"And Grampa?" they locked eyes, "what are these legends you mentioned before?"

"Ach!" was the exasperated reply and he stood up, "it's getting late. Mags will be wondering where we are." And with that he was gone and the answers with him.

On entering the farmhouse Jack rushed up to his grandmother and embraced her tightly. "Thank you for having me and all your lovely cooking." Evan smiled to himself.

Although she did not reciprocate the surprise embrace, it warmed her core, she patted his head gently. "Sit down then."

On the table was a heavy metal pot full of rich thick rabbit stew, with onions, carrots, potato, leeks and barley to thicken. It wasn't Jack's first experience of rabbit; he'd always thought it a dry meat and wasn't overly fond but this was another level of flavour. The dark rabbit had imbibed the juices of the stock, while the heady mix of fragrant herbs made this dish something special. He'd polished off two large bowlfuls with accompanying slices of

The dragon under the hill

buttered bread before he paused to relate, in breathless speed, the events of the latter half of the day to his listening grandmother.

Without noticing, they had covered miles walking over the uneven terrain in the fresh air and with the very early morning and a bloated satisfied stomach full of stew, it was a short time before it all caught up with the young lad and presently he fell asleep, resting on the also sleeping dog. Both curled up in front of the fire. His amused grandparents left him there for a while, finding themselves trying to stifle their laughter before his grandfather lifted the limb frame into his arms and carried him upstairs still dead to the world and put him straight to bed.

Murky deep darkness faced him, when Jack awoke at some random hour of the night. One thought screaming out for his attention, he desperately and immediately needed to pee. It was an unusual occurrence for him but he had been drinking copious amounts of tea all day, he reminded himself keeping up with his grandfather. As any other boy in the world would, before getting out of his cosy warm bed and going to the outside toilet, he first considered any alternate options. Could he wee out of the window? Apart from being an awkward height, he wasn't sure what was below and didn't want to pee on the washing line or some poor, unsuspecting farmyard animal, whose only crime was picking the wrong spot to lay his head down for the night. The jug was already full of clean water and the bowl was out because what if his Nana saw it first thing when she came to wake him? Short of wetting the bed, only the worst and least desirable option was left to him.

His eyes now accustomed to the dim light meant he didn't need to fumble for the candle stub. He slipped out of bed, the bare floor boards initially cold against his naked feet, which woke him further from his drowsy state. He crept as quietly as he could down stairs and before leaving the farmhouse donned his coat and rubber boots. It was a short, straight but urgent run to the outside toilet, where the boy used sound only to aim as he finally happily

The dragon under the hill

relived himself, and relief it certainly was. Exiting the tiny outhouse, closing the toilet door behind him, Jack lined up his trajectory ready to scamper back indoors but something in his thoughts, something like the feeling you get when someone is watching you, called out him to look up to the hilltop and in the direction of the stony cairn.

Not quite as defined as his first night, the stones were still finely silhouetted and stood out against the moonlight, ever imposing as before. Jack looked and continued to wonder about their mysterious story but just as he was about to turn away and head back, a stone moved. His instinct was to flee but he was transfixed, his stomach fluttered as he strained to see.

What he had thought was a stone, on further consideration had a more distinctive shape, was now stood on the apex of the cairn. From this distance and in this light, it was hard to make out exactly what it was. He strained and squinted moving his head to change the angle. Not able to work out any definition within the shape he concentrated on the space around it, the contours left by the profiled outline. Jack remembered what he had been told about evil old Cymro roaming the area and tried to fit that figure to what he could see. It could be the size of a big dog but looked bigger. It wasn't easy to judge but it seemed to be structured differently, a different shape, sharper in its edges, more angular, longer…then it was gone. Even though Jack was looking directly at it, staring intently at the vision, it had disappeared without him registering movement or catching any residue. It was a haunting experience.

Jack stood there for what seemed like hours, on edge hoping to catch another glimpse but saw nothing else. The cold seeping through him and the unease induced by the spectre, drove him back inside the farmhouse at pace and back to sanctuary of his bed.

The dragon under the hill

It was Sunday. The Lord's day. Which was the only day that offered any deviation from farming's routine and it meant a traditional large roast dinner; the vegetables for which Maggie prepared the night before, taking most of the evening. In real terms it also meant a less active day on the farm and the possibility of an afternoon nap, although certain chores had to be done every day. Usually for Jack and school children up and down the land, Sunday evening meant his weekly bath in the family tin bath in front of the fire and he considered himself lucky if he was only second or third into the water. Before all that though, Sunday was chapel and Chapel meant 'Sunday best' clothes. Jack found his grandfather's impatient struggles with his button on collar greatly amusing and was a source of much joy that someone else found the dressing up as uncomfortable as he did.

Under his grandfather's supervision, Jack had proudly coaxed Merlin in from the field the old steed shared with the other horses and harnessed the docile Welsh cob to the little cart, which was a surprisingly complicated affair. After a quick check and tightening of buckles, looking very much the part dressed in their best clothes, two generations of the James family were off, with Heini in the back, wanted or not.

Like most population groups at that time, large or small, life and love revolved around chapel. This was even more true of Wales. The famous 1904 revival led by Evan Roberts had started humbly in tiny Loughor near Swansea but had swept through the land like a holy pandemic for a year and a half. During this time lives were radically changed, communities born afresh and a quarter of a nation found God and added their numbers to the already blessed hundreds of thousands of 'chapel goers'. It is said sporting events were not held that year, publicans complained at the loss of revenue, criminality dwindled and even pit ponies stopped working because they could not understand the instructions given to them without the profanity that usual peppered it. The ripples of those events, even over one hundred years on, are still felt in the land, if only now in regret of how times have changed and what was lost. Congregations are now small and aged, chapels converted to flats and carpet warehouses, their influence dwindling and marginalised and when such an important hub in a community is lost, then the heart of the community is not far behind.

Many, many churches and chapels were seeded in that short time, paid for community and Zoar in Rhywle was one of them. It was not only the spiritual but emotional heart of the area. It was where people communed, shared in their faith and all too often idle gossip. New dresses or the latest hats were shown with secretive pride, comfort given in need and sometimes a shared glance would spark into young love. It was where children were dedicated, lovers married and the final goodbye respectfully said.

The little country chapel was smaller than the Baptist church Jack attended with his family back home in Merthyr Tydfil and was not dominated by the massive pipes of a church organ. It still had the same musty smell, white washed walls, lofty balustraded pulpit and dark wooden pews with little doors at the end. Everyone was met at the entrance by a chapel deacon, rotund and jovial, who shook their hands firmly, exchanged greetings and gave everyone a small, green half brick-thick hymn book.

Pews like these were ever present and a staple of places of worship the land over and were notoriously uncomfortable. A lengthy service often left an aching back and sore buttocks. Idris had told Jack that they were specially designed that way, as your discomfort kept you alert and more specifically to stop older folk and those inclined from falling asleep during the sermon. Although it seemed little hindrance to the grey bearded elder in their home chapel, Mr Fox, whose intermittent snorts after he'd obviously

62

nodded off, were a source of great delight and amusement to Jack and his older brother during the sermon.

Regular churchgoers tend to be creatures of habit and will sit in exactly the same spot for decades, even a lifetime. The spot may offer better acoustics, be warmer or allow a swifter exit or just be the first place they sat the first time the visited. Whatever the preference, habits are soon formed and with them unwritten rules, woe betide an intruder in a long-claimed spot. The James family was no different and positioned themselves accordingly. Once he had followed his grandparents into their chosen pew and were as comfortably seated as was possible to be in these stalls, Jack inspected the hymn book to see if it included any he recognised or even ones he enjoyed singing. To the boy's shock and disappointment, the entire book and its contents were in Welsh and worse was to come, the whole proceeding service was also completely in Welsh.

Children are taught Welsh in school but if you don't speak a language regularly it's near impossible to develop any real fluency. Jack's school-boy language knowledge meant he understood one word in five but not enough to really follow the passionate sermon nor enough to ease his now grumpy dislocated mood. No thought or concession was made for him or any form of translation offered.

The heritage and importance of the Welsh language to its people cannot be overstated and is supported throughout the country with vigour and passion, even by those who don't nor will ever will actually speak it. It is intrinsically linked to the identity of a small but proud nation. However, the truth remains that while in North and West Wales, Welsh is still the first language of a number of its residents - in the industrial populated South, mainly English is spoken as the first language. This means not only is Welsh relegated to a second language by the majorly populated areas but being taught in schools is often the only contact some ever have with it used conversationally.

Jack found the experience painful but finally, and not a moment too soon for the alienated lad, the last hymn was sung, again unaccompanied by music and a deep booming voice of one of the older men closed the service in rumbling prayer, with all the congregation joining in on the 'Amen'.

Filing outside into the court yard, loosening ties and donning caps, the 'second service' begun. The quiet reverence of the meeting was exchanged for an explosion of conflicting noise and voices as people greeted others they had missed earlier and little groups were formed. Friends chatted about the 'good word' the Reverend had given and those who had news or stories shared with others they may not have seen in a while. Jack was quite an attraction, introduced to every single member in turn by name and never in his life had he had his hair ruffled or his facial features inspected so intently and so often.

"O, doesn't he look like his dad?"

"Well, he's got his mother's eyes if you ask me."

"He needs feeding up Maggie, he's skin and bones."

"Now be a good boy for your grandparents, is it?"

Commented the ladies of the fellowship dressed in their home-made floral fabric dresses, pinned on hats and walking Oxford shoes. They cooed, coddled and fussed. The gentlemen were polite but rather less attentive, extending to Jack either a finger crushing handshake or just a curt nod. A few times he was asked his age and when he told them, received a slow "hmm" in response, marking the end of the conversation.

"And what do you want to be when you grow up?" was another multiple enquiry. Jack knew he didn't want to work in the tannery like his dad or join the army as his brother planned but other than knowing things he didn't want to do, he had not given much thought to what he saw himself doing when older. So, he

The dragon under the hill

would simply reply "I don't know". Not even the most vivid of imaginations or best of forecasters could have foretold that a mere half a dozen years later that slight young lad, full of innocence and naivety, would be staring out over a troubled midnight sea listening out for distant explosions, the clouds being momentarily ignited with flashing of horror. Standing on the deck of a supply ship, inching nervously through the perilous Atlantic supply route as part of the embattled country's great Merchant navy in the midst of the horror of a world at war.

Slowly, as time wore on, the after-service communion started to draw to an obvious close and people started to drifted away, with plans made to see each other soon, cheery goodbyes and 'God bless'. The numbers quietly petered out, winding their way homeward. It was then that Jack was introduced to the Reverend Thomas.

"Ah, you must be David and Bronwyn's middle son John?" said the Reverend with a huge smile. "You won't remember me because you were no more than a tot last time I saw you. How are you liking the farm so far?"

Although in slight awe of the becollared figure, Jack immediately liked the clergyman and felt happier to speak to him than anyone he'd met that day.

After some thought Jack announced, "It is very different from Dowlais in Merthyr, so much lovely space. I've learned about horses and sheep. Yesterday we saw a kestrel and Grampa said I could shoot his gun". Behind the talking pair Maggie shot Evan a horrified and furious glare, to which he responded by shaking his head and shrugging innocently, as if to say, 'I don't know what the boy is talking about'.

"This morning I got old Merlin in from the field all by myself and harnessed him to the cart. I do sometimes miss my mates for playing but Nana gives me lots of tasty things to eat."

The dragon under the hill

"You are right there lad," concurred Reverend Thomas, "there many a lady in these valleys who pride themselves on being a good cook, one an expert in baking, one stews, another at preserves but they all bow down to our Mags."

"O, Rhodri!" exclaimed Maggie, "never mind your nonsense. You'll be having a burned offering for dinner if we stand around here talking all day."

Rhodri gave Jack a sheepish look, like a naughty schoolboy, punished but unrepentant. "Yes, Mags" he added playfully.

"On we go then," Evan concluded. "John, jump in the back of the cart, keep Heini company while Rhodri bach rides with us. He needs Maggie to keep him in check, see he behaves himself", he joked.

Jack rather enjoyed sitting in the back holding the dog and letting his legs dangle over the dropped board. It was a different way of seeing the world, not being concerned with what's ahead or their nearness to their destination, just happy to be. Enjoying his immediate surroundings for what they were. Noting wild flowers in the hedgerow of yellow, white and purple; diverse types of leaves as plants invisibly jostled for the light and catching the tones of the country birds and their accompanying songs.

From time to time he could hear the adult's conversation and sporadic laughter – he had certainly seen a different side of both his grandparents around the Reverend Thomas.

Ordered to change his clothes as soon as they got home, Jack spent some time playing fetch with Heini and feeding the geese, all the while keeping a sly eye on the stony cairn, the events of last night very much still in the forefront of his thoughts.

Maggie, true to the Reverend's word, produced an abundant feast for their dinner. Serving dishes piled high with crisp and fluffy roast potatoes, parsnips and sweet roast onions, boiled new potatoes dripping in sage butter, carrots, runner beans, sprouts, peas and centre stage was a roast leg of lamb, studded with rosemary sprigs, perfectly cooked, it's tender juiciness clear to see as it was expertly carved. There was even a choice to pour over rich thick gravy, oozing bread sauce or mint sauce made fresh from the herb garden. The quality and enjoyment of the beautiful fare was matched by the old friend's conversation and gentle teasing which Jack was pleased to just listen to while devouring his share, his lips glistening with the sweet fat from the meat.

"Is...is that rhubarb crumble?" asked an excited Jack, when his grandmother pulled the dish, with its golden knobbly crust, from the oven and placed it on the table.

"Yes, it's a bit hot yet", came his grandmother's reply.

Jack felt almost moved to tears. "Aw Nana," he couldn't stop himself exclaiming, "rhubarb crumble is my very favourite. Oh, I love crumble!" Staring at the dish, owlish in his unblinking focus, as if still deciding if this beautiful apparition was real or not. To the amusement of the others, lad's gaze didn't move from this fare through the whole time it was being prepared, divided up and dished out

When the anticipation spawned from the sight and mouth-watering smell was over and he finally got to plunge his spoon into his bowlful, smothered in steaming custard and taste the crumble, the youngster was in heaven. Savouring the wonderful contrast between the softened tart rhubarb and the crunchy sweet topping, lingering on every satisfying mouthful, trying to make it last as long as he could. Purposefully licking his spoon clean as the sticky delicious topping cemented to it. If his stomach hadn't already been fit to bursting he could have happily eaten the lot.

After their meal, Maggie busied herself organising and storing away the leftovers, cleaning and washing up in the kitchen,

67

The dragon under the hill

refusing all offers of help and assistance, however well-meant or insistent they were. Evan soon succumbed to nature and a full stomach and quietly nodded off in his chair by the fire with a motionless dog at his feet, leaving the boy and his new-found friend alone to talk.

The Reverend gave Jack a synopsis of this morning's sermon when he realised the boy spoke little Welsh and they talked about the boy's family in some detail, about life in Merthyr and for the first time Jack was asked about things he liked. They also established that the lad preferred to be called 'Jack' to which the Reverend agreed.

During a natural pause in the discourse, Jack felt confident enough to quiz their guest regarding a burning question.

"What are the legends about that old hill, grandpa won't say?"

"Hill?" echoed the clergyman.

"Yes, with the cairn at the top there", said jack pointing.

Reverend Thomas nodded, thoughtfully, then said "Maggie. John and I are going for a stroll, walk off your lovely dinner."

"So be it," she said without turning around "take the dog with you, She's getting lazy in her old age."

For a long time no one spoke as they slowly walked up the lane, Heini investigating interesting smells up and down the hedgerow on her own mission.

"Jack lad, I love history, I love folklore, myths, legends, tales and stories. History is a great passion of mine and this beautiful country of ours has a depth of history like few others and it is so important young folk like you learn these things and don't

The dragon under the hill

let them die. So, you maybe sorry you asked as, if you aren't careful I will bore you for hours on local history.

"Now then, before we start, word to the wise, you mustn't talk about any of this around your grandfather, he really doesn't like it. Understand?" said the Reverend conspiratorially.

"But, why?" Insisted Jack.

"Hmm…we'll come to that later Jack, m'lad." They walked further while he thought out loud "where to start…where to start?". Coming to a decision he continued. "You know that the Welsh are descendants of the Celts, who were the original inhabitants of Britain?"

Having been taught something similar in school, Jack nodded, inspiring the explanation to continue.

"For thousands of years creatures and people have lived in these valleys, eking out a living. These people at some point started taming animals, raising crops, developing, building homes, having families and living and dying. Most of it we imagine fairly dull and mundane but interesting, exciting and sometimes brutal things must have happened too. As at the time nobody wrote anything down we have little knowledge of what went on but there are stories that have survived through the years through word of mouth, tradition and place names.

You live in Merthyr Tydfil, which as you would have been taught is Welsh for Martyr Tydfil. The story goes that sometime around the fifth century, she was one of many children of a local King. I think his name was…Brychan. Now Tydfil was one of a group of kind hearted Christians who travelled the area offering help and healing treatment to the needy people in the Taff valley. One day, she and her family were attacked and robbed by a band of marauding Picts, who brutally killed her while she prayed. Her father and brothers later caught up with the bandits and slaughtered them but too late for gentle Tydfil. Later, a church was

69

The dragon under the hill

built at the spot she was slain and the town grew from there that is named after her. Now, we know all this because a bit later, monks thought it important enough to write it down and because of that these writings can be read later by us and we get an accurate account of what went on.

Now, other stories didn't get written down but just passed from one generation to another verbally and in the process of retelling, they inevitably get changed, embellished or even forgotten. So, all these years on the actual truth is anyone's guess.

Take your hill for example and that stony cairn you are so curious about. Some say it's the burial place of an ancient Celtic king, others that it's the tumble down remains of a bygone chieftain's fort but the oldest legend says it's the lair of one of the last dragons in Wales. We'll never really know for sure but most legends, even the most fanciful have a seed of truth in them somewhere. My guess, it's a burial mound of some kind and they only ever did that for nobleman."

"Dragons, really?" interrupted Jack.

"Oh, Welsh custom and folklore is swarming with dragons. Dragons fighting under mountains causing castles to crumble, which is supposedly where the Red Dragon on the Welsh flag comes from. Dragons changing form, dragons living in lakes, dragons creating mountain ranges or their skin folds actually being the hills themselves. Well, even this farm's name is 'hill of the dragon' in Welsh and it's been called that since before your grandfather's great grandfather was born."

"Now what the dragon represents is another thing, could be just a way of portraying things they didn't understand or something shaped by fears and ignorance or maybe there really was some beast around then. It's unlikely but possible, like I said a lot of these legends have a seed of truth/"

They stopped at an attractive vantage point. The Reverend Thomas took off his black jacket and placed it on the grass, gesturing to the boy to sit on it and share it with him.

"Beautiful here, eh lad?" mused the Reverend, Jack nodded, it was beautiful.

"I love this farm and your grandparents are my most cherished friends," said the Reverend, "In fact, I've known your grandfather since we were tots. We ran every inch of these hills as kids", he chuckled to himself as a wash of nostalgia covered him with snapshots of memories nipping, "dur, we got into some scrapes. There was the summer I broke my arm (it still hurts in the winter) after I fell out of a tree we were racing up and the trouble we got in for sneaking a jar of Evan's grandmother's jam and eating it in the barn was legendary. Many a'night we spent out here sleeping under the stars, camping out. Our 'tent' was only one of my mam's old bedsheets strung up but we thought it was great at the time. We went to lessons side by side, sat next to each other at Sunday school and later church. In fact, the only time we spent apart when I went to seminary. I was there when he met Mags, duw, I even married them. I was there when your father and your aunty Cerys were born and throughout them growing up. He's been my best and closest friend for nigh on fifty years and in all that time I only saw him cry or lose his temper once.

You must never mention you know this, like I said before…Now then, he must have been younger than you maybe 9 or 10, we were having lessons from a travelling tutor in the village – that was how it was then, there was no school here as such in those days. During break, your grandfather started telling me how he had investigated some funny movement he'd seen on top of the hill the night before and when he got near he saw a shape moving and crept closer. Now he reckons it wasn't any animal he'd seen before and when he glimpsed it and it moved into the moonlight, he said it looked like the shape of a small, quite real dragon. Anyway, we didn't realise two of the older boys,

71

clueless thugs they were known for being, were eavesdropping and they pounced on Evan. Laughing at him, calling him a liar and a big baby, started pushing him around and trying to force him to say he was a liar, making up stories, dragons weren't real and to take it back, real nasty like. In the end your grandfather lost his temper and gave them each a clout, knocked them both down, despite their size advantage, even broke one of their noses. It upset him though, he ran home crying.

It took years before he really got over it. As it seemed every time he thought people had finally forgotten, some cruel kid would tease him about it again. We hardly spoke about his 'dragon' ever again." Rhodri concluded forlornly.

"Oh," replied Jack, processing all this information. Feeling he could trust this man he revealed his own secret.

"Reverend Thomas, I think I saw it too", wanting to tell the events as accurately as possible, Jack took his time.

"Last night it was, I'm not sure what time but we had all been asleep for hours. I was coming back from the outside loo when I looked up and one of the stones moved. Well, I thought it was a stone until it moved you see and then it jumped right on top so I could see the outline. But tummy was all butterflies it was." Now drawing a picture with his hands. "It definitely wasn't that old Cymro, it was long - not stocky, had sharper edges, pointy like. I couldn't make out what it was for certain and it was gone so quickly but it could have been...I'm not lying, honest I'm not." He added.

"I believe you son." Responded Rhodri.

"Really?", replied a surprised Jack.

"O aye, I believe you saw something. What you saw last night and your grandfather saw all those years ago, well I can't say. Do I believe you saw a dragon?...Honestly, no, I don't. At that

72

distance, in that kind of light, who knows what it actually was. What I do know is you must never go up there looking, especially at night...promise me?"

Jack nodded.

"Good lad." said the minister through a warm smile.

"Dur, all this talking has made me thirsty. Let's go and nag your grandmother for a cup of tea, is it?" Rhodri said, getting up and collecting his jacket.

Jack felt a tinge of guilt as they walked back. He had made a promise to his new friend the Reverend, how could he not have but he knew he would soon break it.

The dragon under the hill

Chapter 7

The following two nights were rainy, overcast and the ground wet and slippery, no good for carrying out the lad's plan but as evening closed on the third night the sky was clear. The moon was already visible and bright, one by one stars were appearing everywhere. The constellations vibrant and pin-point, Orion, Lyra and Cassiopeia; Andromeda, Pleiades and The Plough shone out.

Unlike previous nights, he did not change out of his clothes when he got into his bedroom but wore them under the bedclothes, just in case either of his grandparents looked in on him on their way to bed. Jack waited in the darkness of his room for what seemed an eternity before he heard his grandparents climb the stairs and go into their room. Now even more patience was required – the boy waited for as long as he possibly could for his grandparents to drop off to sleep, before quietly and nervously getting out of bed. Taking great care not to awaken the traitorous squeaky floorboards he crept to the door his footfall gentle and soft.

After tiptoeing downstairs, he crept into the pantry and located his handkerchief full of leftover pieces of roast lamb he'd previously stashed there. He did wake up Heini but on recognising who was making the noise she showed little further interest. Soon his gum boots were on and he was out the door starting the tricky ascent up the hill.

Things look and feel so very different in the dark, distances become harder to judge, open fields become menacing and each footfall treacherous. While the normally enchanting sound of the wind in the trees becomes haunting and eerie. All putting the errant boy ill at ease. He had mentally mapped out the best path to the summit during the day but found it a struggle to

74

find. The lack of light made it difficult for him to find a clear path upward and he often had to veer off to get around an obstacle.

During the long climb, the ground made deceitful by the dim lighting, Jack had a long time alone with his thoughts and troublesome doubts. On at least three occasions he stopped suddenly having decided to turn back but persuaded himself to continue, searing his nagging conscience. He desperately wanted to stick to his grandfather's rules and hated breaking his promise to the Reverend Thomas but he simply had to know what he had seen that night. Scenarios played in his head, his grandfather's disappointed face, his grandmother's stern incredulous chastening 'What did he think he was doing that time of night, he could have been hurt or killed?'; 'What had possessed the boy to act so foolishly?'; what the betrayed Reverend's face would look like and what his parents would say and do to him if he was sent home early - how he would have wilfully disobeyed and let so many people down. It was almost too much for the boy to bare, yet he forged onward.

Heavily conflicted and still wrestling with his choices he finally reached the edge of the small odd shaped field that held the time trodden cairn. To his young eyes, it looked just like a ramshackle chaotic pile of rocks but there were sections where some order remained, that seemed to have some intelligent design behind it. Some remnant that hinted at what it once was. It was definitely very old and the land had reclaimed much of it already. It was partially surrounded by some of the ugliest, hobbled trees he had seen. All battered and twisted from the weather, callused due to exposure.

Picking his way through a gap, entering the clearing Jack was hyper alert. He forced his eyes as far open as they would go to be able to catch the slightest of movements. Focusing mostly on the apex of the cairn where he'd seen the creature stand, nearing, getting a better idea of its scale, at its highest point the cairn was taller than Jack by a foot at least. He listened intently

The dragon under the hill

trying to pick up any sound that would intimate even the tiniest movement. Trying to shut out the wind and its effects on the grass, trees and their leaves, even holding his breath for periods as not to make a sound himself. When he felt he could stand still no longer he decided to pass the point of no return and tentatively approach the cairn.

With his grandfather's words now loudly resounding, warning how dangerous the ground was, the hidden caves and overgrown potholes, he gingerly stepped forward. Testing each footfall a couple of times before putting his full weight on it. Slowly, he crept forward, all the time keeping alert, scanning around and with an escape route in mind. All the time fighting back the clawing unease that the eeriness night brought.

Snap! The boy's heart jumped, his breath stolen from him. In his deep concentration it had sounded like the loudest noise in the world but once over the initial shock he realised he had simply stepped on a twig, snapping it. Jack stopped exactly where he was and waited – if there was anything here, it certainly knew of his approach now.

Stealthily continuing his advance, he eventually reached the mystical cairn. In the dim light, it was difficult to make out much more detail, where or how deep the gaps in the stones went. He inspected it as hard as he could, looking for any markings or signs of recent activity but could see nothing out of the ordinary. Carefully, picking a flat stone, he pulled out his laden handkerchief and placed it on the stone, opening it exposing the meat.

It felt like he had hardly pulled the blankets up under his chin and closed his eyes when his grandmother called him to get up. Dawn had not yet arrived. Yawning profusely, he stumbled downstairs to meet those waiting, he was exhausted. No longer afforded the luxury of a lie-in, he was truly part of the club now and the expectation that came with it. There was normally little said at this early hour. Evan had learned long ago that others, including his wife, did not share his morning brightness, so curbed himself until breakfast. So, they drank their tea quietly, Jack trying to stifle yawn after yawn.

After Jack had laid out the handkerchief with the lamb pieces on it the previous night, he had tiptoed back to the field's edge being very deliberate to retrace his steps and watched the stones as long as he dared. Disappointed and discouraged, he had made his way home and went straight to his bed having experienced nothing to add to his previous sighting.

Through the chores, helping his grandfather, breakfast, what turned out to be a beautiful morning and even through lunch; Jack said little. He felt deeply guilty that he had disobeyed his grandfather and broken a rule. Doubts and accusations voiced themselves and hounded him – what if he had fallen and got hurt or what if he had got caught? And like everyone sporting a guilty conscience, there was a nagging fear that his grandparents knew what he had done and he didn't want to spark them remember to chastise him by saying the wrong thing. He feared that Evan was just waiting for the worst possible moment, when he least suspected it, to confront him and send him home with his tail between his legs.

They had spent the best part of the afternoon repairing one of the snaking dry-stone walls marking the boundary of the farm, which was an ancient expert skill in itself. He watched intently as his grandfather would run his measured eye across the wall, pick up a stone from the pile and roll it around in his hands deliberately, checking it from every angle and sizing every edge, before discarding out of hand and doing the same with another. On odd occasions the stone would be whacked hard with a trowel along some invisible fault line and the stone would split or a jagged edge fly off. This process was repeated until a suitable candidate was found, which to Jack's eye looked no different to the ones

The dragon under the hill

thought unsuitable and it was nestled in the gap in the wall. By the time he stood back to check the fit, the stone looked like it had been there all along. It was not a speedy process but the dexterous repair was indistinguishable from any other part by the end. When completed, Evan announced it was time for their evening meal. Starting their significant walk back, Evan sent Heini on, then looked down and addressed the lad. "You've been very quiet today boy" he stated in a questioning manner.

"Tired I am, Grampa", came the reply.

"O, is it?...Aye lad, farming life does take a lot of getting used to," conceded the old man.

"Yes Grampa".

"Listen lad" Evan started, "your grandmother wanted me to talk to you about something."

Jack panicked! This was it, what he had been fearing. Both his grandparents had known this whole time and this was where they would confront him, get upset and send him home. It was all Jack could do to stop himself shaking and blurting out a profusion of apologies. He painfully met his grandfather's gaze as he continued and braced himself.

"Your grandmother was cleaning your room this morning, very thorough is our Maggie, every nook and cranny, nothing gets missed. When she moved your bed to clean, she found a brown paper bag with what looked like over four pounds of apples in it – there was even green one which we don't grow here, so you must have brought that one with you. Now I've seen you eat apples in a pie and the like, so what's the story boy?" he said kindly.

Jack was awash with relief as the reveal of this particular secret, although embarrassing, was nothing compared to what he had recently done. He did not want his grandfather to think less of him but wanting to be honest and as this was the least of his

The dragon under the hill

current guilts, he opened up. Explaining to his grandfather how it felt to him to break the skin of apples with his teeth, the trepidation and obstacle a simple apple was to him and normally his brother Idris would look after him and slice, quarter or even peel his apple for him with his penknife. He described how his parents didn't understand and that he was frightened that his grandparents would take the same view. Being brought up never to waste food he couldn't bring himself to throw them away, so he'd been stashing them until an idea of what to do with them came to him.

"O, is it? Right." Evan bounced back, giving him time to think.

Evan considered his response carefully and then placed his hand gently on the boy's shoulder. "Well lad, I must confess I've never heard that one before in all my years but you must never be frightened to tell us anything. We will always support you and look after you. Whatever it is we'll always listen and find a solution. You must know that?"

"Yes, Grampa".

"Thought you were going to start your own grocers shop lad, contaminated with a Merthyr apple as well." He joked, releasing the tension.

They enjoyed an exquisite meal of leek and potato pie, which was a banquet in itself. It's creamy filling held the softest potatoes, sweet carrots and chunks of tasty leek all in a thick pastry crust. Jack loved the underside of the crust where it had been most in contact with the filling and gone soggy, absorbing the flavour. While Maggie dished out dessert, which just happened to be apple tart with cool cream, Evan winked at the nervous Jack and spoke to his wife.

"We have solved the mystery of the little apple squirrel Mags"

"O, right" she responded, the clattering of dishes stopped. Maggie gave her hands a wipe on her apron and sat down, giving the situation her full attention.

Evan then went on to relate almost word for word what his grandson had explained to him and reiterated his response, Jack should never be frightened to talk to them about anything.

Jack was touched, not only by the fact that this particular adult had listened to what he had to say so intently and given his words such importance, he could repeat them and their sentiment almost word for word hours later. Also, by the fact he was not mocked or dismissed out of hand.

In a rare moment of openness and tenderness, Maggie reached over and took the young boy by the hand meeting his gaze.

"That's right...Jack" she called him for the first time, "they say honesty is the best policy but to us, it's the only policy. Always tell the truth whatever the cost and we won't be angry with you. Fair?"

Jack nodded.

She smiled "I think I know what you mean about biting apples. I hate the feeling of squeezing wire wool when scrubbing something. When the strands grate against each other...oo it goes right through me, makes my very teeth itch it does." Even speaking these words made her shudder.

"Well, I've got a right twp pair here haven't I?" interjected Evan (in Welsh 'twp' means 'simple' but can be used affectionately). They laughed together.

Despite what he considered a near miss earlier, Jack still snuck out again in the middle of the night and ascended the hill. All he found was his handkerchief exactly where he had left it but the lamb was gone. Replacing the bait, he told himself it could have been eaten by a fox, a badger, crows, a whole myriad of creatures, even old Cymro but he couldn't stop himself from feeling deep down, it was a sign.

The dragon under the hill

Chapter 8

Jack was raised from his slumber by Maggie's impatient call but he found out that not only was it slightly later in the morning than they normally rose but that he and his grandmother were alone.

"Where's Grampa?" Jack asked scratching.

"Oh, he's had to go into the village this morning to run some errands. He won't be long, back about lunchtime." His grandmother informed. "You'll be helping me this morning, when you're ready."

Despite his initial reluctance, Jack quite enjoyed spending the time alone with his grandmother. While his grandfather was like a walking, talking part of the land itself, knowing the answer to any question about it and anything that walked, crawled or grew on it, burrowed under it or flew over it; his grandmother had her own old-world depth of knowledge and cunning.

She knew where the wily old hens were going to lay their eggs to collect them but when it came to collecting goose eggs, it was more about timing than location, making sure they were far away to avoid a noisy remonstrations and angry pecking. She explained how to identify different herbs and the uses they had beyond flavouring food. Herbs to mix into the pig's feed because she'd noticed the sow had a bloated stomach, how to remove different types of stains from clothing during washing and in the vegetable patch around the back of the farmhouse, she was queen. With skill and much success, she grew onions, potatoes, parsnips, carrots and leeks, spring onions, swede and runner beans, garden peas and cabbage; and instigating a smile on Jack's face the unmistakable huge coarse leaves of large rhubarb plants, broad and shading. Weeding and tending her crops

The dragon under the hill

masterfully, she rotated them like an orchestral conductor during the finest of symphonies.

Pulling a leaf from a nearby plant in her herb section, she passed it to Jack. "Smell this. You should be able to tell what it is"

"It's mint", the boy quickly replied, immediately recognising the strong scent.

"The problem with mint", Maggie said waving her hand over the area covered with the plant, "is not so much growing it but stopping it growing. If you let it, it will take over everywhere. You have to keep it in check." With that same knowledge, she talked about the sage, rosemary, thyme, parsley, horseradish, basil, dill and garlic. The best conditions to grow them and how she used them in her famous cooking.

"Nearly everything we eat is provided by this land or the surrounding farms, like milk, butter and cheese from the Bennett's farm next door. We have to buy flour, sugar, salt and a few other things but not a great deal." Maggie took obvious pride in their sustainability.

Afterwards, she took him to the stream to show him where water cress could be gathered, pointing out on their journey wild garlic unmistakably filling the air with its aroma; senna whose seeds can be useful for easing constipation; lavender which she liked to flatten between clothing and bedding after they were washed and put away, St. John's Wort and wild hyssop both of which can help people sleep but the latter must never be touched by a lady with child; she knew where each grew in nature and what each could be used for. Knowledge that only came from decades of walking hand in hand with the land.

They prepared and ate a lunch of thick cut cheese sandwiches with pickles and they laughed together when Maggie caught herself half way through automatically forcing an apple on

83

The dragon under the hill

the boy. They made two spare rounds for Evan who had not yet returned and wrapped them tightly in brown paper.

Using the single hand axe, Jack was busy splitting the smaller logs, set aside for the fire and repeating the process to make thin sticks. He'd been shown earlier to be very careful to keep his fingers away from the blade, tapping the top of the wood with the axe head until it imbedded, allowing the wood to be lifted with the axe and then driving it down into the stump. These smaller sticks would be put on top of the kindling, whole or snapped in half, to start off the fire.

Engrossed in his chore, he didn't notice the horse and cart had entered the courtyard, pulling up near the farmhouse, until Heini appeared, bounding from behind him to be fussed.

"Hello Grampa." Jack said excitedly, ready to launch into a narration of the morning's events.

"Boy", came the curt and serious reply as his grandfather stepped down from the cart. It was obvious that something had occurred to upset him. "Unhitch the horse and take him to the field. I need to speak to your grandmother."

"Mags?" He shouted entering the house, "you won't believe…" then the door slammed shut, so that was all Jack heard of the conversation.

He tried to rush his chore to find out what was going on but haste only made the straps slip and the latches more difficult. By the time Jack had unbuckled the horse from its trappings and put them all away, secured the cart, led Merlin out of the courtyard to the start of the fields and got back, his grandfather was just finishing up his lunch. There did seem to be a slight atmosphere but he had missed whatever drama there was.

"I'll grab my gun and see if the boy and I can't bag a few rabbits, Mags." Evan said chewing his last mouthful.

84

"Be careful then." Was his wife's response.

Jack watched quietly with fascination as his grandfather reached under the ornate Welsh dresser which held all the plates and crockery and pulled out a long wide wooden case, darkened with age. Placing it on the table, on paper Maggie had already laid down in an automatic response. He unlocked the side catches with a loud click and opened the case, revealing the green baize sections and their contents. In silence, he retrieved the headstock first, giving the hammers and triggers a quick check and rub with an oiled rag. He then pulled out the side by side double barrels which he inspected thoroughly, staring into the light through each barrel in turn and then pushing through a rod with a brush on the end, followed by drawing through a small oiled rag which was attached to thick wire, hooped at one end for traction. He collected the last piece of the construct, the forend and slotted it into place, assembling the shotgun. Finally, doubly making sure it fitted together perfectly and functioned as it should. He 'broke' the gun into its unhinged form, opened a drawer and from a box pulled a handful of red 12 bore cartridges and put them in his pocket.

"Come on then," he motioned to Jack, leaving.

His urgent purposeful strides exposed Evan's ill mood and Jack had to run to catch him. They walked in mostly silence for the next 40 minutes, only peppered with the odd exasperated sigh, muttered word or impatient barked order at his dog when she got in the way.

"Away girl!"

Breathing hard, Jack found it difficult to keep up and painfully turned his ankle on a couple of occasions on the uneven ground as Evan strode on.

Nearing the woods that marked the bottom end of farm, as if hitting an unseen wall, Evan stopped. Turning to look down the hillside, like his next words were written there, the farmer took

The dragon under the hill

a deep decisive breath and signed loudly and emphatically, as if letting out all the ill will from where it had been building, unable to stomach its bile any longer. Before finding a suitable spot where he promptly sat down.

"Tired are you, Grampa?". Said Jack.

"Tired, lad? Aye…" Said Evan trailing off, before idly musing, "been tired for a long time now it seems to me. Sometimes I feel like pulling up some of this lovely turf and wrapping it around me, all cosy like and sleeping for a thousand years." His anger and indignation had turned to melancholia.

"Life is a bit like the wind, see boy," Evan continued, "there are times when it blows hard and fast, like a steam train coming at you and catching you up, you close your eyes and brace yourself against the buffet and when you open then again 30 years have passed and there is an old man looking back at you in the mirror, where your face used to be and someone has stolen your knees and replaced them with stiff, clicking bits of knotted wood. Other times the air is still as a stone and not even the gentlest of breezes moves one single blade of spindly grass and that old clock stands still and you can hold those moments nearly forever. Aye, in those moments time can't find you, he's lost you somewhere and can only find you again when you let go. Moments like these."

"What do you mean?" asked Jack, finding the ideas of this oddly philosophical side of his grandfather too much for his young mind.

"Close your eyes lad, soak in in the peace. Hear that curlew calling in the distance? He's a long way from the shore."

Evan could feel Jack's restlessness and decided to move on. Brightly and back to his normal self he concluded.

The dragon under the hill

"All I'm trying to explain to you lad is probably what every old man tries to get across to a lad like you once in while. That life is shorter than you think and to enjoy it while you are young. Make sure you are never too busy or too angry," he added with a hint of confession, "to stop and listen to a lost curlew or know exactly where you are going to place your foot next." They shared a look that communicated enough.

"Right. Where those bunnies hiding?"

Once in a likely area for rabbits, it is the job of a good hunting dog to use its keen sense of smell to track where the animal is by 'working' through the foliage, bushes and long grass. For this, hunting dog's hair is always kept short and tidy and tails are cropped shortly after birth, to avoid getting tangled up in rough plants. To flush the rabbit from its hiding spot so that it runs into the open, where the hunter awaits. The dog must be trained not to fear or be rattled at the sound of the shogun going off, it's no use if the animal runs away at the first loud noise. Should the shot be successful, a trained dog then retrieves the kill for its master and certainly doesn't run off with it or eat it itself. Heini was an accomplished hunting dog and Evan an excellent shot. They had never come home empty handed yet.

"You must be extra quiet and keep your voice low while we're hunting". Jack was told, which he obeyed conscientiously through the afternoon. Evan led him to the boundary of a thick wood, miles away from his precious flock.

The killing of animals, especially in front of you is something hard to get used to. It is necessary and part of life, to eat meat to survive we must kill an animal. This is and how it has always been and will always be and instant death by a shotgun is certainly quick and humane. Although able to understand the simple equation between what they were currently doing and something like the rabbit stew he had gobbled so voraciously the other night, Jack, being brought up in a lifestyle where meat came

87

from a butcher fully prepared and sliced, realised how it is easy to be distant from the reality of where meat comes from and the initial brutality. So, he vowed to be more appreciative of meat in the future. Giving thought not only to the animal itself but to those whose job it was to raise and ultimately kill it. It is an important part of farming to understand an animals ultimate end and therefore to give it the most fulfilling and cared for life possible until that point comes. There is something correct about hunting something that you will eat, a respect, however this is not true of hunting simply for sport.

After the hunt was over they had a haul of three rabbits and one unlucky woodcock who just happened to pop up at exactly the wrong time. When it was obvious that was it and the hunt was over, Jack subtly mentioned to his grandfather his statement on the day they met about shooting his gun.

"I can't go letting shoot this gun, lad," Evan said surprised, "your Nana would put me into the pot next to these rabbits!"

Children have that knack of remembering word for word what adults say to them or in the presence and repeating it back at the most inappropriate or inconvenient moments, which is what Jack did on this occasion.

"You said one of the rules was that I couldn't touch your gun without you there and I could shoot it, if I wanted." The boy repeated.

"I did, I did say that" he conceded. "but thinking about it now..."

The boy pushed home his advantage and wined, "Aw, you did say."

Evan was a man true to his word. "Are you sure? This thing has got an almighty kick to it. If you don't brace properly, you could really hurt your shoulder?"

"I'll do everything you tell me to" replied the very eager boy.

"But you're small and…" said the floundering farmer.

"You did say".

"Ach," exclaimed his grandfather not really seeing how he could not fulfil something he had promised "for goodness sake don't ever tell your nan, she'd kill us both."

"Promise," came the confident response.

"Fine." Finally relenting. "First of all, never walk with your gun loaded or unbroken, it's all too easy to trip and folk have shot themselves dead climbing over fences or tripping up and what not. Second, never, ever, ever point a gun at another person, even if you are sure it's not loaded, you could be mistaken. Also, be very careful with cartridges, it's unlikely but dropped or hit in the wrong place and they'll discharge." Came the lesson.

"Yes Grampa," responded Jack, filled with anticipation.

Slowly and steadily giving his gun to the boy, he stood close behind and put the weapon in place. Jack received the shotgun. It was a great deal heavier than he had imagined but he held it as tightly as he could, sighting down between the twin barrels.

"Right, place the stock on to your shoulder but you must pull it really, really tight because it will kick back hard, so brace yourself. I'll stand close behind you to see you don't fall back."

"What shall I aim at?" the boy enquired, excited.

"See that post there with the clump of sheep's wool snagged on it? Aim for the wool".

Jack raised the gun and aimed.

"Now when you've aimed and are ready to shoot, pull back the hammer to click once this is called half-cocked, then again for another click, now it's fully cocked. Then take a breath, hold it and remember, don't pull or yank the trigger, squeeze it slowly. Be prepared, brace yourself for the kickback, when you feel ready, shoot", Evan said, a tinge of nerves in his voice.

Boom!

Buckshot scattered around the fencepost, topping some long grass nowhere near the woollen target but no one cared. Jack was overjoyed to have fired a gun and his grandfather was relieved nothing untoward had happened.

"I did Grampa, I did it, did you see?" he rambled with excitement. "I held it tight like you said and felt the kickback but I still held it".

"Good lad", replied Evan grateful it was over and to have the gun safely back in his possession, "I'm not sure old Mr Rabbit is going to be very worried seeing your aiming skills but not bad."

Jack was elated.

"But" his grandfather cautioned "what is the main thing to remember?"

Jack thought for a moment before replying, "Not to tell Nana?"

"Correct!"

Maggie could hear them returning well before the old farmhouse door burst open, as both voices were joined together singing loudly and enthusiastically their umpteen rendition of 'Run rabbit run'. Like cavemen coming home from a day of hunting and bringing life giving provisions for the family, Jack and Evan proudly presented the proceeds of the shoot to Maggie, laying them on paper on the table for inspection. She immediately picked up the

The dragon under the hill

single woodcock, held it aloft with two fingers and while scrunching her face asked. "And what am I expected to do with just one of these scrawny things?"

"O, I don't know love. Maybe stick him on your bonnet for church on Sunday". Which made both he and Jack laugh raucously. Unfazed and unmoving, she waited for them to finish, holding her husband in that fixed stern glare, the battle was on.

"Honest Mags, he came right at me and I feared for my life. These woodcocks can be vicious killers. It was either him or me." He joked. Again, spawning laughter from the two. The woman and the glare remained unmoved.

Knowing he had lost, Evan spoke seriously. "Heini flushed it and I instinctively shot it – if you can't think of anything to do with it, I'll clean it and give the meat to Heini."

The offending woodcock was dropped back down in distain and Maggie returned to her cooking. Evan and Jack shared a naughty glance.

After their evening meal of cottage pie, green beans, carrots and a few jam topped Welsh cakes to follow, Evan picked up an apple from the bowl and rolled it in his hands for a long time.

"So Jack," he finally said, "about this apple thing of yours". Maggie stopped what she was doing and sat at the table, knowing what was coming and wanting to share in it.

"Your grandmother and I were talking and she came up with a great suggestion, didn't you Mags?"

Jack looked at his smiling grandmother and expected some form of conditioning, like being forced to bite apples twice a day every day until he learned to get over it.

"Yes," Evan continued "Maggie will borrow Old Nana Price's false teeth for you to use them to bite the apple first and..."

The dragon under the hill

"Evan!" came his wife's reprimand.

"Alright then", conceded Evan, his fun spoiled. "So, there was a special reason I went into the village this morning. I visited Morgan's little hardware shop and got a little something specially for you." Reaching into his pocket he pulled out a small parcel of tightly wrapped brown paper. Jack took it and held it in his hand motionless like a new-born baby.

"Well, open it lad", his grandfather encouraged.

Whatever it was Jack couldn't guess but it was small and heavy. He slowly unwrapped the packet to reveal, to his amazement, a beautiful new gleaming penknife. The folding buck knife was about four inches long with a deep mahogany coloured smooth varnished handle held with four brass pins, with a brass pommel and bolster. Jack placed is thumbnail in the groove in the blade and pulled it out. It was a little stiff but it soon clicked into place. The blade was about three and a half inches long and looked viciously sharp. It even had a small shield embedded in the handle and on it a word was written in pleasing calligraphy, it simply said 'Jack'. It was one of the most perfect things the boy had ever seen, he was awestruck.

"A penknife of my very own", he gushed. "It's the most amazing gift I've ever had" he looked at his grandparents in turn and asked, "Is it really mine to keep?"

"Of course lad," Evan consoled, then turning serious "but you must promise us to be very, very careful with it because it is very sharp and it's not a toy. Don't go waving it about or stabbing things you shouldn't".

Maggie jumped in "One mark on my kitchen table or if we find out you have cut yourself by not being careful then we will have to take it off you."

The dragon under the hill

"Aye", interjected Evan "No carving your name into any of the farm's trees either."

"That is the deal." Concluded Maggie.

This seemed to need a response, Jack putting his new gift on the table, jumped up from his seat and threw his arms around each grandparent in turn. "I will be careful, I promise. Thank you. Thank you. Thank you. It's the best thing ever!"

"Besides", said his grandfather smiling, "at last count you've got fourteen apples you've got to work your way through."

As Jack was admiring his new knife, feeling the weight, caressing the varnished wood, turning it over in his hands like a precious jewel, there was a loud commotion coming from the courtyard. A rowdy series of aggressive honks from one of the geese and muffled through the walls, a man's voice could be clearly discerned shouting "Get off! You stupid creature, it's me mun! Leave it now!"

The Reverend Thomas burst through the door, slamming it behind him and looking harassed and annoyed breathlessly announced "I come here every single week and that blessed goose still goes for me every time...shwmae everyone" ('Shwmae' is an informal greeting, in English would be something akin to 'Howdy')

"Rhodri, I don't know what you ever did to that goose but Elanor doesn't like you one little bit", Evan commented amused by the situation.

"Just promise me that when that goose's time comes, you'll invite me around to tuck in", replied the Reverend.

"O Rhodri" exclaimed Maggie, horrified.

Pointing through the window Rhodri shouted. "One day goose!" Making a ringing motion with his hands.

The dragon under the hill

Jack couldn't wait to show the Reverend his new knife, like a father with a new born son, it was presented in similar fashion with similar reverence. Rhodri was suitably impressed and reiterated the earlier warning for the boy to be very careful. He added that Jack was growing up and part of growing up was being responsible and this was an opportunity to show to everyone how responsible he could be. Jack dearly wanted to tell his new friend about shooting his grandfather's shotgun earlier but knew this was not the time nor the company, so restricted himself to what he knew he could say.

"And grampa took me with him and Heini hunting rabbits and I was quiet like I was told to and I carried them all the way home. Didn't I grampa?" Jack said with machine gun delivery.

"Aye" said Evan "we'll make a good gun dog of you yet, lad"

"Is it? And how many did you get for the pot?" asked Rhodri.

"Three rabbits and a woodcock." Came Jack's proud response.

"A woodcock?" said the Reverend, "What did you shoot that for? You need 2 dozen of the scrawny things to fill a pie mun!"

Evan shook his head, looking away, as if this conversation had nothing at all to do with him.

Maggie interrupted, "Now you lot, get from under my feet and sit by the fire. I'll bring over tea in a minute."

They retired to their usual spots with Jack on the floor with Heini, still fascinated by the knife and its tactile nature. The Reverend Thomas started the conversation off and spoke seriously to his old friend, "I heard about your drama in the village this morning and I did some asking around and I know the Jenkins,

94

The dragon under the hill

the Bennetts, Iestyn and others are also on the same list...no doubt Old Man Roberts too".

Jack remembering this afternoon and his grandfather's usually surly mood after he'd returned asked. "What happened in the village Grampa?"

"Ach", Evan responded with disgust, his annoyance obvious "that horrid little man from the ministry is still around isn't he? And as soon as he spotted me this morning in the village, he came rushing over to me waving a piece of paper right under my nose shouting the odds. Duw, I nearly hit him - llygoden fawr!"

Jack looked at Reverend Thomas who provided a translation, "means 'little rat'".

"Too right", Evan continued "saying that this special paper from London meant that he had permission to come on my land and survey it and we coulndn't stop him, all official like." By now Maggie had brewed the tea and brought it over to the men. She quickly served them then pulled the footstool to her and sat next to her husband putting her hand on his.

"What did you say to him?" Jack asked.

"What could I say lad? I told him we'd see about that and to stay away from my farm but knowing him, this won't be the last we hear about it." He warned. Gabbing the poker and taking out his obvious frustration on the fire with voilent jabs.

Rhodri interjected, "I'm going over that letter with Twm tomorrow but I do suspect it's all legal and sadly, we've got no recourse to let them carry on. What's more we could get in trouble ourselves with the law if we tried to stop him."

"That's not fair!" exclaimed Maggie.

"It's true, obstruction or something, any one of us could be charged with if we got in their way. That's the law". Said the Reverend.

"Well it's a stupid law, if you ask me," Maggie continued, "and I'll be telling Twm myself when I see him next!"

Catching the boy's eye, Rhodri explained "Twm, that's Tomos Jones. He's the local constable see. Only part time like, as his job normally consists of signing fishing licenses or pulling apart a couple of rowdy lads after too many beers in the Tŷ Bont public house but he is the nearest thing we've got to a legal expert around here" Jack nodded.

Rhodi continued, "Mr Deacon from the Ministry will be there as well though, he won't let that peice of paper out his sight."

"I hope he goes next door and Old Man Roberts shoots him" Evan growled.

"Evan!" chastised his wife. Her cutting glance froze Jack mid giggle.

"Well Mags. I was tamping when I got back. I was so angry, I had to take the lad shooting to cool off."

"I know." Maggie conceded, patting her beloved husband's hand.

"As it was three rabbits, one woodcock and a fence post had to pay the price with their lives." Added Evan, winking at Jack.

Jack then launched into a second indepth description of the hunt, the expert way Heini had roused the animals, his grandfather's shooting prowess and he was just as proud to share all he'd learned in the morning he'd spent with his grandmother and her skills with the flora. Reverend Thomas, as he always did, listened patiently.

As the evening drew on, the conversation followed its usual lines and soon it was time for Rhodri to take his leave. After his hosts were suitably embraced and prayer made, he gestured to the boy.

"Walk me out Jack lad" he requested, "keep me safe from that vicious goose."

The evening was surprisingly warm and the air smelled sweet with honeysuckle and hawthorn blossom, a summer breeze teased the hedgerow leaves and whispered a melodic verse through the lane. Clear of the farmhouse, the Reverend Thomas asked his companion, "So Jack, have seen anything since we talked last?"

"I haven't but I'm keeping an eye" replied Jack, trying not to give too much away.

"You do that but listen bach, your grandparents have got a lot to deal with at the moment, so keep on being good and don't give them anything to add to their problems." Jack nodded.

"Good lad, now I'm trusting you watch my back Jack, protect me from the stupid goose."

Jack smiled as he watched his friend disappear behind a high hedge and into the night.

Chapter 9

There, something moved!

Jack's night-sight was fully engaged, nearing the top of his now familiar loping climb to the summit, he had definitely seen something move at the peak of the hill near the cairn. It was a fleeting movement and he could not exactly say if was the same wonder he saw some nights previously. He paused mid step waiting, now exceptionally alert. Before continuing on, having seen or heard nothing further.

This ascent had now become a nightly routine for the boy and his route took him to the edge of the small field from where he would patiently observe the tumble of stones before approaching. He tried to picture the exact point he had seen movement earlier but it was difficult to judge in the gloom and areas of deeper darkness. He did feel it had to be near his undisturbed handkerchief, where each night he had replaced the meat.

He listened. Long gone was the unease and dread he felt up here at night. The darkness and unfamiliarity it brought held no fear for him anymore. The sounds he heard were familiar and only served to pique his interest more. He scanned the entire area, eyes like a searchlight. He had now spent many nocturnal hours in these atmospheric surroundings and felt it become less mysterious each passing minute. He then followed the same linear path to the cairn, believing this route was trustworthy and safe under foot. On reaching the usual spot, he pulled out of his pocket some pieces of cooked rabbit he had fished out from the remains of a stew.

A sudden noise in the shadows directly to his left startled the boy, making him spill the pieces of meat on the ground. A weak, involuntary half whimper half yelp of terror escaped from his

The dragon under the hill

mouth as he spun around to face the direction the sound had emanated from. The vegetation rustled, coming alive, as something big and bulky was stalking forwards. Straining his eyes against the shadow's blackness, despite being used to the dim light, Jack could not make out any details or even a general form, though he had to be looking directly at it, whatever was approaching was invisible to him. For a fleeting moment he thought he saw something catch the meagre light and reflect back, eyes maybe?

"Hello?" he ventured meekly, fear volcanically swelling inside.

The advent of his cracking voice pin-holing the dark night, was like a starting pistol to the skulking, hidden source of the sounds and the spectre launched itself from the invisibility of gloom and like a dart, straight towards where the anxious young lad stood. It was like some of the very shadow itself, some of the soulless black had wrenched itself away and was coming for him at speed with nightmarish force and mass.

Even when the rancorous presence broke cover into the stronger light, the direct illumination of lunar beams seemed to be absorbed by the approaching evil, like a living black hole it was absent of colour, wholly black. It was only when the beast let out a foul and deafening series of deep barks that ripped through Jack's body like buckshot, the boy realised with utter gut rending terror and awe, it was Cymro!

To encounter the monstrous dog he had heard talked about with trepidation so many times was the last thing he had expected. Fear fully ravaged and penetrated his body, distress was ice, numbing his muscles and scrambling his thoughts, a shrill cry went out across the hill that he heard but had no awareness he had made it. The beast was huge, ferally derelict and pounding hate.

The dragon under the hill

Turning to escape from the barking juggernaut, the boy had hardly managed a few steps away when something akin to a steam train rammed fully into him with brutal forces. His body was jack-knifed, folding backwards in half while simultaneously being jettisoned forward, his head snapped back violently and the air forced from his lungs. Winded and in pain Jack clattered forward arms apart, hitting the terrain face first in a hard crumple. He could taste soil mixed with the metallic iron of warm blood in his mouth.

He had hardly landed when the vile dog was already upon him, gnashing and growling in frenzied malice. In the madness of attack, seizing the nearest thing it could and biting down, it grabbed hold of the loose side of a Jack's coat as it ballooned around him. With mighty force and violent jerks, it was pulling at its prey, making it impossible for Jack to get any stable footing. Yelling and flailing madly, fighting to free himself, the prisoner was desperate to get away. Catching the beast a few times with a wild boot but the kicks seemed to have little or no effect. Only when the crazed animal shifted its hold trying to get a better grip, was there an opportunity allowing the lad to pull free from such malevolent clutches.

Still on his back, panting, pushing himself away with his legs and grasping wildly with his hands, clawing the ground the lad tried to propel himself away but he seemed tethered to the ground. Jack tried colossally to get away from the dangerous monster but his exhausting efforts to plough his body away were countered in just one leap. A sledgehammer hitting his chest, the dog was again on the boy, its full weight and size overpowering the lad. A wretched deep growl accompanied its atrocious frenzied attack, Jack could feel the vibrations travelling through his weakened body.

Reaching out blindly to protect himself Jack managed to find the animal's thick collar and held it in tight desperation with both hands. Pushing back as hard as he could, petrified and alarmed at the shear strength of the feral fiend, as with all his

100

tensed muscular effort he only just managed to keep the snarling jaws mere inches away from his face. The stench of the creature's rotting-foul hot breath was hideous and vomit inducing. Slaver dripping from yellowed slashing teeth which crammed its huge mouth, splayed over Jack's face. Its claws tearing at the boy's chest scrabbling for leverage. The relentless, evil animal shook itself wildly, rolling its head trying to get free of the locking grasp.

Screaming, the poor boy wondered how long he could repel the murderous brute as its efforts to free itself grew more hysterical and forceful. Jack remembered his pocket knife but dare not release a hand to fumble for it and even if it could be retrieved, could he open it one-handed as it was still in stiff newness? Cymro made up the boy's mind for him as a final furious twist of his neck while wrenching backwards freed the animal from the boy's clasping fists. Tumbling backwards with the force of his exertion the black dog rolled a number of times, a tangle of legs and demented fury.

Eyes fixed on his assailant, the youngster frantically rummaged in his pocket until he felt the reassurance of the weighty knife. The black beast instantly regained his footing and again was a single-minded mass of teeth and storming insanity, as it came barrelling forwards, barking as it charged at the scared lad. Jack frantically clawed at the edges of the blade trying to catch the nail-notch and get the knife open. His efforts became more agitated and frenetic as the beast neared. His rising panic making his urgent attempts even less accurate.

In rage and venom the soot-black hound bunched its powerful muscles, throwing itself in devilish banefulness and vehemence at the doomed boy. In reflex, Jack threw his arms up in front of his face for protection, bracing for the horrific impact. A loud crack like muffled thunder, a sound like folding wind encircled the scene, thickening the air and instead of Cymro's vicious teeth impaling his outstretched arm, he heard a loud yelp of surprise and pain as it echoed over the hilltop.

The dragon under the hill

Something had impacted the attacking dog in mid-leap with such force it knocked the hefty animal nearly twelve feet away. Jack saw the dog skid to an eventual stop after landing awkwardly, obviously hurt and somewhat bewildered. Cymro was a mad dog in every sense of the word and rabid to its core. Forcing its heavy, brawny body upright, it regained its furious compulsion and readied itself for another attack. Now more cautious, the beast circled its quarry, growling menacingly. Spasming, the canine's hind legs kicked it forward for another murderous charge at the boy, again the roar of a squall was detonated around and this time the full force of the burst of wind was felt by Jack. The gust pitched him forward as something big came from over his head and landed between him and the striking dog.

Jack's breath and clarity of thought left him in that moment. Despite his ordeal, adrenaline and fear; despite the dim light and shifting shadows, there was no misidentifying what he was looking at. With its sharp features, elongated body and iridescence, a prism in the moonlight the reptilian creature was unmistakable – Jack was transfixed, trying to reconcile logic with the reality of what his vision was telling him.

He was snapped back from his stupor by another loud yelp of pain and shock from the snarling dog, obviously having just been dealt a further stinging blow, Jack had been protected for the second time. Then the head of his saviour turned towards him and looked straight at the young boy. In that moment, the entire world was shrunk down and solidified into just those ethereal eyes and nothing more. Huge and bright like molten gold with the universe at the centre, they filled the entirety of all the boy could perceive and hypnotised him completely. Jack had never seen anything with as much lucidity or precision, he was mesmerised and engulfed, caught and lost in a timeless stare, captured wholly.

In his trance he heard a voice. It was not audible or spoken, it was not heard or gleaned but it was forced bluntly straight into his mind, appearing directly into his own inner voice.

102

The voice was so loud and clear and it spoke a single word that was more a command that was to be obeyed, without choice or recourse. It simply said.

"Run!"

Before his consciousness had registered the order and its meaning, Jack was already running. Without looking behind him or paying heed to any noises that hit the periphery of his hearing, in his wake, he descended the hill like the devil himself was in hunting pursuit. Gone was the careful following of the path and precise foot placement, this was a mindless primordial desire to flee.

In his feverish descent Jack misjudged the slope and fell. Crashing, he spiralled downwards, tumbled and bounced as he continually lost his footing, toppling downhill at a plummeting speed. He half stumbled and half plunged as his body lurched and rolled through the darkness towards the familiar shape of the farmhouse and slipping and sliding to safety.

Only after finally reaching the perceived sanctuary of the courtyard, bloodied, bruised, shaking and covered in mud, sod and grass, did the overwhelming emotion of what had happened and what could have happened, hit the panting, sweat soaked boy. He darted into the protection of the outside toilet, locked the door and immediately burst into unrestrained tears, falling defeated to his knees. Letting his shaking body and racing mind give in to the post adrenaline stress and strain, he crumbled into heartfelt sobbing and guttural moans.

He stayed there till long after his flowing hot tears and running nose had dried and his hands had stopped shaking. It was only then he started to feel the pain from the received battering, each limb and body part starting to register increasing discomfort. It was still too raw an experience for him to process but he was sensible enough to know he could not go into the house in the state he was in, so he made sure he was fully in control of his emotions before slipping back to his room.

He took the chance of lighting his candle stub in his room. It is amazing how in our efforts to be deceptive, we can be at our most devious and shrewdest. Jack cleverly jammed his clothes at the bottom of the door to stop any light escaping and alerting anyone who might see. He quietly washed off the dirt and now dry blood from his face, scuffed elbows and knees, before checking himself over properly. Beyond numerous cuts and a mosaic bruises, as far as he could discern, he had suffered no real damage. Amazingly, not one of those vicious attacking teeth had punctured his skin during the bitter strike.

Jack crawled aching into bed, blowing out the dancing light. He stared wide-eyed at the ceiling, still waiting for this heightened adrenaline to give way and allow the seeping drowsiness he needed take over. He knew that he had been so very lucky this night, he could so easily have been really hurt or even killed by the evil coal-black hound.

He also knew, with all his heart and understanding that when all was concluded and defined, there was only one amazing, unbelievable, mind blowing but undeniable truth – tonight, he had seen a dragon.

Chapter 10

"N-N-Now..now, Mr James I say, let's be calm here! Be reasonable!" Came the panicked, high pitched squeal of Mr Deacon as he slowly backed away from the farmhouse door, eyes pleading and wide. Pushed back by the cold Damascus steel barrels of a shotgun resting heavily and squarely on the bridge of his hooked nose. Holding the other end of the firearm, looking very stern and annoyed, Evan let fly with a barrage of Welsh at the rigid man. Maggie stood directly behind her husband glaring unblinking at the Ministry's man, with obvious disgust she made no effort to conceal, while Jack stood to Evan's left gaping blankly at the frightened man. Secretly trying to hide his immense amusement at how events were unfolding.

Calmly watching the proceedings, Tomos Jones, the area's only policeman, in full constable's uniform stood with his hands in his pockets, making no attempt to defuse the situation or to rescue Mr Deacon. He simply translated.

"Mr James, says 'He is perfectly calm, very calm in fact and thinks he's been very reasonable in the circumstances because he hasn't shot you yet.'" The constable tried to convey this with as little emotion in his voice as possible.

A few short minutes earlier the scene had not been quite so dramatic and confrontational.

An eye-catching black and red Austin 7 saloon with its grilled long bonnet reflecting the bright morning sun and shiny, spoked, silver wheels mirroring the surrounding greenery, had chugged up the dirt track leading to the farmhouse of Bryn Y Ddraig farm. Pulling up loudly and spluttering to a stop marking an inexperienced driver, at the edge of the courtyard four men climbed out. The first being Mr Deacon with his insipid rat-like features underneath a black, large brimmed trilby hat. He wore an

105

even duller and less impressive dark, pin-stripe suit with polished black brogues that he despised getting the tiniest bit dirty. When he wore this ensemble, the petty little man felt he was donning his uniform, one that commanded respect. He adored the sense of privilege and power the paper in his pocket gave him and couldn't wait to brandish it in the face of these 'insolent yokels'. How he had relished receiving the legal order, which to him were as sacred a text as Moses receiving the commandments from the mount. In private he caressed the embossed envelope and had read every word a dozen times.

The second man to alight from the vehicle was Twm, whose presence had been requested by the Ministry to see that the survey went ahead unhindered.

The two other men were younger and simply dressed in casual trousers and plain shirts with the sleeves rolled up. As soon as they got out of the car, they had a good look around to get their bearings. Deep in conversation they then opened up a large topographical map over the bonnet of the car and began to intently study it, coming up from its depths on occasions and pointing intently at the landscape.

Without acknowledging the surveyors he'd brought or looking behind him to face Twm, Mr Deacon demanded "With me, constable."

With his hat in one hand he strode straight across the courtyard fetching his cherished Government edict from the scabbard of his jacket pocket to wield it like a superior weapon, with the other hand. Without breaking stride or knocking he arrogantly pushed open the farmhouse door and unbidden, lurched inside.

"I have here Mr Ja..." Was all he managed of his haughty prepared speech, before an angry but well-prepared Mr James stopped him dead and forced him back out of the house on his heels with his waiting shotgun.

This went totally unnoticed by the two surveyors, as one continued his study of the map the other was unloading various cases and instruments from the car's ample boot.

The standoff continued.

Mr Deacon tried to use his trump card. "You are...you can't" he stuttered "I am empowered by law to come on your land!"

This elicited another guttural response in Welsh from Evan, unmoved.

Constable Jones, still a by-stander, happily continued his role as translator.

"He says 'It certainly doesn't grant you the right to barge into his home'" The constable thought and continued, looking at the terrified suited man, scratching his chin thoughtfully. "He's got you there Mr Deacon, the mandate you have gives you access to the farm land for purposes of surveying. Not to enter any of the private buildings on it. As far as the law is concerned, you just broke into this man's house."

"This is utterly ridiculous!" the spiteful man spat in protest.

There was a short conversation between Evan and Twm in Welsh, which was interrupted by the increasingly worried Ministry man squealing, "What's going on now? Just get him to lower his weapon man!"

"O, sorry Mr Deacon", Twm continued, as if he'd forgotten he was there, "as the village's local law enforcement officer, I was just discussing the legality of shooting someone who had broken into your house with this homeowner. I informed him that although I did witness the aforementioned break-in and he would be well within his rights to press charges, that if he did discharge his firearm at you then, that would probably be deemed as not coming under 'reasonable force' due to the time that's passed since the break in".

Mr Deacon was becoming more and more frustrated and exasperated with this farce and his oily face was becoming redder and redder. Jack was enjoying it for the entertainment it was. Knowing enough Welsh to understand that what his grandfather and the Constable had discussed was nothing remotely like the translation given. Completely in cahoots they were winding up the little Englishman completely. He also knew that not only was the shotgun not loaded but even the most casual observer would notice that the gun's triggers were completely missing. He further entertained himself by miming sighting down a gun at Mr Deacon and shouting "Bang!" which caused the impish man to jump, startled. This was the proverbial final straw for the incensed official.

"God damn it man, do something!" He yelled at the policeman.

"Now then, there is no need to blaspheme now, there's a good gentleman". Constable Jones chastised with a stern authoritive air, raising his voice for the first time. There was now a sense whatever fun there was to be had, was over. Twm grabbed Mr Deacon by the arm and led the bewildered official away from the glaring family.

"About time you gentlemen go about your business and don't inconvenience these good people any more than is necessary, I think. Don't you?" The officer instructed.

Mr Deacon was incandescent in his resentment at the suffered humiliation, furious his moment of triumph had been turned into a rolling catastrophe. How he hoped these 'inbred local idiots' would get their comeuppance. He would live for the day when the Government forced these fools off this land and he would be there to watch the bulldozers destroy that petty white building until not one brick stood on another, if it was the last thing he did.

After watching the men leave the courtyard and confer with the waiting surveyors where to start their work. Evan closed the door and placed the gun on the table, laughing.

"Duw, at least we put the wind up him, eh boy?" Evan announced jovially.

"Serves him right for being so arrogant. Fancy just stomping in here like he owned the place. The cheek!" Maggie added incensed.

Jack laughed and laughed – the picture of Mr Deacon's face, as it changed from overconfident conceit to cross-eyed, whimpering distress with the barrels of the gun perched on his nose, would fuel Jack's merriment every time he thought of it or told the story in later years.

Still laughing, Jack started to put on his rubber boots, before being questioned by his grandfather.

"What are you doing lad?" he asked.

Jack thought it was obvious but answered, "I thought I would go out and see what those men are doing."

"No, you won't", came the surprising but firm response from his grandfather, "leave those men to their business." Seeing Jack's disappointment and confusion, Evan elaborated.

"We've had our fun with them this morning and pushed it as far as we could, with Twm in tow but if any of us do the wrong thing while they are taking their measurements or whatever they're doing, then it could go bad for us." He continued kindly, "it's not that I don't trust you lad but better safe than sorry, even Heini is staying where she is until those men are done."

The dragon under the hill

Looking down at the faithful dog he spoke in a playful voice, "because you know this vicious beast eats Englishmen for breakfast." Stroking Heini's head.

Evan went back to cleaning his gun and Maggie continued peeling potatoes, the very activities the wretched Mr Deacon had trespassed on earlier.

Jack, like most children his age, hated to be told that he could not do something and despised having plans he had made checked or thwarted. Crestfallen and forlorn, not only was Jack at a loss of how to fill his time indoors and he was incredibly curious as to what surveyors actually did in processing the land but mainly he wanted to sneak back to the hilltop to inspect last night's battlefield.

"Grampa?" the boy whined, "but I've got nothing to do in here." As if this argument was the magic key that would get his grandfather to change his mind.

In clinical response to the boy's whimpering complaint, Maggie put down her small knife she used for peeling, wiped her hands in her apron and walked over to the large Welsh dresser that dominated the room – no self-respecting farmhouse, cottage, terrace house or any dwelling in this land would be found without the ubiquitous Welsh dresser, the more ornate and imposing, the better. She opened a drawer, collected a few things from within and presented Jack with some writing paper and a couple of short pencil stubs.

"It's about time you wrote home, isn't it?" Maggie questioned. "You write a nice letter to your mum and dad in your best handwriting", in a teacher like tone that made it clear, this was not an idle request.

"I don't know what to write nana," the boy pleaded, his reluctance evident.

110

"How about you start by telling your mother how you got your clothes so filthy and caked in mud last night. It's going to take me ages scrubbing later to get them clean, if I can." She responded.

Not wanting to lie to these lovely people but seeing no other option in the circumstances Jack proffered.

"I fell last night coming back from the loo. Sorry nana." A lie which he backed up by displaying a selection of the cuts and bruises he had gained last night. The best lies are based in some truth he supposed.

This seemed to placate his grandmother, "you've lots to tell them and maybe when you've finished, after lunch your grandfather will take you into the village to post it."

Jack looked up at his grandfather for confirmation, as he had not yet explored the village and longed to have any excuse to be outdoors.

"Aye lad" Evan concurred, "do a good job now and I might let you drive the cart n' all"

This was enough motivation to start the boy scribbling.

A few hours later, having been into the village to post Jack's letter as agreed, his grandfather making good on his promise to hand over the worn leather straps and let Jack drive the cart – although he suspected old Merlin knew the way well enough and the reigns were just for show. Jack and Evan, the dog in tow, returned from their tour of the village to find Twm completely alone in the farmhouse, happily drinking tea sitting at the kitchen table. His commanding Policeman's tunic folded on the bench next to him and his starched shirt half unbuttoned, sleeves rolled up. All trappings of authority laid down, to visit with his old friends, just as 'Twm'.

"Shwmae boyo" said Evan in greeting.

111

The dragon under the hill

"Shwmae Evan, hello John" replied the guest. "Maggie has just popped to feed the pigs some peelings."

The travellers disposed of their coats and outdoor footwear and joined their guest. Evan settled himself at the table, "I thought you'd still be out with your new friend and his cronies?"

"Well that's the thing" Twm recounted, "they've all scuttled back to where ever they are staying, the Ty Bont is it? Saying they'll have to come back another day."

Twm was just about to explain further when Maggie came back in from her chores and seeing her husband home, bid them pause until she had made a fresh pot of tea and could sit and listen with them herself. This suited the constable as he enjoyed having the audience and told stories in his own unrushed meandering time.

"That ratty Mr Deacon was spitting feathers for hours after your encounter this morning," Twm began, finally able to recommence his tale, "how I kept a straight face when he came backing out of here with your shotgun barrels like a pair of spectacles perched on the bridge of his big nose, I can't say. The look on his face was a picture, I thought he'd 'cach' his pants. I mean, any fool could see there were no triggers mun."

The group giggled and sniggered together, relishing the recent memory.

"Aw, especially when this one by here" pointing at Jack, "pretended to shoot him and he jumped in the air like a scolded cat! I had to bite my lip." The laughter at Mr Deacon's expense continued.

"Anyway, he was tamping mad after like I said and was ranting and raving to the surveyors about the 'stupid Welsh locals' and how he 'couldn't wait to see you kicked off your land'. Really

The dragon under the hill

nasty like", scrunching his nose as if irritated by a foul stench, to emphasise his point.

This brought scowls, the shaking of heads and tutting from his audience.

"To be honest, the two young surveyors are nice lads, as it happens and were having none of his nonsense. They were professional like and just wanted to get on with their job. They started at the bottom field, you know, wanting to do the far edges of the land first. Well to be honest, once you'd blocked out Mr Deacon who was still flapping his gums about this and that, it was really dull. They'd look through that instrument thing, take a little measurement, write it down, move the stick, take another measurement, write it down, move the stick. Same down the valley to the edge of Taflen forest and then they wanted to go right up top, to the cairn. Something to do with making big triangles and working out distances"

Jack's heart began to beat faster, anxious of what they might have seen there. Evan addressed the constable "You warned them of the dangers of going atop the hill though, didn't you?"

"O aye" came the reply, "told them all about the hidden potholes and overgrown caves and that they'd be better off giving it a miss but that only seemed to get them even more interested. I mean, they'd tripped up enough times between them and were stumbling all over the place getting there. Not used to it see."

The others nodded, for those not acclimatised, walking along the uneven slopes can take some getting used to.

"But there was nothing I could do to stop them," he looked at Evan, knowing how he felt about that portion of his land, "my job is to make sure they don't get interfered with, so to speak. So, I led them right to the very top."

The dragon under the hill

He paused, raising his finger for emphasis before adding theatrically.

"And then they came across it" Twm said mysteriously, pausing there.

Jack was the first to jump in with some urgency, "across what?"

Twm chose that moment to finish the dregs of his tea, exasperating the waiting boy. Looking at Evan he asked.

"Did you know the 'Beast of Rhywle', that evil dog, old Cymro was dead?"

"No!?" said Evan, shocked.

"Oh never", responded Maggie in her customary fashion.

"How is that then?" Evan asked.

"Well we finally arrive at the very top, duw they were like kiddies in a sweet shop these lads when they saw the cairn but when we got around the other side to the boundary of Old Man Robert's land, there he was. The big black vile thing was lying there, stone cold dead. The brute was all torn up like, even had all his innards ripped out. They were spilling out everywhere."

"Ach y fi!" exclaimed Maggie, (which is a wonderful Welsh guttural phrase conveying disgust) pulling a face.

Twm carried on his story. "Thing is, we've all seen dead animals and after they've rotted for a bit or if something's been at them, the first thing they go at is the innards but this was like a slash or something, a really clean cut, right from his tail to his throat. And he hadn't been dead that long by the looks of him, a day or so it seemed to me".

114

The dragon under the hill

Evan jumped in thoughtfully "Mm, there are plenty of creatures around and about that will start eating a carcass but there is nothing in these hills that could take on old Cymro. He probably died of natural causes and then the foxes got at him."

"That's the only conclusion I could come to as well", agreed the constable. "Unless you've got a bear on the farm Evan."

"The only bear around here is this one, when we try to get him out of bed in the mornings," joked Evan while placing his hand on the top of Jack's head and giving him a gentle shake.

"Well at least these hills will be a lot safer now without that monster prowling around the place" added Maggie.

"Horrible to see though, especially as the crows had already had his eyes" continued Twm, "both the surveyors were on their knees throwing up their breakfast, sick as dogs they were. While that stupid Englishman, Deacon, was shouting the odds how you had done it on purpose. 'Slaughtering animals in a macabre fashion to obstruct the work going on.' He kept saying. Anyway, there was no way these poor fellas were good for anything after that, so they called it a day and said they'd return when they were feeling better. I practically had to carry both of them down the hill, green to the gills they were – hard not to laugh. All the while Mr Deacon was ranting on, pee-heeing about this and that. Duw, he's an angry little man and he hates you with a passion." Nodding at Evan.

"Let him." Came the stony reply.

Tomos finished his tale with, "they all piled into the car and sped off...lovely car it is too. I felt like a Lord when I got to ride in it earlier, must have cost over £170 but it's borrowed it is. From the Ministry, one of the lads let slip."

The dragon under the hill

"Have you been over to Old Man Roberts to give him the news yet?" asked Evan, bringing the conversation back to the matter at hand.

"What? Without you?" exclaimed the constable incredulous, "No fear! You are the only person who he doesn't try to shoot!" this statement and his high energy delivery seemed to really tickle Maggie, who erupted into laughter. Maggie rarely laughed so freely but when she did it was charming, musical and infectious

"If you think I'm going there on my own, especially wearing this uniform, you're as mad as that old dog of his. I'd come back with more holes than a tea strainer," said Twm, smiling at Maggie's merriment.

"Right," Evan announced, "let's get on with it, we're wasting daylight. Twm, we'll grab some shovels and bury that animal first and then go over and give Old Man Roberts the news."

As they got up to leave, Jack made movements to join them. Twm put a hand on the boy's shoulder, "son, what's up there is no sight for a young boy to see, better you stay where you are." Causing the boy to sink back down.

As he was putting on his coat, Evan reinforced the constable's message, "Aye, you stay here boy. Mags, wrap up half a dozen of your nice Welsh cakes for us to take, will you? We should be back in time for tea."

"Righto" obeyed his wife.

"Unless Twm gets shot, then we may be a bit late", he joked.

The dragon under the hill

Chapter 11

"Leave!"

The loud authoritative voice compellingly filled Jack's head, grabbing hold of his very will and it took all of the lad's mental strength not to mindlessly obey straight away. It was like riding a bolted horse, having to wrestle control back and keep on the desired path. With great determination and no small help from his own young stubbornness, he managed to push aside the echoing adamant voice and impose his own spirit.

"I...er...I only, I came to say, 'thank you'" stuttered the boy to the invisible voice "er...thank you for rescuing me from that dog."

As much as he searched, straining his eyes, which was harder to do in the light rain that peppered the dark hill and listened hard, the boy could not detect any sign of where the creature was and although he recognised the voice from the night before and knew who it must be emanating from, he did not understand how he could 'feel' and understand it's message without hearing it spoken out loud.

"Leave! Leave this place!"

The second time the command seemed more urgent, had more drive and strength. Powerful in overwhelming influence, blinding Jack to all other stimulus. He had already taken a few steps before he checked himself and stopped. With firmness of his conviction the resolute boy stood his ground, eyes shut and fists clenched hard.

"I will not leave! I need to know", he was shouting now, "I...I need to know why? Why did you save me?"

The dragon under the hill

After the second ticked with no response, "Why?" he screamed, to nothing and to no-one.

There was a long period where nothing could be heard except the rain tapping on the leaves and the singing of the long grass stirred by the curling air but stubbornly the boy stood his ground. Then he heard the voice again.

"The beast was...broken. Cracked, in its mind. You are innocent, a child."

Jack was elated to get even this titbit of insight. The voice had no accent or discernible timbre but there was something ancient about it, something world-weary and sagacious. It had a cracked tension like the first time you speak after waking in the morning. The speech pattern awkward, an unnatural staccato, as if very word was excavated out of the very stones from around them, as if its author had not used words for a long, long time.

Still a part of Jack doubted the whole situation, logic telling him there must be some other explanation, making him constantly second guess what he had seen and experienced. His head was whirling with thoughts, a sea of questions and spurring curiosity. He had difficulty focusing it all down to coherent questions. Had he really seen what he was sure he had? Is the voice real or just in his head? What if it's all true? What do you ask a living breathing legend? What enquires do you put to a creature thought myth? What do you ask a dragon?

Jack arranged his eddying thoughts and composed his most pressing and human of questions.

"Are you real?" Jack asked out loud.

He waited. Time passed and the rain, although not heavy, was beginning to penetrate his clothing by shear concentration of moisture and the gruff breeze started to pierce his layers of

The dragon under the hill

protection, cooling his skin. Jack started to shiver, the shield of his excitement fading.

Not knowing how many minutes had elapsed, the boy knew he could not wait any longer – it seemed the reluctant dialogue his hidden correspondent had entered into with him was now abruptly over.

Jack produced some chunks of salvaged meat from their most recent meal and placed them on the usual stone, took one last long look around the cairn then started off on his return journey down the hill. Reaching the edge of the field and spying the very distant farmhouse, getting his bearings, he was halted. At last, a belated reply.

"Are you?"

Biting his bottom lip, in gleeful elation, carefully the youngster navigated the sodden land down to the farmhouse.

Heading towards the sanctuary of home, a beacon in the darkness, Jack's mind rested on the events of earlier that day.

On another night, the rain and fact there was very little moonlight would have given him second thoughts about making his way to the hilltop but not only had he been cooped up in the confines of the farmhouse for most of the day; more importantly he had an intense need to validate his experience from the previous night. He needed confirmation that it wasn't all in his head, some apparition invented to help him cope with the trauma of Cymro's surprise attack. Some scrap of corroborating evidence, marks in the ground, a trail, something.

These things had played increasingly on his mind during the dull afternoon waiting for his grandfather and the constable to return. In the mediocrity of helping his grandmother with preparing the meal and other chores, gave Jack a lot of time with these thoughts. The whole experience was oddly joyless and lacked the

119

interest of the previous occasions he had spent time alone with her. At the very least they were getting more and more familiar with each other and more at ease in each other's company.

They set the table with the beautifully crisp, aromatic, homemade meat and potato pasties, fresh out of the oven, the crowning glory at the centre, like a great holy shrine. Filling the place with warm mouth-watering smells, crying out to be devoured.

With impeccable timing, Evan and Twm returned from their assignments, the latter's invitation to dine with them implied and accepted, never needing to be verbalised.

Over the meal conversation was shared but they omitted any further detail of Cymro's demise, state of his body or the burial, only to confirm what the constable had told them earlier. Talking mostly in playful detail about their apprehension about eventually going to see Old Man Roberts.

"True to form," Tomos regaled, "he saw me coming a mile off and I was in his sights before I got anywhere near the place." Taking another big bite of his third huge pasty and giving Maggie a very appreciative nod as he chewed loudly open mouthed, crumbs spilling down from his animated face. "Duw," said Tomos interrupting his own story, "you make the best pasties Maggie, beautiful pastry…and I love the best when the juices have run out during cooking and have got a little burned. Nice tang."

Patiently and pretending not to notice their guest's sloppy eating, the other's waited for him to continue.

"Anyway, where was I?" Tomos began, still chewing, "Old Man Roberts has got me in his sights and knows by this point I can see him too, so he shouts 'Clear off you…' and then he used some ripe language that I would never repeat in such gentile company, 'or I'll blow your'…" stopping himself there, he fought hard to find the most appropriate word to convert the original to.

120

Coming up with, "'I'll blow your...gonads...off copper!" he looked around the room, checking their reaction, finding he had chosen well.

"He would have n' all, if Evan hadn't made himself known to him at that point. He still wouldn't let me any closer. My, that man hates any authority figure and you then went in didn't you?" Passing the storytelling duties on to his friend, like handing over the speaker's conch.

Evan nodded as if that was all that was required.

"What did you say to him, love?" Maggie asked.

"Well he wasn't happy to see me at first, especially not with 'shiny buttons' over there with me," gesturing to Twm, "then again, I've never known him happy to see anyone. Duw, he soon melted though and was like a little lamb when I presented him with your Welsh cakes Mags. He must have scoffed three in one mouthful without chewing", he exaggerated for Jack's amusement, making eye contact with the boy, charmed by the tale.

"I had him to sit down, telling him I had some bad news and tried to tell him the Englishmen surveying my land had found his dog dead. I never got to finish the sentence. As soon as I mentioned the Englishmen he was back out of his seat like a shot, shouting and cursing about those 'invading, land stealing' so-and-so's and looking out from behind his curtain raving about if they come on his land 'he'll give them both barrels' and that 'so-and-so of a copper better stay away n' all otherwise he'll get the same'. You know, his usual jolly self. In the end the only thing I could do was tell him bluntly that his dog was found dead. I only told him the basics, no details like, only what I could of the truth, that we suspect it was of natural causes. It wasn't a young dog by any means."

"How'd he take it?" said his wife, softly.

The dragon under the hill

"Aw, he started to sob a bit like, shock I imagine. I mean he didn't see much of that thing, half wild it's been for years but he did raise it from a pup and was some sort of company for him on times, I suppose", came the response.

Twm interjected, "I think he quite liked the thought of the brute roaming around the place terrorising the area and putting the wind up folk too. If ever a dog and owner were alike in personality it was him and Cymro"

"No doubt," continued Evan, "so I offered to make him tea or something but he only wanted a nip from the whiskey bottle. I poured it for him then he told me to 'clear off and take PC Plod with me'. So, I left him to it."

"Aye, what can you say? We came straight back here then" ended Twm, who was collecting errant crumbs between his fingers before ramming them in his mouth, giving serious thought to taking on his fourth massive pasty.

Jack, as now was his habit, slowly and carefully peeled and cored an apple with his new penknife. Not only did he become more proficient in this activity but he often practiced opening and closing the folding blade. This worked out its initial stiffness and eventually he could open it easily with one hand. He loved his penknife and it had fast become his most prized possession.

After their repast was complete the off duty policeman, declared his need to go, thanked his hosts for their kindness and before bidding the group goodnight did an hilarious impression of the frightened Mr Deacon backing out the door with Evan's shotgun on his nose.

"I'll be seeing the Reverend first thing to pass on what has happened and as soon as I hear anything more about the surveyors and when they plan to return, I'll let you know. Nos dda all." Then he left to a chorus of goodbyes.

The dragon under the hill

Hardly had the door shut when Evan chuckled to himself, "He's a good sort, old Twm but duw can he eat? I'm sure he was swallowing those pasties whole. Count the knives and forks Mags in case he's gobbled some of those." Maggie just smiled as she cleared the table.

It was the early hours when Jack had finally crept into his bed having discarded his wet clothes. He shivered waiting for the little cocoon of bedclothes to warm up his cold body.

He thought about old Cymro and the fact that he had been so easily dispatched by his saviour. What did the constable say, 'sliced from tail to throat'? He thought about what the voice had said about the dog being 'broken' in the head and what that meant and how did it even know? He was glad he had not seen the animal's carcass after all, the image may have been too brutal a sight and tainted his desire to get to know his rescuer. He wanted to believe that Cymro's death had been quick and humane. That the being had killed the dog without pre-meditation or malice but there was no other recourse to save Jack's life. That no pleasure was gained from the experience or that it represented any desire for violence for its own merits. He needed to believe that the creature had pure motives in what had happened, done out of altruistic protection, for the sake of his view of the entity and for him to continue his visits.

His head, a lexicon of rotating questions that he wanted to interrogate the voice with but his lasting thought as he slipped into the arms of Morpheus, the Greek god of dreams, was that he, little insignificant John Richard James of dirty Dowlais in Merthyr, had spoken to a real dragon and when had anyone ever done that?

123

Chapter 12

There was a tentative knock at the room door.

"Mr Deacon, Mr Deacon are you there?" Said the caller.

Mr Deacon recognised the voice as was one of the surveyors. He continually got them mixed up, one was Eric and the other Oliver or Ollie. Even though they were not related, to him they could have easily been twins. Since their joint arrival three days ago they seemed interchangeable, although this was probably more down to his dismissive and belittling attitude towards them than any actual physical similarity. Both had better breeding, a better education, better qualifications and prospects than he did. Therefore, he spitefully and unkindly took every opportunity to remind them he was squarely in charge of the assignment. He had immediately commandeered the Ministry car they had arrived in and treated it as his own.

"Enter", said Mr Deacon with as much self-importance as he could muster, not even bothering to get up from his chair.

"Er…hello…I…er" stuttered the surveyor, Mr Deacon took a punt and guessed this one was Eric. He looked at the caller stone faced.

"I just…er wanted to inform you that…um…yes, we are both feeling rather better…yes.. Ollie is collating the figures from today…er…it was a good start I thought." Continued Eric.

"A good start? Really?"

Mr Deacon's response surprised the surveyor and knocked him off his stride.

"Bu…But in the circumstances…after what happened." Eric's voice was pleading.

Mr Deacon stared silently, enjoying his ability to make the younger man feel uncomfortable, when he had felt sufficient time had passed he pressed.

"Let's be clear, your behaviour today was completely unprofessional and embarrassing and that goes for both of you. May I remind you we are representatives of the Ministry?" He scolded.

"Oh, I rather think...er...that is rather harsh. I mean, you saw..." was the stammered response.

"Never mind excuses", cutting off the visitor, he got up from his chair and squaring up to the surveyor, stabbing him repeatedly on the shoulder with a bony finger, he ordered "I don't want to see a repeat of that again, I expect better from you both tomorrow. Understood?"

"Um, but you...", Eric managed before succumbing to the stern glare of the littler man, "I see...yes, of course Mr Deacon," the stunned man replied and turned on his heels and left.

As the door clunked shut, Mr Deacon smiled. There was no need for him to do that, to speak to the young man in that manner, except for the fact he found it hugely satisfying and sweetly enjoyable.

When he had first arrived nearly a month ago now, to this tiny blank seemingly inconsequential spot on the map, Clarence Ormerod Deacon had seen this assignment as merely a stop gap. A simple task that would take a few days and he would get back to head office with a feather in his cap. A celebrated success, allowing him to lord it over his peers and get noticed by his superiors. He had rarely been given an outside commission before this one and was eager to prove himself with a quick and simple resolution, to be recognised as a man destined for great things. There was a girl, there always is and although she dismissed him along with the plethora of other suitors at the Ministry, that were

125

The dragon under the hill

forever circling her, finding any excuse to chat at her secretarial desk or bring her some treat or trinket, like she was some pecking hen. He knew that this victory would make him stand out from the crowd and she would see him for what he was and winning her in front of all those jealous others would be simple steps.

Having seldom been outside of London before, he had actually looked forward to his first visit to Wales. He was vastly confident in his abilities and expected little confrontation and nothing his powers of persuasion or a fat cheque could not overcome. He also vastly underestimated the locals he would encounter, their intelligence, strength of mind and ability to co-ordinate.

Three men were dispatched from the ministry at the same time, all with the same objective. To look at an area in the wide open spaces of rural Wales chosen for a possible Ministry site for military use, make sure the land was suitable and then purchase the sections. The Ministry was becoming increasingly worried regards the reports coming out of central Europe the rise of Fascism and other extreme right groups leading to countries becoming xenophobic and unstable. In response it wanted to quietly make what preparations it could for any trouble.

One of the three was dispatched to a region somewhere in North Wales, one to the Sennybridge area of the Brecon Beacons in the South and he was given the site to the West. Little did Mr Deacon know that the other two deals were going wonderfully well. While he'd been dealing with the locals, the North site was close to signing and the Sennybridge deal was freshly completed. This knowledge would have infuriated the resentful man.

Initially, it had all gone so well. Starting off in an upbeat and straight forward manner, he had travelled to the village, secured lodgings over the only public house, the Ty Bont (the only place in the village that provided any), where initially the locals

The dragon under the hill

had been jolly, attentive and kind. He had been able to deal with the fact that no one in the village, not even the village post office, which was to be found at the back of Morgan's shop, had a telephone or telegraph equipment. So his progress reports had to be tediously handwritten and sent by post. He had also found ways around dealing with the boredom that was created by there being very little to do in the sleepy village, making his reports overly long and salty.

It was when the residents found out who exactly he was, who he represented and the exact nature of his commission, that things changed acrid and bitter. The friendly morning greetings and nods in the street were replaced with icy stares and blinkered ignorance. Every interaction he came across converted to speaking in Welsh, whether it had started that way or not and many people who had previously conversed with him happily in English now pretended not to understand anything but their native tongue. Plus, he was convinced most translations he received, when he could cajole someone to giving one, were not only erroneous but also mocking him right under his nose.

Slowly as the trip had been extended and extended, days turning into weeks, he met more and more hostility and resentment. Chalking up more and more unpleasant encounters and less and less civil tones. Turning it from a perfunctory job to be done, into something increasingly personal. With every toxic stare, ignorant rebuff and turned back, his mood, humanity but mostly his sanity had been whittled and chipped at. He had been shouted at and bullied, laughed at by children, scream at by farmwives, physically intimidated, had his lapels grabbed; he'd been threatened with shooting, had shotguns waved in his face and knives brandished (even if the brandisher had demanded he actually stab her), he had been frog matched through gates, chased off land by dogs and out of one a courtyard by a goose; he had been frightened, despised, and sent to Coventry; reviled, vilified and painted a public enemy. Often, he'd been scared for his safety and hated the fact that these people had made him feel powerless and frightened, even if it was just for fleeting moments. The local constable and Reverend had still been courteous and professional and he had tried to deal with them more often than not as spokesmen for the people or to convey a message that he knew would be passed on but he knew even they were working against him and laughed at him behind his back.

Clarence Ormerod Deacon's problems stemmed not only from his task and personality but mainly his lack of empathy. Ploughing into the situation with arrogance and a sense of intellectual superiority, he had given no time to researching the area, it's people or culture. Failing to empower himself with enough information, he was unwittingly, grossly unprepared for what he was attempting. He did not come near to understanding how important the land was to the people he was asking to leave it. He did not even consider that each farm had been built on the sweat, blood and bones of grandparents and great grandparents and so on and the sense of belonging that generates. Roots that run deep.

This was not easy land, it was not gentle and the weather often raged against those taming it but like anything that cost, anything that was hard work, it engendered great loyalty and affection. How could he appreciate that these people could no more give up their farms and homesteads, any more than they could deny a piece of themselves, turn a deaf ear to a crying baby or hurt those they loved? They were forged out of the soil and stone, rooted in the earth like the wind shortened trees, counted their life by its seasons and would never nor could ever agree to walking away, however much he pressured, cajoled or bribed. Given this context, no amount of money, no splendid alternative or dogged badgering could have any effect on their entrenched position.

Never trying to understand any of these things, empathise or appreciate the value of what his requests to leave actually

The dragon under the hill

meant, Mr Deacon had lost his battle well before it had begun. Now he just didn't care. The accumulation of this negative treatment just twisted his shallowness, fed into his deep-seated insecurities and piped into his own self-loathing.

Now he saw every refusal as a personal slight. Every local was an inbred village dwelling idiot. Every interaction, even pleasant, to be treated as suspicious. Every building an affront to be torn down. He resented the wasted time he'd spent in this backward place, this job keeping him away from his comfortable home and life in London and especially, at this point, how it reflected on him to his employers. Even the small comfortable room he stayed in, with its view of the village square to the front and unfolding vista down the valley at the rear, had turned from a cosy sanctuary to a cold and mocking prison cell.

He hated this place, he hated the people and he had singled out Evan James as their ringleader and despised him the most. More than he thought he could hate another human being. He thought 'that wicked man' to be the devil himself dressed in a wax jacket solely responsible for any wrong or ill he had suffered and would suffer.

Take this morning's events. He knew the local constable was only going through the motions of seeing that his work went unhindered. He was staring down a barrel of a shotgun for goodness sake and nothing was done to intervene or even rebuke his attacker. He should have been able to at the very least press charges instead of the debacle it was, with that inept policeman in collusion with his loathed assailant. Didn't he have a legal document from Westminster allowing him on that land? Didn't these fools understand that? Didn't any of these Neanderthals have any respect for authority? Didn't they realise what an opportunity he was offering them, to get out and away from this horrible place, he was doing them a favour? Didn't they want to do their duty, it was their country calling after all?

The dragon under the hill

Any dreg of sympathy or droplet of affinity with these people disappeared with what he could only see as the rank heinousness killing of a poor defenceless dog and arranging him on display like a ritualistic sacrifice, just to intimidate and upset the surveyors was a horrific act beyond the pale. He wishe those young surveyors hadn't reacted so weakly and even worse foolishly blurted out that the car was borrowed to the constable, as he was enjoying how it made heads turn and was sure he was the envy of all who saw it, thinking it was his.

He was now going to show them, he was going to demonstrate his real power and start the process of seeing them humbled and gaining his vengeance.

Writing out at some length his latest report to the minister's aide, with relish he exaggerated the opposition his group had received, recounted in great detail the dead dog incident and made great play of the weapons that had been pointed at him including the threats made. He specially over blew this morning's incident and the danger he faced, he insisted on the ministry backing him up further, that his work could not be completed without armed soldiers to back him up, preferably with him allotted more overarching authority. Even fanaticising about leading them through the village and onto the James farm, like some venerated pied piper.

Sadly, this Ministry worker did not know his history and the other occasions in the not too distant past when English soldiers were marched into local disputes in Wales. Each time based on a belittling of the people and a haughty indifference to their cause, the response a heavy handed over reaction, making things worse and leaving bitter blood soaked stains on communities and history. From the Merthyr Uprising of 1831 and the climax of the Chartist rising nearly a decade later, to the rolling Rebecca riots and the Tonypandy miners in 1911, still known as Churchill's shame. The addition of troops only exasperated each situation and made the chances of the confrontations ending in

130

bloodshed almost inevitable and civilian death certain and abundant. In the days when 'an attack on a soldier was an attack on the King', simply defending your home or family, fighting for basic human rights or your livelihood or even an unjust case of mistaken identity meant prison, deportation or a hangman's noose was to follow. The voice of each quashed rebel, singing nationalist or like Richard Pendeyrn, a martyr's last words still echo and inspire.

With this knowledge of plentiful mistakes by other little men, maybe then he would have given second thoughts to his request and his blatant exaggeration of the facts of the situation but probably not. The man was now driven by spite and spite alone. In such a state, someone can lose themselves completely and end up so far from who they once were. If ever Clarence Ormerod Deacon had been kind and gentle, a temperate and considerate person, then those aspects of his nature had had slipped away. Lost to him in the heavy fog of insulted rage.

Having finished his report, he placed it in an envelope and addressed it, he leaned back in the chair that was at the little table and smiled a crumpled, insipid smile. He would post the letter first thing in the morning, come back and rouse those two bungling, bumbling surveyors from their room next door and get them back over to 'that man's farm' to finish the job they started. He galvanised himself to take whatever abuse that was dealt out to him, ignore the sniggering behind his back because he knew that he had started events in motion that would wipe the smiles from his enemy's faces. He could not help but think with salacious relish, 'my day will come'.

Chapter 13

In the bright morning sun, sporting their 'Sunday best' clothes, the James family descended from the cart. Evan tethered the horse and they trooped towards the little chapel, exchanging merry greetings with all they encountered on the way.

A small queue had formed near the entrance, as each chapel goer was individually greeted and given their hymn book. While they were waiting patiently a booming voice called out.

"Jack! Jack, over here boyo!"

It was the familiar voice of Reverend Thomas calling Jack over to where he stood. A young girl stood by his side, his hand resting fatherly on her shoulder.

Jack obediently approached the pair and got a ruffling of his hair from the Reverend in leu of a greeting for his efforts.

"Bore da Jack, are you well lad?" asked the Reverend.

"Good morning", came the reply "very well thank you". The young girl just stared.

"Now then lad, I know you had trouble last time you were here because...well, the Welsh was bit fast for you", Jack knew the Reverend was being kind to him, overestimating his Welsh language skills in their mixed company, "so I've got you some help."

Looking down at the girl, he smiled, "Jack, I want you to meet Lily here. Lily Hegarty...or Lil for short."

The youngsters nodded to each other suspiciously, as most do when forced together by adults, especially if they are the opposite sexes.

132

The dragon under the hill

"Her grandparents come from Ireland originally but we'll forgive her that." Laughing at his own joke, his companions did not share his mirth. "Their farm is a couple down the valley from where your grandparent's live. She's about your age and has an excellent vocabulary. Fluent in both languages see. She's very kindly agreed to sit with you and translate the service for you. Won't you Lil?"

"Yes, Reverend Thomas", came the youth's reply.

Jack felt unusually nervous entering the chapel with Lily and while joining his grandparents in their pew he couldn't help but notice the two young surveyors that had come to their house the day before, sitting attentively at the back of the chapel.

Scowling, he said out loud, "What a cheek, those two coming here like!"

His grandmother quickly rebuked him, "now boy, all are welcome in God's house, don't forget that, you".

The truth was that not only were both the young surveyors, Eric and Ollie, devout in their faith and were accustomed to church attendance on Sunday but unlike Mr Deacon, they enjoyed the locality and were very interested in all aspects of the culture they found themselves immersed in. They were eager to learn, about the land primarily but also about the people, language and history, grateful for any knowledge or experience.

They had been warned earlier in the day by Mr Deacon to expect nothing but hostility and ignorance from the local people, once he had got over his rage and disbelief when they resolutely informed him that because it was Sunday, not only would they not be working but they would be attending the local chapel. 'Hadn't they just had the whole of Saturday off to get some needed supplies from Cardiff?' He had argued but they would not be swayed.

The dragon under the hill

In reality, not only had they been warmly greeted at the door when they arrived early but at the end of the service they had even received two separate offers from different farming families to come back to their home and have Sunday lunch with them. They were extremely tempted but reluctantly had to decline the offers because they knew this would leave Mr Deacon all alone for lunch at their lodgings and despite them not really enjoying the man's acerbic company, they did not like the thought of leaving him to eat alone.

Although they did not understand more than a few words during the entire meeting, they had rather enjoyed the vibrant hymn singing, being impressed by the gusto, easy harmonies and shear volume the congregation mustered, despite its size. Highlighting a cultural difference between the neighbouring lands, singing in a group situation, like church, an Englishman will pitch his voice until it gets lost in the crowd, only then being both blissful and satisfied. While if a Welshman even gets even an inkling that his voice is getting lost in the crowd he will sing louder to rise above it, only then will he be blissful and satisfied.

They were impressed by the passion and earnestness with which the preacher spoke, what the Welsh call 'hwyl' which is a complex word referring to a burning inspiration, spirit or a fervent belonging. Avidly quizzing the Reverend afterwards regarding what he had actually said, they happily received a repeat performance, this time in English.

Jack was transfixed but his eyes and focus was not on the animated preacher but on his new companion.

The Reverend Thomas dramatically gesticulated his meanings, expertly bolted out words for emphasis and lowered his voice to caress and mould some crucial point. His powerful oration both stirring himself and those listening. Her eyes fixed on the pulpit, Lily lilted and rolled out the translation in soft spun tones. To the young boy, her voice was like warm sunlight reaching out

134

and touching his face and the lightest of breezes gently lifting and tingling the hairs on his arms. He hardly realised he was staring unblinkingly at her, finding himself marooned in what he saw, he felt weightless, a mass of tingles and wisps.

The way her raven black hair caught the light, caused a sea of tiny halos to glide up and down her loose curls, her eyes equally dark had a gravity their own. Leaving him defenceless, drawing him into to them and to the bottomless chasm there. He was lost, shipwrecked and adrift in them. He had never studied anything as hard as he did Lily's face that morning, rapt by her flawless cream, alabaster skin. Those thin but inviting cherry-blossom lips were giddying and he was equally rapt by the way the very end of her nose moved when she spoke. She smelled of lavender and fresh Camay soap and in her little floral dress she shone angelically. Like staring at the sun, she burned her bright image on his retinas. To this young boy she was loveliness, she was the high cap-stone of beauty and he was falling into her effortless magical allure and could not or would not struggle.

For her part, she thought very little of Jack. She harboured a little crush on the Reverend as did all his female parishioners, would do anything for him and saw this solely as a favour, a chore. She had been unimpressed when she eventually met Jack, especially after the Reverend had spoken about him in very glowing terms. To her he was a small scrawny lad, totally unremarkable, ordinary in looks and speech and as she was growing into a woman now, certainly not worth a second thought.

Dismissing him out of hand did mean she missed his strong mindset and personal qualities, although admittedly not immediately obvious at that time. In years to come he would show a tenacious determination in all his hand found to do, including, she would realise later, matters of the heart.

It was an odd experience for Jack, saying goodbye to her at the end of the service and seeing her leave with her family, the

The dragon under the hill

angelic visitation over. Everything seemed dull; dim and slightly distant, something ached within him that he did not understand.

It was well into the afternoon. After their substantial Sunday roast dinner, Evan was lightly snoring in his chair, the only movement a projection of the flickering light from the fire dancing across his frame, his faithful dog doing the same at his feet. Maggie was peeling apples for another one of her baked delights, while Jack was intently drawing on some brown paper he'd found, with a tiny stub of a pencil. He was in deep concentration trying to capture every aspect, even the smallest detail of the creature he'd encountered.

All three, even the slumbering Evan, were startled as unheralded, the farmhouse door was opened but quickly relaxed when the familiar voice of Rhodri shouted his greetings.

"Woke you up b'there did I old fella?" he aimed at Evan.

"Look Heini, a burglar! Bite his nose off," came the half-hearted reply. The dog for her part did not see any of this as her business and stayed rooted to her roost beside the flames.

"Tea, is it, Rhodri?" said Maggie getting to her feet.

"After Mags, I've come to take the boy for a walk…yes and the dog", he announced, pre-empting Maggie's next sentence.

"'Ave him," Evan said, still dozing, "but please don't lose any bits of him as his mum will be cross".

"O right," Rhodri impishly raised his right hand, "I solemnly swear to return the young chap in the condition in which I borrowed him and not to break him."

Evan nodded satisfied as the pair left.

The dragon under the hill

"What do you think that could be about?" Evan asked his wife languidly.

"Well, obvious isn't it?" She said smiling, "didn't you see the way he was looking at little Lily Hegarty during the meeting. They boy was catching flies his mouth was open so long."

"O, is it? I didn't notice, me" came the half-dreamt response.

"Typical of you, if one of your lambs lost a lock of its fleece, you'd spot it a mile away but when it comes people, you're as blind as a bat. You mark my words," she continued, her smile broader, "that lad is smitten."

During the post service hullabaloo this morning, with the surveyors being present, the inclusion of Lily and the normal bustle, Jack had only a fleeting moment of interaction with the Reverend to exchange pleasantries but in that brief moment, being the man he was, Reverend Thomas had picked up that Jack wanted to speak to him with some urgency and privately.

Heini, although reluctant to join them was now patrolling the hedgerow, following her nose on some random quest known only to herself. Reverend Thomas expertly curved around the conversation, like he was approaching a nervous horse.

"Was the service better with you understanding the sermon?" was the opening approach.

"Yes, I think so." Muttered the lad, not having the heart to admit he couldn't even recount what the subject of this morning's sermon was.

"Lovely young girl, Lil is, don't you think?" watching the boy avidly for the slightest facial movement.

The dragon under the hill

Jack was derailed and not a little embarrassed by the question and felt his face warming, struggling to answer.

"O Yes", then catching himself corrected himself, "Ah, I mean...I mean, what? I don't know...I didn't really notice." He managed to stammer when he recovered some of his composure, when deep down his heart was singing a sonnet and painting masterpieces in her honour.

"Aye, lovely girl" the preacher repeated, almost just to himself.

They reached the spot where they had sat a talked previously, it was some minutes before anyone spoke.

"So my boy, is there anything you wanted to talk to me about?" he asked directly, thinking that Jack wanted to discuss his obviously burgeoning feelings for the girl he had just met and seeing his earlier discomfort, realising the boy wasn't going to get there by himself.

"Um...what? No...no... I don't think so," his mind still on a certain girl and milky-white skin and sloe-black locks. Then his brain snapped into gear, wrestled from its floating stupor and he was jolted from his enchantment to teeth, claws and mighty myths.

"Oh! Oh, yes!" he yelled coming to himself, "I saw it! I actually saw it!" then he was off and running, animated with story-telling hands. "It's real, it's actually real. I saw it up there, right up there, I can show you and then..."

His friend had to interrupt "Whoa, lad. Slow down. Now start again, from the beginning. Who did you see?"

"Grandfather's dragon," came the plainly spoken reply.

"What?" exclaimed the clergyman.

"The dragon" repeated Jack calmly.

138

"No? What? You saw it, actually saw it?...Are you sure it wasn't just a shadow and you just think might have been it?"

"I was as close to it as you are to me now". The Reverend Rhodri Thomas stared directly into the boy's eyes, there was no way he was lying.

"You'd better tell me the whole story, starting from the beginning then boyo", he encouraged as they both sat down.

Jack then hungrily told the whole story from start to finish, like a starving man devouring every word in bites far too big to chew and swallow. How he was very sorry to break a promise and disobey his grandparents but following the night he had first seen movement on the hill-top and spoken about it, he had visited the cairn every night to investigate it and leave some meat. There was no way he could not.

He depicted, in colourful detail, the traumatic night he had been set upon by the deathly black hell-hound Cymro, coming out of the blackness. How the beast was near to tearing his face off before something rescued him. He described the sound of what he later realised must have been large wings and then the moment Cymro tried to come at him enraged, only to be intercepted from nowhere and swiftly and easily killed. In faulting language, he attempted to convey how the fabled being had looked, those two golden eyes that looked directly at him and into him. He struggled to explain having the animal's voice speak directly into his head. Jack went on to portray his further visits to the cairn to seek out his rescuer and thank it. He outlined their 'conversations', including the most recent, last night.

"I went up again last night despite the rain," the lad continued, "it took a while for it to answer, it's not very friendly and hard to get to talk. It always starts by telling me to go away, 'Leave' it says, harsh like but I stand my ground. Then, as I'm asking something, it will just stop, like it has had enough. No matter what you do or say after that, you'll get nothing back"

139

The dragon under the hill

He looked up, trying to remember word for word the most recent exchange, "So anyway, last night I asked him where he lived, had to wait ages, then he said 'Under'. So, I suppose it means in the cairn or caves somewhere under the hill. And I asked him how long he has been there and all he said was 'Before man'. And that was it".

His companion took a deep breath and slowly exhaled, giving himself time to compose himself and a suitable response.

"Duw, duw, duw" was all he could come up with before there was another thoughtful pause.

Clearing his throat, the Reverend launched into his response.

"I'm very disappointed in you for breaking a promise you made to me and it was very wrong of you to disobey your grandparents like that. Sneaking around like that at all hours in the dark, in such a dangerous pace. I understand your curiosity but that's not an excuse. How do you think your grandparents would feel if something had happened to you? How would they know where to find you? It was a silly thing to do and I expect more of you Jack"

"I am sorry, I couldn't help it. I had to," pleaded Jack.

"Ach, I forgive you lad and no harm was done but we won't mention it to your grandfather just yet, he may not be quite as quick to forgive and as for Maggie..." he warned. He thought some more before speaking more softly to the forlorn boy.

"I believe you in what you are telling me, I certainly don't think you are lying, I just find it hard to believe it. Does that make sense boy?"

Jack shook his head. Being a preacher, the first analogy that came to mind was a biblical one.

140

The dragon under the hill

"Take that bit in the gospel of Mark chapter 9 if you remember it, where Jesus offered to heal a boy and his father said, 'I believe, help my unbelief' – it was like the boy's father knew in his heart that Jesus could heal his son but because he had not seen a healing or Jesus perform one, he struggled to imagine it with his head. Do you know what I mean?" expanded the clergyman.

"I think so." Jack replied. He scrabbled in his pocket and fished out the brown piece of paper he'd been working on so industriously earlier. Handing it to his companion, he pointed to the main image. "Here, that's sort of what it looked like."

The Reverend looked at the crude drawing and it was certainly a depiction of a dragon. It couldn't be mistaken for anything else that roamed these hills but it must be the imaginings of a sleep-deprived, eager boy. Forcing himself to see patterns and shapes in the gloom and half-lights and convincing himself of the origin but he does seem so utterly convinced and there were some oddities about how old Cymro had met his end.

As the image was studied the boy rambled, "I'm not a very good drawer. Dad is good at drawing, he can draw excellent rabbits and foxes. Whatever you like…"

"How big was it?", was the interruption.

"O, hard to say because it's long you see but in body…maybe a bit bigger than old Merlin the horse" guessed the boy.

"And this is definitely what it looked like?"

"Only for a second I saw it mind but yes, that's what it was like?"

"Are you sure boy? Could it not have been something else?" The Reverend felt he was floundering, struggling to get a foothold in the situation.

The dragon under the hill

Jack pointing to his picture relayed, "Small head, long body, like this

"You must have found it all a bit frightening, son?" said the Reverend in a caring manner, finally finding his feet.

"Scared stiff, I was shaking after that night with Cymro," he didn't admit to the flowing tears though, no young lad wants to be thought as a cry baby. "but when I go up now, I don't feel scared at all."

"Anyway, I should probably come with you next time, I think" ventured Reverend Thomas.

"OK" responded the boy "but it hardly talks to me, give me a couple of nights for it to get used to the idea."

Was this the boy stalling to think of a story or a genuine request, thought the Reverend.

"Look son, I don't like the idea of you clambering up there and rooting around in the dark on your own and continuing to deceive your grandparents is bad enough."

"I'm safe on the path I've found, honest I am," trying to convince the clergyman he continued, "I'm sure if you went with me first off nothing would happen. Then I'd look a fool and you'd think I'm a liar..." feelings ambushed the boy and he found himself getting upset, "and I don't want you to think of me as a liar." Now nearly in tears.

"Alright lad, alright" he relented, before whispering to himself "I must be mad, Maggie will kill me for sure".

"I can't believe I'm saying this but I'll give you until around the end of the week and then I'm coming, ready or not. You must be extra, extra careful and if anything happens, you run straight home." Said Rhodri.

142

The dragon under the hill

"I'll be careful, I'll be safe."

"Fair enough," the preacher conspired, "I'll meet you around about here, midnight on, say, Friday? Fair?".

Jack nodded his agreement, glad that he was believed but apprehensive about what might happen.

The Reverend let out a huge sigh, wondering if what he had done was the best course of action and urgently praying quietly in his heart. 'Lord keep that boy safe!'

"So" said Reverend Thomas changing the subject, "back to young Lily. I'm told you are quite taken with her."

Jack's blindsided look of horror at being found out so easily made the Reverend laugh raucously, hugely enjoying the youngster's discomfort, he did not push the boy further.

"Right", announced the preacher, "let's head back and see if whatever Maggie was making with those apples is ready for us to scoff."

When they returned, the table was already laid and both Jack's grandparents were sitting around it. The dog being first in through the door went straight to greet her master.

As soon as Evan saw the others enter, he blurted out.

"So lad, what's this I hear about you and a girl."

Without skipping a beat Jack scarpered straight passed them to his room, taking two steps at time in his hurry to escape the horror of his embarrassment, the adults laughing mightily behind him.

Even though she had laughed as heartily as the rest, Maggie was the first to curb the kind of good-humoured cruelty all families dish out in these circumstances.

The dragon under the hill

"Aw, bless him. We mustn't tease him too much now. I'll take him up some crumble in a minute, that'll cheer him up." Despite telling the group off and trying really hard, she still could not suppress her massive smile.

The dragon under the hill

Chapter 14

It was raining quite viciously and the ululating wind churned the droplets so they were dispersed in all directions, nothing compared to the average fury and turmoil from the weather the hill experienced in the winter months but a forbidding and harsh environment nonetheless.

It had certainly crossed Jack's mind, while still in his bed, to stay exactly where he was and give his nightly excursion a miss. To stay in the warmth and let his thoughts dissolve in the wistful mystery and wonder of 'the girl'. Met only this morning, she already consumed him, eating his mind in voracious bites. Was she really all she seemed or the shimmering aberration of love struck youth? Before he knew it, his mind had wandered and meandered to Lily's harbour where he could cast anchor and gently lullaby with the roll of the bobbing sea.

Rousing yourself from a warm bed is hard enough at the best of times, especially from a beautiful dream or cosy thought but knowing you don't have to and to do so is to face horrible wild weather, plus a hill climb in the dark, is height of impediment. His burgeoning determination continued becoming more steal-like as he found himself downstairs putting on his rubber boots before he could argue with himself.

Jerked out of his concentration the boy yelped in shock and fear as something unseen touched the back of his leg. Spinning around in weightless panic, eyes grasping frantically in the gloom for his assailant, Jack almost lost his footing completely. Only to find instead of some horrific night terror or apparition, stood the placid expectant face of Heini looking up at him for attention. Jack stifled his angry need to shout at the animal, holding a hand over his pumping heart he managed to contain himself to a whisper through gritted teeth.

The dragon under the hill

"You frightened the life out of me then, you silly girl," the unrepentant dog continued her wait for attentional undeterred. "Duw, my heart of pounding b'here!"

"Go on now, lie down," Jack ordered, after finally giving the dog a few cursory scratches.

Struggling with his boots he sat at the table to catch his breath, where just a few hours previously, he had spent another wonderful evening with his grandparents and their old friend.

His grandmother eventually persuaded him to come down from his self-enforced exile in his room and join the rest for a repast. With the duel promises that he would not have to suffer any further teasing and there was freshly cooked apple crumble and custard to be had.

Struggling up the slippery hill clutching his coat tight around him and bowing his head against the wind, he warmed himself by remembering the conversation around the table as he ploughed through seconds of his beloved apple crumble. He remembering being impressed by the easy way they talked about their feelings when his grandparents first met, first impressions and well won hands. Feelings of attraction and romance were new to him and when it came to his own experience he found it difficult to capture them in words.

He had really enjoyed when his grandparent's attention had turned to their guest and teased Rhodri for him not yet taking a wife.

Rhodri tried to maintain that he was 'married' to his parish and didn't have time for a woman in his life but his old friends knew him well enough to push home and obtaining real and honest answers from him. He confessed about sometimes being lonely and giving the matter thought from time to time. It would be nice to not go home to an empty house and have someone to spend

The dragon under the hill

the evenings with and no one wants to think about growing old alone but most of the time he was busy enough that he didn't mind.

Jack was especially amused when his grandparents took turns in naming eligible suiters for the Reverend and although he did not know who these ladies were, as the names were listed he was greatly tickled at the clergyman's response to each individual name. 'Too old', 'Too young', 'Too much like her mother', 'Too much like the heifer she milks', which caused hilarity from Jack but got the Reverend a sound telling off from Maggie. 'Too bossy', 'Too icy' and a surprising 'Too noisy, she never shuts up. You'd chew off a couple of your own toes just to have something to stick in your ears to have a bit of quiet', which instigated a riot of spluttering laughter even from Maggie. Although, she did reclaim her righteous indignation long enough to exclaim the 'Oh, Rhodri!' he was expecting again from her. Sometimes he just pulled a face and shook his head but on a few occasions he had nothing to say, which told a story of itself.

Jack had enjoyed seeing the tables turned on one of the adults and Rhodri wriggle and squirm with discomfort, even if it was by deliberate design. He was grateful to see such open friendships dealing with subjects that can cause deep awkwardness and lasting embarrassment.

"Anyway", teased Evan, "she'd have to be deaf to put up with that snoring of yours and have no sense of smell to wash your stinky socks. I'm sure I've seen some of your socks roaming the village on their own."

"O, you cheeky so and so," responded the clergyman in mock indignation. "Well, I've been insulted now, I'm going home with my tail between my legs." This was all part of their usual repartee but did bring the evening to a close.

The terrain and his footing demanded his full attention as he snapped back to his present. A few times he had to release his grip from his coat lapels to extend his hands to halt a slide through

147

The dragon under the hill

the wet grass as he lost his footing but he had been up and down the hill so many times in the dark, that he was in no real danger and his boots could probably transverse the course on their own now.

Reaching the apex, he did his usual checks and listened out for any activity. Unable to stay still long due to the irritating rain he entered the field, quickly circled the cairn, looking all about him for any sign of movement or life. At the usual spot, he placed some chucks of meat and called out.

"Hello! Hello! It's Jack. Are you there?". The wind was battering his back as he was more exposed now.

"Leave!"

Came the now customary response.

Jack had to remind himself to fight the urges that the voice stirred within him to simply obey.

"Sorry, I won't leave. I don't mean you any harm, I only want to talk!" He shouted, competing with the strong wind.

"Leave this place!"

The voice seemed louder and the urges stronger but again the tenacious lad stood against it, as he stood against the gusts that threatened to topple him.

"I have brought you some meat" he announced, before forging on, "I know you are real. I know you are there...How is it I hear your voice in my head?"

After a pregnant pause, Jack got a response.

"You are young. You are still...open".

The last word seemed carefully chosen. It was still impossible to tell anything from the tone or inflection, it was like

148

The dragon under the hill

the very stones were speaking. Each syllable chiselled painstakingly made audible by the grating of adjacent rocks. Encouraged, Jack pressed on.

"My name is Jack and I'm twelve and this is my grandparent's farm."

Still trying to see any movement in the night, Jack asked.

"What's your name and how old are you?"

This time the response came slightly quicker than before, which seemed like progress to the boy.

"We do not measure time as you. I have been here since the days when all was...ice." The voice becoming less staccato and more fluid.

"I am called...Krait."

"Krait...Krait" Jack repeated, trying out the strange word, forming his mouth around its foreign feel.

"Are there more like you, Krait?" the boy asked.

The powerful wind, whipping the rain against his face made him wish things would progress a whole lot faster but he was utterly fascinated.

Like someone using an old antenna, he was afraid to move in case he lost the reception. The precious contact kept him rooted to that spot in the ground.

"Ah..." there was a pause like a held breath, "I have not heard my name spoken in so very long, it seems foreign to me now." The voice stated before answering the boy's question.

"I am...alone."

The dragon under the hill

While Jack was digesting the answer he'd been given sadness began to touch him, the creature spoke unprompted.

"Once" started the voice, "there were many in this land. Now? I do not know."

"What? All alone? Are you...are you...the last one?" Asked the surprised youth.

As he talked to Krait, Jack begun to find meaning in the pauses, a feeling he had not noticed before, accompanying them. This pause felt melancholic and forlorn.

"It has been countless winters since I have encountered another. Not since..."

"Oh, I am sorry. That's really sad." Commented Jack feeling Krait would not be finishing that sentance he should break the silence that had lingered, sensing he had brought up a subject of great significance and pain, that had been deliberately buried for a long, long time and was not surprised when he heard the next statement.

"Leave now." This time the words were not supported by a command, this was gentler, a request.

"I will go but I will come back again tomorrow." Jack stated.

"As you wish."

Hurriedly making the journey back down from the inhospitable, weather-battered hill-top, Jack felt he understood so much more about the being that called itself Krait and the way it imparted its words to him. The creature was obviously highly intelligent and had been alive for who knows how long. It knew how to communicate with assurance. Not in a traditional way, where words are formed and sound is heard but by somehow sending out its meaning, its feeling, transmitting somehow like a

150

The dragon under the hill

radio mast. So, that someone who was 'open' as it had been described, could experience it straight into their head. He supposed being 'open' was like owning a radio set proficient enough to pick up on the transmission and maybe some people had too many thoughts of their own in their head to be the same way.

Unlike radio, it seemed like it used the person's own vocabulary to speak with them and during the times when it appeared to be working out the right word, it was searching their mind for the most accurate word in their language, so the communication went both ways like a cable. Now he was getting used to the link they shared, maybe the creature could spark feelings within the boy, to convey its own sentiments. Jack did not think himself emotionally immature but like all lads his age, he was a long way from being self-aware enough to understand complex feelings, let alone put them into words.

He couldn't imagine the things the being had seen, lived through and experienced. There must have been a time when more of these noble creatures existing, spawning all those Welsh legends and tales thought mythical. Ruled the land and soared from one apex to another, mountain tops being their perch and the whole valley covered in one expanse of their wings. They must have been the land's potentates, so mighty and lethal. What must have happened all those years ago? Krait and his kind had slipped so easily and firmly into myth and legend. How could something so wonderful, so other-worldly and powerful, end up cowering in solemn insignificance alone in a cave under his grandparent's farm?

Jack decided to add it to the list of questions he would ask next time before approaching the subject of having another visitor. Right now, all he cared about was getting into the warm and maybe pinching a few spoonfuls of crumble from the pantry.

The dragon under the hill

That night Jack found he felt different as he clambered into his bed, like he'd grown two inches from the boy who left the same bed hours earlier. Difficult for his young mind to define but he definitely felt there was more intensity to his senses, he was more 'aware'. More aware of his body, his thoughts, his emotional being; more aware of his room, its sounds and its smells, the tiniest detail in his sight from the width of a crack in the plaster near the window to the image refracted through a water droplet making its way down the window pane; more aware of his surroundings, the wind and the rain pestering his window, the noises made by the animals in the night and even the sense of where he and they existed in the length of the valley. His mind seemed more expansive and sharper and his memory surer and more detailed. He wondered how much of this was down to his recent experiences, how much due to him growing up and how much attributable to this mental link developing with the incredible creature. Maybe it was just a lack of sleep and too much stimulation.

He soon coasted into a fitful, troubled sleep. His mind haunted by glimpses of colours, fragments of images and bits of dreamscapes, none of which were familiar to him and none of them clear enough recognise or were too fleeting to really register. Ever essence filter to darkly to make out like blacked out windows. There were feelings attached to the cerebral flashes but too intangible to be named or retained.

When he woke sweat-soaked in the pre-dawn half-light, bed clothes tangled around him, his neck muscles hurt from where he must have been clenching his teeth hard against the night and his dreams. He wrestled himself free, washed the sleep from his face and found himself receiving the blessed comfort of the crackling flames of the fire he built as his grandparents stirred.

The dragon under the hill

Chapter 15

Today was a day of letters.

A man who was without the self-awareness of a small boy, Mr Deacon, was slowly painting himself as a pantomime villain in the area. He had just received a letter from the Minister's under-secretary. The stiff, official letter mentioning that the Ministry was both surprised and concerned at his report (especially his request for troops), was torn open and read voraciously. Thinking it both overkill and a sign that this task may be too much for him the letter concluded that they had still decided in this instance to agree with his personal recommendation and assistance would arrive in a couple of days. This acquiescence to his demand, blindly elated Mr Deacon and reinforced his now entrenched, anti-local position and the small war he now felt he was fighting against them. In his state of alienation and blinkered vision, the criticism and concern that followed in the letter fell away unnoticed.

Due to his dismissive attitude towards the two men, Mr Deacon failed to notice and probably could not even conceive that the surveyors themselves also sent in daily reports, as they were instructed to do so, reporting to the same Minister. Owing to their upbeat and more discreet disposition, their reports were invariably more akin to the real state of affairs and were treated as such. They often unwittingly contradicted Mr Deacon's accounts when the Ministry compared them. At best they gave a much different perspective to the situation and at their worst, reflected a situation their operative was fast losing control of.

Eric and Ollie read the Ministerial response that Mr Deacon had just received in turn, as he had shoved it under their noses at the first opportunity, wide-eyed with pride. They were firstly alarmed at the mention of soldiers and even the suggestion they were needed here but being capable of more clarity of

153

thought than Mr Deacon at that moment, they recognised the Ministry's subversive tactic. His superiors were clearly, as the expression goes, 'giving him enough rope to hang himself'. They obviously suspected something would go wrong in this situation, tipping point coming at any moment and were making sure only one person would be squarely and solely to blame.

The surveyors did feel sorry for Mr Deacon and did try to talk him around from the path of mental deterioration he was on, providing wise and reasonable counsel but his moronic, jingoistic dislike of the locals and the petty way he waved around the communication made it hard to.

Even their attempts to gently discuss his interpretation of the situation where shot down as he became increasingly angry that these 'upstarts' didn't share his joy and the discussion was ended with an abrupt snap.

"Oh, just shut up, the pair of you!"

Constable Tomos Jones also received a letter from his superiors but it was received in the opposite humour. It made it clear that Mr Deacon had complained about him to the Ministry behind his back and they had, in turn, shared the dissatisfaction with the area head of the police force. This displeasure had been passed on to the Chief Constable who had dictated the correspondence to the local officer.

"It's like trying to protect a barking, biting dog from little children's ankles. They've got it the wrong way around. It's the community that needs protection from him, mun!" He complained to the listeners around the James's kitchen table. Holding the offending letter in his disgruntled hand, he proceeded to read from the affronting article.

"I mean for goodness sake, listen to this rubbish, 'It has been brought to our attention...'" he looked up, "Aye, they mean that blooming clown Mr Deacon has been crying like a baby."

154

"Slimy toad." Commented Evan.

"Then it goes on, er...where was it.... aye here we go, 'you have been accused of dereliction in your duty to offer the sufficient protection we expect you to extend to a Government operative and his team.'" Twm looked up from the page in wide-eyed astonishment.

"Dereliction! Blooming dereliction! I'll dereliction him..." ending in a splutter as words failed him.

Pointing out the window in some random direction, as if the accused was standing before them in a courtroom dock. "He's the one who's been going around upsetting people and acting like he was blooming king and should be obeyed." He continued incredulous. "He's the one who's been making enemies left, right and centre. All this is his own making mun!"

Maggie joined in the righteous indignation, "Tell those high and mighty bosses of yours how the horrid little man burst into our house!"

"Aye", pitched Evan "I could have been having a bath and he would have seen me in all my glory."

"O, Evan, don't make me laugh because I'm tamping angry, I am." Said the unhappy visitor.

Evan, realising that this dissection of the letter, phrase by phrase, was in danger of going on indefinitely and feeling a change of subject would benefit his friend said, "So, where are the surveyors and your best friend?"

Without taking his eyes from the letter, the constable hooked his thumb behind him and explained. "The young lads are taking a few more measurements down this end, then I have to take them up the valley to the boundary, then back up to the top...another big triangle or something. Mr Smug-Face is prowling around somewhere near." He then looked at his watch. "Actually,

155

The dragon under the hill

I should probably go and catch them now." As he donned his policeman's hat and was closing the door he announced to the room waving a fist, "It's all I can do not to give him a right clout right on the…" The rest of the sentence was lost behind the closed door.

"Poor Twm" said Maggie as he left.

Jack for his part was mostly ignorant of the whole conversation that had just gone on, even though it had taken place in front of him. When the constable had arrived early this morning, as well as brandishing his own letter, he had brought a letter for Jack too. It was from his mother and was a reply to the letter he had sent her.

Jack had never received a letter addressed to just himself before and even though he immediately recognised his mother's flowery cursive writing, to the youngster it was as important as a letter from the King George himself. His instinct was to eagerly rip it open but remembering his treasured blade, he carefully and neatly sliced the envelope with his penknife. He had consumed its contents for the third time, by the time Twm left and he had an opportunity to relay them to his grandparents.

"It's from mam" he began, "thanking me for the letter I wrote. She says all the family are well and her and dad are missing me. They are glad I'm enjoying my time here and say they hope I'm behaving and doing as I'm told, and ask after your health." He summarised.

"Any real news," enquired Maggie.

"Nothing much to tell", Jack responded, "Desmond is toddling around, into everything. Idris says 'hello' and said he finds it hard to sleep without me snoring next to him. Here," handing the letter to his grandmother. "Have a read for yourself."

156

The dragon under the hill

This is what Maggie had been secretly waiting and hoping for and she devoured the letter.

"I'm going to reply right now" said Jack, eagerly grabbing some paper, enthused by this new thrilling feeling engendered by getting a letter all his own, seeing his mother's looping handwriting and imagining her and his family as she described them, "and I'm going to put my drawing in it for dad to see."

Finding it easy to start, he soon found his writing grinding to a halt as he did not know how to approach either of the two major things that were going on in his life or even if he could. He decided just to mention, in as matter-of-fact manner as he could, his experience of chapel and having someone near his own age translate for him. He wanted to let his hand continue writing and from it, flow out how this imperious beauty had ensnared and captured his heart, how he was feeling the distant forward call of manhood blossoming because of the eddying pulses she had stirred within him. However hard he tugged against it, the noose only got tighter. If he tried to push her from his mind, her elfin face would rebound at him all the stronger.

But above all the intensity of his first real infatuation, he wanted to scream and shout and scrape the pencil down the page with all his weight behind it to write big, bold and vibrant – **I have met a dragon!**

After lunch, the intention was to continue their effort to stay out of the way of the surveying group and take a trip into the village as a family but they gallingly found that the surveying team's Austin 7 saloon had been parked in such an awkward way as not to allow room for their cart to exit the farmyard. They suspected that Mr Deacon had done this deliberately as some small vindictive victory.

On seeing this Evan called out. "Jack, run off and find Twm and get him to move this car will you? They'll be over at the end of the northernmost field…over there" pointing.

157

The dragon under the hill

Jack took off running in the direction he'd seen indicated, a man on a mission. Although he had not been that far over that side of the farm before, the terrain was familiar to him by now and he leapt and sped across it, a mountain goat in his sure-footed lope.

When he found the group, Mr Deacon and one of the surveyors were way off in the distance. Twm was sitting on a gate still re-reading his letter, still trapped in his own world of indignant ire. While the other surveyor was nearby looking through the theodolite making notes, blinkered to anything else.

"Excuse me sir." Interrupted Jack furtively.

"Oh," exclaimed Eric with some surprise, snapping out of his bubble of figures and triangulation, "hello there young man. What can I do for you?"

"Hello sir, my grandfather is asking if one of you can move your car because we can't get the cart out of the farmyard. We're all off to the village you see." The lad explained.

"Oh, how inconvenient, that's a poor showing from our chauffeur this morning eh? I happen to be the one currently in possession of the key and will happily accompany you back and rectify the situation immediately." He said obligingly. He gestured towards the rest of the group his intentions and followed the waiting lad.

As they walked back, Jack noted the stumbling way the surveyor walked across the land, like a sea-sick man, compared to how he himself now bounced along, like he'd been in this environment all his life.

Being worried about the surveyors attempts to map the top of the hill and how it might affect the creature, Jack tried in his simple, childish way to take this opportunity of being alone with one of the investigators to steer him away from the cairn.

158
The dragon under the hill

"Excuse me sir. You know not to go up the top where the cairn is, don't you?" Jack declared. "There are all sorts of hidden potholes and overgrown little caves that you could break a leg or fall down and they might never find you." Using his grandfather's words as dramatically as he could muster.

This did not have the desired effect the naïve lad was intending, as the surveyor's eyes lit up at the mere mention of the hill-top.

"Ah, yes, it is fascinating. Absolutely fascinating. It's a very unusual rock type for the area at the top there, very porous and not only do we not know the age or origin of the cairn itself but we suspect the whole top area of the hill is a honeycomb of caves. Fascinating." Eric rambled, now on a subject he delighted in. "Can't wait to investigate further."

"But, you shouldn't go there. There are dangers." Jack meekly suggested, but Eric's curiosity had been vigorously stirred.

"Oh, I shouldn't think so," came the now distracted reply, "not if one is careful. Potholing is not my area of expertise you understand but we may need to get some help, an expert in that field perhaps" Jack was crestfallen as he continued. "In actual fact, I don't think we have anywhere near the correct equipment to survey that area and may need to revisit a few times."

The thought of strange men clambering over the cairn and investigating the caves there horrified Jack. All he could think about was Krait and how this should not happen but his young mind could not summon any suitable ideas by which he could prevent it. He felt powerless and frustrated. Although, a treat was soon in store.

When they got back to the farmhouse and his waiting grandparents, they were so taken with Eric's contrite apologies and genuine interest in the farm and its history that he earned himself an Ollie and invite to stay for tea that very evening. In

The dragon under the hill

return, the young surveyor suggested that rather than just move their vehicle a few feet and clear room for the cart to pass, that he would compensate them for their inconvenience by giving them a ride into the village and back in the car. Like any young man his age Jack jumped at the opportunity to have a ride in an actual car and a lovely, shiny new one at that. His grandparents, however, took more persuasion, while Heini after one sniff flat out refused. Soon with Jack occupying the passenger seat and his grandparent's tentatively in the back, the James family were conveyed like royalty through the small country lanes. The inside smelled strongly of new leather, the seats were cloud-like in comfort as the hedgerow flew passes at speed. The vehicle's shock absorbers and suspension dealing with the bumpy dirt road effortlessly (especially in comparison to the old cart and it's aged leaf springs), giving them the smoothest ride they had every experienced into the village. It was the talk of the area for years after. The day a shiny, regal car loomed into town and Evan and Maggie James calmly stepped out, like it was an everyday occurrence.

While they carried out their errands and faced a bevy of questions from anyone who witnessed their recent transportation, Jack stayed with the driver while he waited. He bombarded Eric with questions about the vehicle, how it ran, how fast it would go and what every knob, switch and button did. The boy relished every second, drinking in the smells, the feel and experience.

That evening they sat down to a meal of succulent lamb chops of dinosaur proportion and numerous vegetables with a mountain range of mashed potato to scale, accompanied by the usual glossy thick gravy or homemade mint sauce.

Eric and Ollie had eaten well at their lodging, they thought but nothing compared to the quality, flavour or quantity of food they consumed that evening. It was the same ingredients, they assumed but the taste volume seemed to be turned up somehow.

160

The dragon under the hill

Clearing the main meal plates away, to acclaim from her guests, Maggie embarrassed her young charge by announcing, "There is apple crumble for afters, unless this little one has scoffed the lot on the sly", turning an icy stare but a playful wink to Jack, who for his part had the decency to turn suitably red and offer a sheepish look.

As they continued cordially around the table, Evan was happy to answer his guest's many questions about the land. To talk to a farmer about his land is to talk to a mother about her new born babe or a Captain about his ship. With pride and authority Evan told them about the land, it's falls and faults, where it was likely to bog in the wet and where best to hide from the wind. He recounted the farming history of the farm and as much as he could bring to mind regarding the whole valley. Maggie would chip in with the odd correction or extra detail. The surveyors for their part lapped up this education and felt a shared genuine affection for the land and respect for those who cared for it.

The tone did change slightly when they asked what Evan knew about the cairn and its history. All they could elicit in response was his usual warning of its dangers and not to go there. Although, when the young men recalled their experience of finding Cymro, he did fill in the black beast's back story.

The young men did manage to lift the mood mightily by talking about the cairn but more specifically the hill's cap and its internal structure. If their theory regarding the nature of the hill and specifically the rock type was proven correct, then it would mean that in all likelihood, the land would be unsuitable for the Ministry's uses. This gladdened and encouraged the James family no end. As they left, wishing their hosts a fond farewell, Eric and Ollie promised to keep Evan and Maggie in the loop, without Mr Deacon knowing. They would by no means lie to him, if asked but felt the land owners had as much right to this information, if not more.

161

The dragon under the hill

"Krait! Krait, are you there?" Jack's breathless voice called out the moment he had crested the hilltop. There was a short space before he heard a reply, although he had sensed the approach before the words arrived.

"I am here."

The boy's eagerly anticipated nightly routine of squirrelling away some meat, making the pretence of going to bed and then waiting until his grandparents were asleep, seemed to take an age this particular night. Time crawled by, tucked up in bed fully clothed just listening, running through his head the things he needed to communicate and the questions he needed answers to. How to approach the subject of the Reverend coming with him and to use the method his grandfather had taught him when approaching a horse for the first time to metaphorically wheel around to the subject. Eventually, Jack felt safe enough to leave his bed, retrieve his stashed meat and commence his journey.

There was a flood of familiarity, not just in hearing the voice in his head but in a connection being remade, like slotting in a missing jigsaw piece but intense, like attaching a wire to a live power source. The nuances of the words were clearer to him now, they were not found tonally or in inflection but in his own feelings and how they were triggered.

"I've brought you some more meat." Jack started.

"There is no need", said the voice, "your morsels are pleasant but I feed myself...sufficiently"

Jack thought himself quite silly now, of course the creature was proficient of feeding itself and wouldn't need anything brought. How foolish of him, dragging up little bits of meat as if the titbits made any difference to a creature the size of Krait that had existed for longer than he knew. Something as formidable could eat exactly what ever it wanted. This threw him off his pre-

The dragon under the hill

established course of conversation and he struggled to get his thoughts back in order, the creature through broke the muddle.

"Why are you here child? Why do you come back?"

"I wanted...I needed to know what was here. I saw something and I just had to know what I saw."

"Curiosity." Stated Krait, "and now?"

"Now?" Repeated the boy, "this is the most amazing thing that has ever happened to me?"

Taking the initiative Jack bumbled out the first question that he could muster.

"I would like to know some things, if that's alright with you?" He gabbled.

"Ask."

"Are you a male or a female?" as soon as it left his lips, Jack was concerned this was an impertinent question and could cause offence, wishing he'd phrased it better or had used the preamble like he'd planned.

"As the majority of my kind, I am male"

This answer brought up more questions in itself. The young lad's mind was used to the one male of the species to one female dynamic. Although had he been more observant, the farm around him offered up many different examples. To the boy's relief, Krait obviously picked up on the confusion and offered an explanation, as best it could.

"We 'Naga' (for that is the name we call our kind), when we lived free among the clouds, would live in a large gathering and at the centre, a...nest".

The dragon under the hill

As the voice continued, Jack closed his eyes finding he could see hazy images of what was being spoken about. Like looking through smoked glass at a movie screen, he could depict aspects of the vision and the movement, just not the finer detail. He did not know if it was just his own vivid imagination or another consequence of this deepening bond he felt with the creature.

"Inside the nest would be the only female. She would lay many eggs. When their time came, she would hatch another male. Seldom, and only to seed another grouping, would she hatch a female."

Jack was picturing the scene while listening but this last detail ejected a question he hadn't indented asking, "How does she know which is egg is which? Are they different shape or colours?"

"Temperature determines, the eggs themselves are identical. A male will hatch when incubated near the female but to hatch another female the egg must be held to the heart, the warmest place, at all times, until the hatching." Krait explained with patient delivery. "The new hatchling is then greeted by each of the Naga in the group individually, this sets the 'bandha'. A bond but so much more, a true connection, a unification and when complete, the infant becomes part of the gathering."

This at once intrigued and mystified Jack, who searched his mind for an equivalent example.

"Oh, like bees you mean – in a hive? I read about bees in school. There is a queen bee and all the others are called her drones, I think." Pleased with his train of thought.

"Hive? Yes, a hive. Unlike the…bees, Naga males do not serve the female but we share an essence, a shared 'hive' mind. We can, should it become necessary, work together for the good of the group. If the nest is under threat or if we are needed by another but we are very much free and equal. We are separate

164

The dragon under the hill

but we are one. Completely and utterly accepted for what we are because we are completely known If one sees, all can see. If one knows, all can know. If one feels, all can feel. We are distinct but we are one."

"Like, how you can speak into my head?" Injected the lad.

"Only much, much more" there was a wistfulness emotion with the voice that Jack picked up on. The creature must be remembering what it was like being part of an extended family, part of an extended consciousness, to know and to be intimately known. What can it be like to have been part of something so all encompassing, all immersing, wholly absorbed and what must it be like to feel it no longer, to have it taken away from you, ripped away? The beginning of that thought frightened Jack to his core.

"It was your 'family' but not my like family, you knew what the others around you were thinking and don't have times when you don't understand each other." Said Jack.

"Yes".

Jack could not decipher the complex muddle of emotions that surrounded that single word, so finally asked the question he had been building up to. "What happened to all the other ones like you?"

There was that cold, detached silence again, that Jack had experienced when he had first tried communicating with Krait. Jack became aware of the loneliness and exposed nature of his surroundings and realised for the first time that the wind had chilled him down to his bones. Had he gone too far with his questioning? Had he stirred up too many painful memories and trauma? Getting impatient the boy called out.

"Krait? Krait?" Again that sense of separation, until the silence was broken.

"Enough! Go now."

165

The dragon under the hill

This was the 'command' voice that Jack had to be stubborn against and concentrate hard on what he wanted to do and not what he felt he had to but there was hurt there too.

"But, I...I came to warn you. I have to tell you, men are coming to investigate this whole area. It may not be safe for you. I don't know what to do." Jack felt the frustration and exasperation hit him in a wave and he started to tear. The cold wind whipped the fresh moisture from his eyes, chilling his face.

"Men have come before. Men will come again." Was the flat response.

"But this is different! They have special equipment for measuring the land and caves in the rock. They were talking about bringing in trained men to climb down into the caves." He explained with some animation.

Silence.

"I tried to talk them out of it and explain to them it's dangerous up here, so did my grandfather but they have permission from the government and we can't stop them...I can't stop them" he continued. Feeling powerless, he was physically and emotionally spent.

Nothing.

"I have a friend. He's a good man. I will bring him with me next time I come. He will help." Jack announced. The response made him jump, startled.

"Dare not! Bring no man here to me!"

It was clearly anger but Jack, to his credit, fought his corner.

"But he is a Reverend, very clever too. I like him and he wants to help."

166

The dragon under the hill

"It is of no use, he will be as deaf and blind as them all." The voice still crystal clear in opposition.

"It maybe he will come without me, it's better I am here with him, isn't it?"

Back to the coldness and nothing.

Jack listened and waited for the refusing voice to argue and deny but again nothing. It was clear there would be no more communication tonight.

As his adolescent mind was whirring and formatting the information he had received, he descended homeward. The things he had felt and seen, although through a glass darkly, moved him in ways he struggled to apprehend. This newness of empathy was a journey as hard as the mountain he climbed home.

He had got answers to a number of his questions and broached the subject of Reverend Thomas coming with him next time. Although the discourse had ended on one side not wanting to talk anymore, Jack steeled himself with equal determination, he would be back to try again.

The dragon under the hill

The Ty Bont, Rhywle was not only the village public house but it was also its hotel, bistro, stable and bus stop. When needed, a makeshift part time auction house, meeting room, concert hall and in less noble days a courthouse and worse.

Once a medieval tithe barn, the building had stood in some form or another on that spot for hundreds and hundreds of years. At the time of construction many such barns existed across the land. Churches and monasteries were far more powerful at that time, had more hold over the locals, were more voraciously greedy and would tax the surrounding farms 10 percent of what they produced. It was this produce or 'tithe' that was stored in their tithe barn. However, some places like Rhywle used it more communally. Where each farm gave what they could, especially in times of harvest and plenty, so in times of hardship; a bad winter or a family down on their luck, the contents of the barn could be called upon and shared.

Although a larger building than most in the village, the Ty Bont's exterior was much the same as every other structure around the small square. Built from solid stone and white-washed with lime, dark slate on the shallow pitched roof and its windows and doors thick wood, almost as dark. It's windows and doors were larger than most homes as they were a later improvement to the building, certainly long after its conversion to its current uses. The only signs that that marked it out as something different were the massive double doors to the side of the property, marking the entrance to the stable and the single small sign that hung over the main door on a simple wrought iron bracket. The weather-beaten sign had once depicted a beautiful hand painted fresco of the river and the old stone bridge over it, the inspiration for its name but now it was hardly visible through the flaking paint and the once

The dragon under the hill

bright words 'Ty Bont' were faded nearly out of existence. It creaked loudly in the wind.

Inside smelled smoky, a mixture of lingering pipe smoke from a puffing patron and the soothing fragrance of the crackling wood fire giving a homely glow in the large stone fire place. Behind that, the hint of stale ale, metal polish and the lingering sparkle of dust.

The large grey flagstones were uneven and worn river-stone smooth by countless hours of hard brush scrubbing and a myriad of footfalls, some steadier than others. The bar as it was, was little more than two huge planks of oak supported waist high by two stocky columns of stone. The wood had gained a quaint charm and deep rum-dark patina over its life, seasoned and worn by countless spilled flagons, served drinks and slid tankards. The shelving behind displayed the wares, spirits of various kinds, some deep mysteries lacking any labels and bottles of homemade lemonade and dandelion and burdock pop with which an excited child could spend a rare penny earned. Large screw top jars weighed down the biggest shelf, stuffed with pickled eggs, pickled onions and pickled pig's feet ready for eating by some daring customer or for the less adventurous of tastes, packets of crisps each including a little packet of salt. Ale was delivered from the brewery in barrels each month and locally made cider stacked in kegs in the inner courtyard.

Above the always burning fireplace was a huge painting of a hunting scene, where great twelve-point stag stood majestic in the foreground. Horse bridles, reigns and polished horse shoes and gleaming horse brasses decorated the walls. Scattered around a few tables with accompanying benches and in the corner a pounding grandfather clock, that was the owner's pride and joy. While pewter tankards, each one monikered and claimed, hung on hooks above the bar.

The dragon under the hill

It had been owned by the same couple for the last 40 years or so, Bowen Morgan and his little wife Megan. 'Bod', as he was known by all, another of those monikers whose reason and origin had been lost to history, was a veteran of the Boer war and after his medical discharge had sort out the quietest and most peaceful place he could to escape the noises in his mind and deafening echoes that still made his hand shake from time to time. With his perfectly rounded gleaming bald head and magnificent huge grey walrus moustache, he patrolled the bar with an eternal grouchy manner that was oddly charming due his ocean deep voice.

His wife, Megan, provided the jovial amiability for them both, a rotund woman almost spherical, she ran the guest house side and provided meals and pastries for guests and locals alike. She was often busy 'around back' in the kitchen cooking, baking or preparing her own sausages from scratch with fingers that resembled the finished product.

Opening times were very fluid at the Ty Bont, as Bod cared about profit more than any set of rules or social norm. A pint could be purchased from opening time onwards and opening time was whenever you could rouse Bod from his bed. Closing time was when the last punter was dragged home by his irate wife or Constable Twm had finished breaking up a squabble or altercation he'd been alerted to.

Rhywle was a pious little place on the whole, only a small percentage of its residence took 'the demon drink'. Sometimes a travelling folk music group would be hosted (for a small entrance fee) and those evenings were always well attended, the angelic harp being played enrapturing all who listened. The majority of the pub's income came from the summer months. When dozens of migrant workers would descend on the village to help in the harvesting of various cops; from wheat, barley and rapeseed to potatoes and apples. Crammed in to every available spot, including the stable, they would all be found a place to roost

170

The dragon under the hill

'somewhere' and enough food and drink was sold during those weeks to bolster the rest of the year's meagre takings. The three current visitors were a real unexpected boon.

One lone drinker sat near the bar sipping his second whiskey of the afternoon, while Bod busied himself polishing the bar and tables. Mr Deacon liked the landlord and landlady as they were among the few people in the area who didn't show him distain or baulk at his presence. As far as Bod Morgan was concerned, this was a paying customer and that was all he cared about, 'like' didn't come into it. He would happily serve the devil himself if his money was good.

Mr Deacon was not normally a drinker and when he had first arrived all offers had been met with a very professional, "not while I'm on the job" but after the true purpose of his visit had been revealed and he had been in receipt of some unpleasant encounters, he had succumbed. Now, increasingly, it was becoming habit, a way of dealing with his fast-declining mood and a crutch to cover his slide into depression and delusion. These days a request was hollered to the 'bar-keep' as soon as they come back from the working day and if not in is his room working on his reports, Mr Deacon would drink alone long into the night. Ollie and Eric were concerned about this behaviour and the recent development of Mr Deacon even skipping meals in favour of drinking and solitude. The statement of his immaculate turnout was declining with less frequent shaves and a more haggard look. They had tried to encourage him to spend time with them, distract him and even confront him directly but he was fighting his own war of his own making and losing more of himself each day.

This evening there was the important work to discuss regarding their findings at the James' farm and their various options of approach and their need to get an expert in to investigate further. Mr Deacon showed little interest in the conversation until the word 'James' was mentioned, then he went on his usual rant about 'that' man and how he'd have his

171

comeuppance soon. It was the surveyors turn to tune out then and they decided to go ahead and organise things themselves.

The gloriously sunny day had morphed into a still, lucid summer night. Jack clambered atop the hill not knowing that for the first time his grandparents had been alerted to his late-night sneaking about but had brushed it off as a late toilet visit or more likely, a foraging mission to the larder for a stolen spoonful or three of crumble. Fortunately for Jack, Evans' idea of 'jumping out and scaring the lad' was shot down by his wife and they had soon gone back to sleep.

The trio of Evan, Jack and Heini had spent the morning relocating the flock further down the valley to some fresh grazing pasture, echoing the old drovers drives of years gone by. The afternoon fence maintenance was a lot more taxing. While Evan could expertly drive and embed a nail with two distinct hammer blows, poor Jack bent as many as he nailed and lost count of the times he painfully caught his digits.

"You're supposed to hit the other nail," his grandfather would say, each time.

Although trying his best, he knew his mind was on other things. He wanted to have clear his approach to tonight's conversation and how he would try and convince Krait to allow the Reverend to help.

Now, standing at the top of the exposed hill in the night's dark blanket, those planned thoughts seemed distant and of little use.

He had thought of dozens of ways to start the conversation, arguments and counter-arguments to win the creature around, until he had reached the point that he didn't know where to start.

172

The dragon under the hill

He decided to follow his grandfather's example, to stop, pause and take a breath. He allowed himself to be taken from the bustling marketplace of his thoughts and become aware of his environment. To be calm. Feel the solidity of the ground beneath his feet, feel the soft summer breeze whisper around the nape of his neck and there, just at the edge, he could feel another presence. He needed no further evidence that he was not alone on the hilltop.

Tossing away his agenda the young boy begun to share his heart. Sharing honestly what he had dared not share with anyone before.

"I didn't want to come here in the first place," Jack began, "when mam and dad first told me I would be coming here for the summer, I couldn't understand it and thought they were trying to get rid of me. I couldn't think what I had done, I don't remember being naughty or cheeking back, that I should be punished. I asked them loads of times could I not come here, wanting to spend the summer with my mates, I was. Playing football, swimming up the ponds or camping up Pontsarn. Up there we got rope swings n'all."

That sense of another entity sharing this with him grew.

"After I got here, everything was so different, I didn't know Nana and Grampa very well and I missed home loads. I didn't want to be here, I couldn't sleep but still had to get up really early. I had no one to play with and had to do chores, I wanted to go home."

As he shared he could feel empathy like a knitted blanket slowly encompass him as his companion listened quietly.

"Then after bit when I got to know my grandparent's a bit better, I liked them then and Heini the dog and enjoyed the farm a bit more. I was interested in that old cairn see, kept coming up, curious like and then you saved me from that nasty old dog and I

The dragon under the hill

met you and I met the Reverend and…" He was about the talk about his good friend and repeat their need for his help when he was interrupted.

"What was that there? I felt something…strong", said Krait.

"What?"

"There, there was a flash of something, someone?"

"He's my friend, the Reverend, the one I'm telling you ab…"

"No", the voice interrupted again, "not the man, someone else."

While listing the positive things about this place and the people he had met, Jack's mind had unintentionally flickered to Lily, unbidden she had illuminated his thoughts and Krait must have sensed the warmth.

Jack with reluctance stated, "Oh, the girl? She's just someone I sat next to in church. The Reverend asked her to interpret for me as my Welsh isn't very good." After a pause, "she's no one really."

"What you say is not true. I do not wish you to be false with me." There was a blush of anger there that cautioned the boy.

It was Jack's turn to be the reluctant talker, to pause for a long time.

"Her name…is Lily", he sighed. Like a criminal confessing a long guilty crime the boy conceded.

In a faltering, ragged way Jack described as best he could how meeting this strange magical girl and ignited feelings within he had never felt before, how he struggled to understand them,

174

The dragon under the hill

even put a name to them. He felt muddled, not a little embarrassed and unclear about what to do about it all.

"I never had any time for girls. Playing with dolls and jumping rope, hopscotch and always giggling, silly like but Lily is different…" Jack realised he could make out the shape of Krait the other side of the cairn, with those gold studded eyes fixed on him. The creature's approach had been imperceptible and silent but brought strange comfort to Jack in this emotionally exposed state. "I don't think she likes me though."

Even without their increasing emotional link, the sadness in that statement was tangible.

"This is something this…Lily, has communicated to you?" Krait asked.

"Well, not as such…"

"Someone else, your friend maybe, has communicated it to you?" Was logically projected.

"Oh no."

"Then how do you know this thing?" The being asked.

"It's the feeling I got", stated the boy.

"Feeling?" echoed back. "You 'felt' you didn't like it here or your grandparents, when you first arrived. Yes?"

"Yes."

"And those feelings changed, did they not?"

The point being made Jack thought for a while, was there a way of knowing for certain and what could he do about it? In the end he confided.

"I just don't know what to do"

175
The dragon under the hill

"I know little about the ways of men. It is simple for the Naga as all is shared." Krait felt obligated to help the boy as best he could. "What I do know is that while hunting, if I do not capture my quarry, I go hungry. I am not promised another chance."

Jack listened intently, trying in his child-like way to translate these thoughts to his situation, as his companion continued.

"Take the opportunity when it is presented to you."

"But…but, I don't know what to say", Jack pleaded.

"Does it matter what you say, she will either respond to who you are or she will not", came the response, lacking emotion but clear in its logic.

Jack was in uncharted territory and the thought of him 'talking' to Lily, filled him with heady, swirling fear.

"You will have to be…brave." Krait added, picking up on the lads' unease. "You can be brave."

This was delivered with such confidence and unequivocal assurance that imbibed Jack with confidence and self assurance in levels he had never experienced before.

"I can", the lad agreed.

For a time they remained together in their shared experience until Jack, remembering his mission broke the silence to bring up the subject of the Reverend.

"I would still like to bring my friend, the next time I come…" half way through his sentence Jack became aware that as he was speaking, quietly and instantly his new friend had slipped away and was gone.

The dragon under the hill

Jack made his way home and filled with the living froth of joy smiled to himself.

"Well, at least he didn't say 'no'".

The dragon under the hill

Chapter 17

"Now, that is interesting news", said the Reverend Rhodri Thomas.

He had come to visit with his oldest and dearest friends about mid-morning. Normally it was the Reverend who would be passing news and updates on to Evan and Maggie but on this occasion, following the young surveyors' visit they were able to enlighten him.

"Seems we've been right all along about how dangerous the top of that old hill was. Like a honeycomb, they reckon, due to this certain type of rock." Evan repeated.

"If confirmed," qualified Maggie.

"Aye, they've got to have it all confirmed like but these are bright lads and they seem sure it's the case. Well that makes the land useless for the Ministry then. They can't have soldiers and the like disappearing down great big holes all of a sudden, now can they?" Proffered Evan.

"No brother" Rhodri answered, "but let's not get ahead of things, counting our chickens and all that." He cautioned.

Sipping their tea in an odd moment of silence, the break in conversation seemed to jog the Reverend's memory.

"O, I completely forgot what I came to tell you," he announced excitedly, "those two nice young surveyors had gone to Twm, on the quiet like because they were getting a bit worried. Seems things are getting to Mr Deacon and he's starting to lose the plot a bit."

"Hopefully he'll get lost completely" added Evan, half under his breath.

178

The dragon under the hill

Rhodri continued, "Sad to say, he's been hitting the bottle quite a bit these days, things getting to him like but they were mainly concerned because he's been sending his reports to his seniors at the Ministry and they are getting more and more exaggerated. Anyway, you won't believe he only went and asked the Ministry for armed soldiers to come here and support him."

"What?!" Evan and Maggie said together, in loud consternation.

"Aye, played up to those above him, that he was being threatened with guns and knives all the time and was in fear of his life. Really lathering it on apparently." Related the clergyman.

"What!...I mean we had a laugh with him and there was Old Man Roberts but he tries to shoot everyone," said as if this was just an old man's endearing quirk, he exhaled loudly, "soldiers. That's blooming ridiculous." Evan was incensed.

"Hang fire now, listen to the rest of it," Rhodri calmed.

"So, a few days later he's waving this letter around from the ministry and shows to the lads. The letter was saying the Ministry are not happy with the idea but are going to send him what he asked for."

Disbelieving shakes of the head were gleaned from Maggie and her husband, finding it hard to contain their incredulity and anger.

"The way the lads tell it, Mr Deacon was cock-a-hoop, expecting a whole army to turn up under his command, so he could order them about. Something akin to martial law. Oh, he was boasting how he was going to show us locals then and if we stepped out of line, boy, we'd watch out because we'd get it...your name being mentioned of course."

"O, I would be offended if it wasn't," injected Evan.

The dragon under the hill

"So, there he is now, our own little Napoleon waiting outside the Ty Bont early this morning at the allotted time for his own personal militia to arrive and we hear a transport truck coming a mile off, one of the big military ones." Doing his best to describe the scene and build up the tension level, like a good story teller.

"And when his expected army finally arrived, he goes around the back to see them all file out from under the canopy, speak to the commanding officer and what not, only to find the back of the transport completely empty. Then, a couple of soldiers pop out of the cab. It turned out all they sent was two young raw recruits up from Brecon Barracks. Two!"

"Two lads" echoed Maggie.

"Aye, and one of them is Iestyn's nephew Alyn. Not exactly the invasion force he was hoping for, I wager." Related the clergyman with no little amusement.

"O, I bet that Mr Deacon was absolutely furious, being made to look a fool like that", sniggered Evan.

"Too right, he didn't half go a funny colour and was bouncing around the village like a rubber ball, in an incandescent rage he was, real Old Testament style anger so to speak. Duw, if looks could kill, we'd all be dead. He started off shouting, then he was pacing up and down talking to himself, very animated he was and finally, gently rocking mumbling to himself. I think he's gone this time." Described the Reverend in a slightly more serious manner.

"He's painted himself into such a corner. I can't help starting to feel sorry for the man." Sympathised Maggie.

"Now, let's not go too far Mags, is it." Stated Evan.

"I overheard Eric telling Twm that he would be contacting the Ministry telling them it's all got a bit much for Mr Deacon. Let's

180

The dragon under the hill

face it, he's no friend to any of us but we wouldn't want to see him in the loony bin, really. Anyway, I imagine they will all be around here sooner rather than later, so best behaviour now," advised Rhodri.

Evan gave his old friend the most innocent look he could muster, "who? Me? Wouldn't dream of misbehaving".

"Righto, Mr Innocent." Rhodri replied, "that being said, I thought I'd take Jack with me today on a few of my parish visits, get him out from under your feet."

This was thought a good idea by all and a stern look given to Evan when he asked if the visits might include the Hegarty household.

"And Rhodri", Evan shouted as they left, "watch you don't lose him, we've grown attached to the lad, learned his name n'all."

Jack had wondered how the Reverend spent his time when he wasn't preaching or visiting the James' farm but as soon as they were alone there was only one subject he wanted to approach.

By silent mutual agreement the companions waited until they were clear of the farm before speaking. To Jack's surprise, they had turned the opposite direction to the village on the country road, the only direction Jack had gone previously.

"How goes it lad?" Was the opening salvo.

"Very well, thank you." Said Jack politely.

"Now, you mustn't think our beautiful little sleepy village is always so dramatic Jack" the Reverend began, "normally the most exciting thing that happens around here is when Old Nana Price's horse escaped from its paddock last year.

The dragon under the hill

Oh, saying that, there was that time some fellows came up from Bridgend and shot Iestyn's horse," the memory triggering laughter.

"No," rebutted Jack, "they never came all that way to shoot someone's horse?"

"Well, misunderstanding it was, joke gone too far like," clarified the preacher, "we often get groups coming up from the town's down south, visiting farms to hunt for rabbits. Normal protocol is they knock the farmer's door and ask can they hunt on their land. Now, to a farmer rabbits are pest and they are more than happy for any kind of cull. So, the farmer might say something like, 'yes but stay away from the bottom fields where the lambs are' or 'of course and me and the wife like a rabbit, so drop one back if you have plenty', you know that sort of thing.

Iestyn keeps a few cows for milking and on this day one of them had fallen, nasty like and broken all her legs. He had sent one of his boys off to get the butcher to take the carcass away but the cow was still in pain. So, when this group comes up from Bridgend, one of the chaps is tasked with going up to knock his door asking to hunt on his land with their shotguns. Iestyn says they can shoot on his land if they put the cow out of its misery and explains the cow is behind the little wall at the end of the field.

The only thing was, this chap is on his way back to his mates and thinks he'll have a bit of fun. When they ask him what the farmer said, he pretends to be all upset and angry shouting the odds, that the farmer had been rude to him and he was sick of these locals and he was going to teach the farmer a lesson. All the time walking towards where Iestyn told him the injured cow was laying.

All the while his mates try and calm him down, he refuses and says he's going to shoot one of the farmer's cows in anger, to

The dragon under the hill

teach him a lesson. His shocked mates try to talk him out of it but by now he spies the injured animal.

He pulls out his gun, gets the cow in his sights and shoots the animal dead. As you can imagine his mates are stunned but one of them gets the wrong end of the stick and shouts, 'yeah lets really teach the farmer lesson and shot his horse as well', and shoots Iesyn's best horse dead!"

Jack erupted into laughter, followed by his companion, who would giggle every time he tried to talk about the aftermath of the incident.

Eventually, regaining his composure the Reverend spoke with warmness about the community he had spent his entire life in. "I love this village lad, with all that is within me, not the land. I don't have that affinity with it that the farmers do, no, it's the people I love. I have held the hand of every baby born and the hand of everyone taking their final breath. I love every cheeky child, sullen youth, strong man, beautiful woman, hardworking father, loving mother and cantankerous old person. God has given me this flock and I am of all men blessed. They are salt and light in an ever-darkening world." He seemed lost in those thoughts for a moment before being present with his companion.

Jack couldn't help but admire the clergyman for his passion and commitment.

"You aren't like I thought a Reverend would be", the boy said.

"O, how's that then lad?"

"Well you like to have a laugh and don't talk about the Bible and God all the time. More like a normal person." Jack tried to explain.

"Normal person I am lad," Rhodri replied laughing, "although I do know what you mean. There are those who think a

The dragon under the hill

collar or some other garb makes them special, better than others but to me this, "tugging at the dog collar around his neck, "is a mark that I'm a servant first, here to serve me flock.

As for talking about God all the time, well I am somewhat of a specialist on that subject but there are often other things that friends need to talk about. Don't here me wrong boy, God is more real to me than you are and my faith is at the total core of who I am. The older I get Jack the more I understand that knowing when to be quiet is just as important as knowing what to say."

They walked together quietly for a time, while the Reverend's words still misted and wafted around them like starlings waiting to roost.

"Anyway, let's go and visit Old Nana Price, she is something of a local celebrity around these parts. The old dear lives in the second farm along and is not well. We'll call in, perk her up no doubt." Said Rhodri

He looked down at the lad and smiled, before adding "Er...I'm only thinking out loud like but the Hegarty farm is next door to the Price's and I did say I would call in but we won't if you don't want to, son."

"O, I er...well, if you promised" responded Jack. Not being able to help himself he added "will...will Lily be there?" he asked as casually as he could.

"Who? O, little Lily," he teased, "I don't know. Thinking about it, she will probably be there, cooking with her mum or something. Why do you ask?"

Jack knew the Reverend was teasing him and enjoying his discomfort but didn't have the armoury to meet his embarrassment full on and just mustered a meek, "No reason I suppose but we could say 'hello'". Remembering last night's encouragement, Jack repeated to himself to 'be brave'.

184

The Reverend Thomas decided he had made the boy cringe enough and launched into the subject at hand. "So, I haven't forgotten, are we still on for tonight?"

"I think so" came the unsure reply, "I mentioned it last night and he didn't exactly say 'no' but by then he'd stopped talking to me."

"O, why is that?" questioned the intrigued adult.

"Well he does that sometimes. When he doesn't want to talk to you anymore, he disappears."

"Really? You keep calling the creature 'he'" the Reverend observed, "you've learned some more about it have you?"

Jack took his time to best describe his recent experiences with Krait. Finding out his name, his gender and what they called themselves. He struggled with his adolescent vocabulary and mix of unnameable feelings to put into clear words the link he had felt between him and the creature. The images he had glimpsed, the feelings that had been promoted and the way the longer the link went on, the more generally aware he became. More conscious of himself as a being, a rational presence interacting with other sentient beings all with their own thoughts, feelings and personal view of the world; more conscious of his environment and his place it, how everything seemed brighter, clearer and more important; and more conscious of his actions and how they can affect what surrounded him and ultimately his small space in history. In trying to describe the creature's old life, Jack tried to use as many of Krait's words and descriptions as he could remember, knowing he did not understand the concept of a 'hive' mind enough to explain it himself. He ended with the soul crushing story filled with pathos of knowing a creature who may well be the last of his kind and the grief of having lost such an incredible amount. Jack left out last night's conversation and what was shared regarding his feelings for Lily, although it was a key step in him feeling closer to the creature.

The dragon under the hill

Rhodri, for his part, was astounded by most of what he heard. If the boy was making it all up, then he had an incredible imagination and overdeveloped ability to self-deceive. He couldn't help noticing that Jack had changed, it was undeniable. Admittedly this could be down to the natural changes of a young man that age or the experiences of being here and being with his grandparents on the farm. Whatever the cause, Jack was gaining maturity and self-awareness that could not be ignored.

The best example of this accumulation of new experiences and its positive effect on the boy was the fact that when he and Reverend Thomas eventually returned to the James farmhouse for a much-needed meal, Jack was clutching a little piece of paper very tightly in his hand. In Lily's own handwriting none the less, was her postal address for him to write to her.

No one would have described him as suave and sophisticated when he met the object of his affection for the second time but he was able to get past the inertia of his bashfulness and marshal enough boyish charm to speak to her and give her some doubts about her first impression of him.

Jack ran up to his room to take his precious new-found treasure and place it as securely as he could among the things in his small suitcase, while Rhodri told Maggie and Evan about what the pair had been up to. They had strolled down to Old Nana Price's who was having a good day and was quite lifted by having him and Jack visit and then they had called to the Hegarty farm.

When they had got to the farmhouse Lily and her mum were making bread together and despite the meeting between her and Jack being perfunctory and cold at first, things did warm up as it was suggested Lily show Jack around the farm and they spent more time together.

"The little chap came into his own then and turned on a bit of charm from what I saw" continued Rhodri, "by the time he'd

186

The dragon under the hill

finished she had written down her address with an agreement that after his time here was done and he went back to Merthyr, that he would write her and she would write back."

"Go on lad!" Evan added, in the same manner he would instruct and encourage his sheep dog in herding the flock.

"Remember now," cautioned Maggie, "give the teasing a miss from now on, is it." As Jack was heard clattering down the stairs to re-join them.

"Krait! Krait! Are you there? It's Jack!" Jack realised he probably didn't need to speak any words out loud, that the mental communication, he knew, went both ways but could not easily change the process of communication he had spent his life using. So he yelled hard into the night as loud as he could.

Two figures stood against the blustery wind, it was not a pleasant night, certainly not one to find yourself on top of a remote hill in the dark. Grateful that it wasn't raining at least, both wrapped their coats tight against the inhospitable conditions.

No reply was heard.

"Krait! Listen, I know you were against the idea of me bringing someone here but he's here to help." He conceded. For his part the Reverend Thomas stood watch, his eyes concentrating on every spot and shadow he could see looking for any movement, any indication of life.

Still nothing.

The Reverend Thomas was finding the wind and biting cold harder and harder to bear. His hands and feet had already been chilled as he waited for what must have been two hours in the field for Jack to join him and together they could begin the

The dragon under the hill

climb, the younger eager to lead. The longer they stayed here the deeper the cold bit.

"Krait, I only want to talk to you, I know you are there." He was pleading now. Partly not wanting to look like a liar in front of the Reverend but also because this relationship as it was, was truly important to him.

There was still no response.

The pair exchanged several looks, which imparted a great deal of meaning as it was clear that their time there was coming to an end in disappointment, having seen little in way of results.

Jack decided to attempt to reach out with his emotions as well as his voice this time in one final attempt. Closing his eyes and concentrating on the way the connection he'd had previously felt. He centred on that feeling of union and tried to push his emotional need to be heard out, before yelling.

"But I've brought my friend to talk to you, he's a good man!"

The words had hardly left Jack's lips when a hurricane exploded around them both, a deafening thunder-clap echoed and blustered, the force was hard to stand against, taking all their resistance. A shrill shriek drilled into their subconscious, piercing into their primal fears which was screaming at them to run. The noise seemed to be coming from everywhere, including their own heads, leaving nowhere to escape to. The dizzying squall increased in power and intensity. Then with a sound like the snapping of a thousand trees, suddenly it was before them.

Appearing like a mighty heraldic archangel appearing in all its fearful, awesome glory, majestic and horrifying; clawed feet clasping the stone of the cairn, wings fully outstretched, wide and powerfully kinetic. It reared up, magnificent in form, dominating the vista. Mixing the terrible and beautiful, the ancient and mystic in

188

splendid alchemy; it was like staring into lightning, burning into their retinas. Its actual colour was hard to define, as the creature moved and breathed it caused a ripple to travel mesmerizingly through its scales like a wave, each scale changing colour as a different aspect was shown. From the deepest infinite black, like torn space, to moonlight silver glinting as the very stars, to summer sunset oranges and reds, then ghostly in blinding white. As it simmered it gave the effect of disappearing and reappearing before them which added to its ethereal magic and wonder. A celestial breach, inspiring debilitating awe and reverence, demanding attention, reptilian tail whiplashing the air behind it. Immutably and totally awesome.

Those stupefying huge golden eyes glowing and glowering from its small horned head, like burning dwarf stars piercing the darkness, ensnared and haunted those watching. Here was a resplendent, absolutely live, glorious dragon and he was far from happy with his intruders.

"Man!" Bile, fury and disgust filled Jack's mind, he reeled backwards as these feelings stormed and raged into his mind. The Reverend was motionless, mouth agape.

"Man!" The creature repeated in louder, more painful thoughts, their immenseness drawing real fear from the boy. For the first time he was scared of the being.

"You bring man here! You dare not talk to me of a 'good' man," the infuriated punitive words came at him, then like a broken damn, words torrented forth.

"Was it not man who killed all my kind, wiped out the Naga? Was it not man who mercilessly killed my entire gathering? Were they not 'good' men who crushed unborn eggs under foot, slaughtered the squealing hatchlings in the nest and drove their wood and iron into the heart of our mother as she cowered trying to protect her young?" Came a barrage of rhetorical questions, with each outburst images flashed in Jack's mind depicting the

189

horrors and travesties that were being described, shocking him and turning his stomach. Though so many years had passed, these things were still blood raw and feelings now unbottled, gushed forth so powerfully felt they threatened to swallow their author completely.

The Reverend was too closed off in his mind to be party to any of this information or emotion and only saw the mighty threat of the creature and instinctively placed himself between Jack and the dragon, in a misplaced act of protection which went mostly unnoticed.

"Was it not 'good' men who refused to share the land with my kind when they found us in it and mindlessly hunted us to extinction? We tried to live in peace with them but they would not, we tried to communicate with them but they would not hear, in the end we could only try to fight back but we who were left were too small, were too few and it was too late." With this statement it was like the majority of the creature's fire and bluster was spent, a much sullener air was tangible. It was accompanied by the creature crumpling from its ferocity and dread inspiring pose, to enfolding the cairn, like a defeated foe in submissive subjugation.

"Was it not man who took away from me all that I had and all that I knew? Was it not 'good' men who ripped apart the only place I ever belonged and those I belonged with, who tore out my heart and made me less then alive, a remnant of who I was and knew. Hounded me relentlessly from mountain to hill, year after year, causing me to live in seclusion, hiding, careful of my own breath, feeding off scraps and rotting flesh as not to be found. Only to creep out in the cloud of night, no longer to challenge the sun in the skies. Each moment spent alone, haunted by screams of the past, hounded by innocent blood and taunted by echos." The voice now a swarm of pain, loneliness and built up heartbreak. "Was it not 'good' men who wiped my kind from their place in history and stowed them away in fables and tales? Was it not man who has caused me to be alone for lifetimes and maybe the last

190

of the Naga?" Krait's stare changed from blazing eyed wrath to tortured anguish and deserted pleading.

"What is it," Krait asked, "to be the last or your kind? To be forever alone." The despair was heart-breaking. "Alone." Like a mighty roaring wave expending all its energy and was a trickle flicking the shore, the creature deflated.

Neither human needed to hear the voice to understand the change in the beast, they moved from their defensive pose and Jack quickly explained in breathless urgency what had been recounted to him. The stunned clergyman needed many parts retelling and took a long time and a lot of persuading to accept that they were in no real danger.

The two human companions, feeling tremendously out of their depth, both slowly approached the forlorn creature, who seemed physically and emotionally drained from his powerful outburst. Not daring to touch it, Jack reached out as best he could.

"We are so, so sorry for what was done to you and your kind." He looked at the Reverend who nodded and whispered, "You're doing fine lad, keep going".

"You must hate mankind and you should..." there Jack could find no other words.

Finally regaining his comprehension and acumen the Reverend Thomas stepped in.

"Krait? I believe that is your name, you are right. Your rage and accusation are right. I knew nothing of what was done to you and your kind but I do know throughout history man's capacity for evil and cruelty seems to know no limits. We have killed for land, food, women, the promise of riches – even for ghoulish entertainment; murdered for power, money and the regard of men; we have started wars because of skin colour, ideals and beliefs but so often we have killed for no reason at all. Men have thought

The dragon under the hill

themselves 'good' when they have tortured and killed women and children, thought themselves righteous when they committed unspeakable horrors on the innocent, thought themselves on the side of light and incurred the Almighty's name, when their actions have grieved God above.

Since the first day, man's selfishness has sown pain, planted suffering and harvested death. Man has a tragic legacy of mindless destruction and there seems no end to the depths he will sink for his own ends, what seems right to him at the time. His inhumanity to his fellow man is seemingly endless and that's before you get to what he had done to nature and the creation in it. Yours is far from the only amazing species we have deemed not worthy to share our world with and driven to extinction and as man grows and expands, our needs greater, things will only get worse and more perverse. Only his ingenuity and methods will change, man will only get greedier, voracious in his hunger for more and more. Like locusts, man swarms and devours all he sees and in the end, will lose sight of all that is important...but...

Human beings are capable of unbelievable acts of love, kindness and self-sacrifice; capable of creating beauty and stirring such feelings of joy and wonder, capable of amazing ideas and creations and may one day touch the very stars. With God's help we can do good to one another, care for our surroundings and save one another but for what was done to you and to your kind, in the name of mankind, from one sensing, feeling species to another – I am sorry.

I know it doesn't mean much compared to the enormity of what you lost, I can't even begin to comprehend the extent of what was taken, what it must have felt like but I know it was wrong and on behalf of mankind we, here now, ask you to forgive."

There was a long broiling moment, when the only sound was the dipping wind, starving them of their body heat. Then, after

The dragon under the hill

many thoughtful minutes the voice finally spoke, Jack offering interpretation for the clergyman.

"How can you ask such a thing?" Mustering the remnants of rage and injustice.

It was the Reverend Thomas's time to play the silent card, he just met the creature's gaze.

"You know not what you ask."

Rhodri's years of counselling and caring for his parishioners kicked in and he spoke gently to the creature, like he would one needing his calming advice.

"Oh, I imagine it is near an impossible thing I'm asking and have no right to either but it feels like you have been carrying this hurt for a long, long time and it's been eating away at you inside, like a festering wound. It has trapped and consumed you until what you have now is not life. Look at it this way, maybe it was for this very reason this lad found you."

He walked closer and lowered his voice, softly and kindly he spoke "Maybe it's time to let go."

Jack, in the stream of the connection, felt a multitude of emotions being wrestled with, saw clear images of the members of Krait's gathering and the group's mother. Each one was being given a personal and freeing farewell as the dragon slowly and carefully made his peace with his past and its trauma. Fires of rage were extinguished and wounds were sewn shut as this sentient being bravely broke free of century old chains. Another lengthy period of quiet followed after the Reverend had last spoke but he waited patiently and openly.

Like the softest breath of breeze, "I can still hear them," bled out.

The dragon under the hill

"And that will never go away but forgiveness is a journey, healing is a journey. Each time you make a deliberate choice to forgive, it will get easier, it will hurt less." The clergyman counselled.

"I know now what I have always known but have hidden from myself. There will never be justice. There is no vengeance. I should have died with them then but I will live and I will honour them."

Then even Rhodri heard the powerful, decisive conclusion. "I forgive."

Not only did he hear but also got a taste of the ripples of relief, release and feeling of losing a great weight that was being felt.

The three sentient beings did not move, did not speak, they just were together in that momentous moment.

Acting surprising coherently in these extraordinary circumstances The Reverend Thomas broke the silence.

"Krait. There is something important, I know Jack has tried to tell you that men are coming to this very cairn. They are investigating the land. We can't stop them but we want to protect you."

"Let them come", came the stoic reply, "they will not find me."

"We certainly hope so," said the Reverend, needing to cut the conversation short as he was suddenly very conscious that it was the early hours of the morning and he was still far up on a hilltop with a twelve year old boy who must be freezing and exhausted. "Thank you for speaking with me, I must take the boy home now."

"I will see you again soon," added Jack.

194

The dragon under the hill

"As you wish."

Then with a frightening speed the beast was gone. There was no sound or sense of movement, it was just there one moment and in a blink...gone. Leaving the two companions bewildered.

The Reverend Thomas put his arm around Jack, looked around and blew hard and long, then uttered slowly and wearily, "well, that was certainly something." Which he knew was the understatement to beat all understatements.

As they descended they discussed some of what had gone on and what they would do. They agreed Reverend Thomas, after some time to think, would talk to Evan and tell him the whole story, they would take things from there. Until then, Jack should carry on as normal.

While he was nearing home after his long walk the dawn started breaking. The Reverend Thomas reckoned that the poor lad would have barely had a single hour in his bed before his unsuspecting grandparents would wake him for a busy day at the farm. He himself longed for the warm surrender of his bed and the silence of sleep and its oblivion.

The dragon under the hill

That next day was a surreal experience for a lot of the village inhabitants with an abundance of unmet expectations.

Mr Deacon very much had conceived a plan for the day, fully expecting to march onto the James farm ahead an impressive troop; Evan spent the day expecting a visit from the group led by Mr Deacon; Jack was on tender-hooks every moment, expecting the visit from the Reverend Thomas and the revelations that would follow; while the Reverend himself fully expected to visit the James family after having spent most of the day undisturbed in bed, catching up on his lost sleep.

None of these expected things happened.

The Reverend Rhodri Thomas, after the unreal night he had experienced, had plummeted into his inviting bed and was immediately enveloped by warming blankets and soothing unconsciousness. Any worries that the unprecedented encounter and what it meant, would play on his mind keeping sleep at bay where unfounded. He was completely drained having given so much emotionally, it had been years since he had felt so tired and weary.

He had slept solidly, unmoving like a dead man, although his unconscious mind was afflicted, boiling with dreams and images sparked by the previous night's events. Filled with blinking visions of mighty winged creatures soaring and circling mountain tops. Then the hate-fuelled, scowling faces of angry men clenching with evil intent. The prodding and harsh thrusting of spear, halberd and lance; the stab and slash of sword and dagger, the smash of axe, hammer and stone; the screeching of utter anguish, the smell of iron and blood and the sickening stench of death, followed by hollow nothingness.

The dragon under the hill

Still in the turmoil of dream state, the thudding of the weapons and stamping of boot became louder and more urgent, a horrid timed percussion. His consciousness slowly seeped back and with it, the realisation that the hammering clashing sound of the weapons performing their horrific task, was coming from elsewhere and transformed into the noise of his front door being urgently pounded on, waking him.

"Alright mun! I'm coming! I'm coming! Duw..." He yelled, as he made his way, blurry eyed through the manse, wrapping his checked dressing gown modestly around him.

"Who's breaking my door down and waking me up? I'll..." he continued to shout as he hefted the thick heavy door open, to be met by the upturned face of a boy, sweaty and reddened from running.

The Reverend Thomas immediately recognised the chap as Albany Price, the oldest boy in the latest generation of the Price family. Although not yet nine years old, he was built like half a grown man and was constantly either running or fighting, mainly with one, or all, of his three younger brothers. Your typical loveable scamp with his thick curly mop of dark hair and all-encompassing mischievous toothy grin, only marred by his habit of stealing sugar from the pantry by the handful. He never ever wore shoes, the last pair bought for him had seen their laces tied together before being launched some distance into the local river, for which he received a sound beating from his exasperated mother, as they were a poor family. This act of rebellion was mainly done as an excuse not to attend school, which he despised. He was hardly able to read but was a distinguished professor when it came to the flora and fauna of the countryside. He had a large collection of 'blown' birds eggs and was as adept at tracking an animal in the snow as any man.

"Please Sir, Reverend sir," said the lad looking very uncomfortable, obviously performing this task under duress, "mam

The dragon under the hill

says… 'can you come straight away as Nana has taken a turn for the worst and was asking for you?'" Straining his memory to convey as accurately as he could the message he had been intrusted with.

This spawned an immediate change in the Reverend from groggy annoyance to serious and commanding.

"Right", came the clear response, "your mam sent for the Doctor?"

"Yes Sir, little Roy is doing it now."

Royston Price was his nearest sibling, a year or so younger but not nearly half as wild and the main foil for his skirmishes.

Like most little villages and isolated communities, they had no Doctor of their own and with no telephone or telegram in the parish to contact the surgery for a physician, there was a typically colloquial solution. Those in need would track down a little squat man called Dai Fennel who was perpetually covered in oil, usually found at home, in the pub or down the shed, tinkering. Who would any time of the day or night, quickly don his leathers and goggles, fire up his 1934 James twin 2 stroke motorbike and splutter and putt all the way to Beulah and raise the Doctor. For this community service there was no official charge but it was expected that when you saw Dai next you would 'see him right' with either buying him a pint in the Ty Bont or taking round a plateful of something tasty to eat. Due to his efforts and the physician running his own car the Doctor would usually attend within the hour.

"Good, now you run back and tell your mother I'll be there as soon as I can", the Reverend ordered. With great relief, task complete, the lad turned on his heels and padded off quickly in the direction of home.

198

While dressing, the Reverend struggled to order the many thoughts that were vying for attention in his mind. He put aside the events of the previous night and its connotations to concentrate on the task to hand. It was not an unusual thing for him to be knocked out of bed at any time to meet the needs of his congregation but this request had a sense of urgency and he knew the walk to the Price farm would take him an hour and a half at least. An idea struck him.

Seeing the shiny Austin 7 still parked, glistening outside the Ty Bont, the Reverend Thomas shot up a quick 'Thank you, O Lord' under his breath before knocking the door.

"If I have to come up there, I'll pour a saucepan of freezing water on you. Now get up!" This was the third time Jack had been called by his grandmother to get up and come downstairs to start the morning. For his part, the exhausted lad was mostly awake and trying hard to force his body into obedience. Getting it to actually move from the warmth of his bed was a difficult fight taking real effort. The annoyed shrill calls of his grandmother the impetuous he needed for that final push

Eventually, he slithered down the stairs, in a boneless body he still felt detached from. Met with a scowl from his grandmother and uninvolved amusement from his grandfather, he felt some form of conciliatory effort on his part was required.

"Sorry Nana, I just don't feel with it today. I'm knackered," he said pacifyingly.

"Horses are knackered, people get tired or exhausted." Came the corrective response from Maggie, "sit down and get some tea in you, perk you up".

With that statement Jack knew that was her way of closing the issue and he was forgiven. He sat down at the kitchen table and stared blankly as his grandfather chatted unperturbed about the plans for their chores today. Mindlessly, Jack sipped his already poured tea. Like bricks slotting and cementing together forming a sturdy wall, Jack's awareness and reasoning started to return to him and with it that heightened perception of himself and his surroundings. His self-awareness, self-confidence and assurance of his place in the world filtered into him like crystal clear pure water through a mountain's rocks.

"Well, well, they still haven't arrived." Evan's voiced observation was the first words that either had spoken in over an hour, resulting in Heini trotting back to them, her interest taken away from following some scent.

They were in the process of busying themselves fixing the gate in the west field, where the wood had rotted from its constant contact with the wet muddy ground. Man and boy together but alone in their thoughts, each of them lost in their own mind, own meditations and looming expectations.

"What's that grandad?" Jack asked, the spell of his own thought's enchantment broken.

"O, that General Deacon and his little army," Evan replied, "I was expecting the invasion today but there's been no sign."

"Good." Was the lad's curt reply.

"No doubt lad, but with some things in life it is better to just get it over with – like pulling a tooth." Came the thoughtful response.

Jack didn't verbalise his question but he was expecting the Reverend Thomas and was wondering how that expected invasion hadn't taken place either.

Evan took off his flat cap and wiped some sweat from his face, looked up and stared intently at the horizon. After a long time

200

in thought he frowned deeply, drew in a long breath and quietly announced in a sombre tone.

"A storm's coming".

Near the old stone humpbacked bridge which had carried travellers over the river for centuries, was a picturesque small patch of meadow, covered in short grass and little wild flowers. This was where the two young soldiers had chosen to bivouac. Setting up camp with their small green tent facing the reed edged river, which acted as their washing facilities, water supply and source of entertainment. Sitting in the early light waiting for their tea to brew, they could watch the elusive water vole nervously forage, a dipper diving for fish and the colourful kingfisher hunting dragonfly from its perch.

Just out of basic training and raw as they come, they were elated to be on special duties and away from the monotony and routine of the stuffy barracks.

Mr Deacon had already been there for over ten minutes and he still had not stopped complaining about their presence.

"I mean, what am I supposed to do with you two? Tweddle Dum and Tweddle Dee are hardly going to scare these people into compliance." Mr Deacon ranted.

To the two young servicemen, this verbal haranguing was nothing compared to their Sargent Major putting them through their paces on the parade ground each day and was like water off a duck's back. They just stood next to each other, holding their newly provided but heavily used, Lee Enfield 303 rifles at ease until they heard something that required them to respond.

"Now this one chap, James, we are going to see today, he's the worst, he's their ringleader," Mr Deacon continued with hot distain on his breath, "last time I was there he pushed a

201

The dragon under the hill

shotgun in my face and threatened to shoot me! While the useless local policeman stood on and did nothing." He growled.

Thankfully, if the soldiers had learned one thing in training, it was how not to burst out laughing when you know you should not, no matter how funny the situation is found to be. Not only did they both know Evan's good reputation but Twm had already told them the story at great length, especially the bit about the triggers being missing but it was his impersonation of the shocked Mr Deacon's face with the barrels resting on his beak-like nose, that came to mind now and was causing them to struggle holding back their amusement as they were still being spoken to. They both held it in magnificently, knowing full well, if one went, the other would follow.

"So, I want you both to be on your guard for this man, he's capable of anything and above all, watch my back. My safety is your priority. Is that understood?" He said in his best, authoritative voice.

"Yessir!" Came the automatic, reflex response.

"Right, now that's understood, follow me, we'll rouse those other two buffoons and make our way there." Then he strode off in the direction of his lodgings with the two uniformed lads trying not to catch each other's eye while amiably trailing up the hill behind him.

As the little troop neared the Ty Bont, Mr Deacon's strides became less and less confident and his face more and more confused. On reaching his destination, his beady eyes scanned the area and his rage was immediate and incandescent, released in one primal scream.

"Where the hell is my bloody car!"

The dragon under the hill

"Thank you for coming Reverend," was the immediate response as Rhodri let himself into the Price family farmhouse, "duw, you got here fast. Were you on your way already?" Elsie asked, who was the mother of Albany and his brothers.

There was no ceremony or formality in any of these homes. No door was ever locked or barred, only strangers knocked and if you called on someone when they were out, you waited until they came back. This was doubly true of the local preacher who was the additional member of every family.

The Reverend immediately noticed, there was no sense of panic or sense of fluster in the farmhouse, just a calmness and feeling of timely acceptance.

"Oh no," he answered, "funnily enough I was fast asleep when Albany knocked my door – dead to the world I was. He fair knocked my door off its hinges." The Reverend Thomas explained, "those surveyors the government has employed to look at the land are actually nice lads as it turns out and one of them, Eric, gave me a lift over here in their posh car."

"Oh, that was kind," said a surprised Elsie, "why didn't you bring him in for some tea?"

Rhodri already had his hand on the door handle of the small downstairs room that had been converted into Nana Price's bedroom shortly after she had fallen ill and called over his shoulder, "he couldn't stop Else, he had to take the car back in case it was needed." As he entered the darkened room.

Elsie straightened her house dress, caught up with the Reverend following him into the room.

"She didn't have the best of nights. She had a few sips of tea first thing this morning and we managed to pray together but since then she's not been conscious and breathing is very shallow." Elsie explained.

The dragon under the hill

"Is it?" Came the reply, the Reverend Thomas turning to his host and putting his hand gently but firmly on her shoulder and spoke kindly "I'll sit with her a while then." Elsie recognised this as her cue to leave, as the sombre clergyman carefully seated himself in the chair near the bed. Reaching out, he took the cool hand of the old lady, her fragile skin paper thin and silk smooth and in his musical lilting voice spoke softly and lovingly of heaven and eternity.

By the time Dr Hawkins arrived at the Price farmhouse, she had already quietly and peacefully slipped away. There was sadness in the home, of course, but it was mitigated by the certainty of their faith and the knowledge of a very long and full life, well lived.

After the Doctor had officially pronounced the death, he signed the certificate, shared his condolences and returned to his practice. Then tradition and the community took over.

As is customary, the body is washed and 'laid out', sometimes on a table used especially for such occasions or on the deceased's bed. The more superstitious would cover all mirrors and keep the bowl, cloth and water used for the washing under the table, to be thrown out in the street only after the funeral. White curtains and linens are hung, coupled with a lit candle in the window, lighting the way, harking back to an ancient belief that a spirit called Margan would conduct the deceased's soul to the other side.

The night before the funeral called the 'Gwylnos' meaning 'vigil'. The mourners would stay by the coffin, pray and tell stories regarding the deceased's good nature. The funeral itself varied from area to area but mainly due to the fact that families were large and people had so many relations, funerals in Wales were traditionally huge affairs. Each town and village had its own set funeral route called the 'burying lane' which the procession would always follow. Family members only would carry the coffin to the

204

The dragon under the hill

chapel where they would be met by the head mourner. In some areas women did not attend funerals at all and certainly would not be going to the graveside for the actual burial.

Old Nana Price's funeral was the biggest the village had seen in years.

As the Reverend later recalled in service, she was originally of tough as nails, fierce Fishguard fish-wives stock and if you want to know exactly how tough the legendary women of Fishguard are, ask the French.

Known as the last invasion of Britain, during the Napoleonic war an expedition force was sent from France to Bristol. Getting blown of course, the ships containing 1400 French soldiers arrived in Fishguard Bay meeting small resistance from the town's few canons. On the 23rd of February 1797 a few small boatloads of invaders made shore nearby but due to ill-discipline and poor rations they mostly just scavenged and looted. The locals, including the women, soon armed themselves and responded and the French quickly surrendered. One 47 year old cobbler's wife, Jemima Nicolas, armed with only a pitchfork and sheer audacity, rounded up twelve French soldiers, single handedly. Locking them up in St Mary's church before returning to the battle. From then on, she was known as 'Jemima Fawr' a local heroine, which translated, is 'Jemima the Great' and lived to be 82.

Even among that stock, reaching the milestone of one hundred and four years of age was something. Old Nana Price's longevity was legendary and her death made the newspapers.

The Price boys, dealing with the first significant death in their young lives were the only one's needing any real consolation, again this is where the Reverend Thomas was invaluable. Answering difficult questions and telling stories about their great grandmother to make them laugh, finishing with the reasonable statement.

The dragon under the hill

"Well, she was 104 and had fourteen children, outliving twelve of them."

Eric rounded the corner changing into the lowest gear and immediately knew his day had taken a turn for the worse. Where the vehicle would normally be parked, stood the two young soldiers and an obviously outraged Mr Deacon, face a hideous sunburned red. He was primed, like a barrel of gunpowder and ready to loudly and dynamically explode.

True to form, before the vehicle had come to a full stop nor Eric exited, the tirade begun. This went ignored until the car was securely parked and Eric had alighted.

"Where on earth have you been?!" Burst from Mr Deacon, anger flowing like lava.

Eric took a deep breath and stated calmly, "The Reverend Thomas asked me to give him a ride to see Old Nana Price, who is gravely ill and I was happy to oblige."

"Who the hell is Old Nana Price?!" Yelled Mr Deacon, louder and higher than before.

Before Eric could respond himself, Alyn, one of the static soldiers piped up jovially, "Oh, everyone knows Old Nana Price round here."

"O aye, well known, she's 104 you know." Said the other in agreement, nodding.

"Did they say how she is?" Asked Alyn, totally oblivious to the explosion standing near.

This sent Mr Deacon headlong into a temper of such fury and confusion that he was momentarily unable to form words and was a red face spluttering and spitting imbecilic mess.

The dragon under the hill

Up until now Eric had been courteous and often subservient to Mr Deacon but he was quickly losing all good will towards to man and added, "She is the matriarch of one of the main farms you've been trying to buy for weeks and has been ill for a while now, if you'd taken more interest in the locals you might have got further than you have."

This lit the firecracker. Faces appeared in windows and doorways drawn by the wrath and venom of Mr Deacon's ensuing volcanic rant, even Ollie heard it from his room. He bounded downstairs to the scene to find his friend being poked in the chest while being yelled at mercilessly, inches from his face.

"Say, what's all this about?" queried Ollie, breaking the flow of the raging tirade. But this was only a temporary state as he found the bluster turned in his direction as Mr Deacon vented and shouted his complaint about his ruined plans. Ollie's next statement stopped the outburst dead, like hitting a brick wall.

"We wouldn't be going to the James farm today anyway," piquing the curiosity of those listening, "we received notification from the ministry this morning that the cave specialist and equipment will be arriving tomorrow and the final decision on the land is his."

Mr Deacon's eyes flashed from side to side as he processed this information and its connotations before he reasoned, "I received no such communication."

"No? We did. Maybe if you'd involved yourself more in the planning, instead of drinking, you'd know more" responded Ollie, whose patience with the mean little man had been completely eroded so felt no sympathy in bursting his illusions. "We receive regular communications from the ministry."

The implications of this hit Mr Deacon like a rock, compressing and quietening him instantly.

The dragon under the hill

Chapter 19

A sapped and fatigued, Jack had hardly finished the last mouthful of his evening meal when he excused himself and went to bed. He desperately needed sleep and ditched his usual routine of keeping his clothes on and waiting for his grandparents to go to bed before escaping. He quickly undressed and slid under the blankets and left waking up for his nightly excursion to fate.

He need not have worried, as the copious amounts of tea he had consumed with his grandfather that day, filtered through and he was awoken in the night by the urgent pressing of a mightily full bladder.

Having no idea of the time, he lit his candle stub and took it downstairs with him to better interrogate the old clock. By the flicker of the candle the old clock read ten past one in the morning, which by Jack's quick calculations gave him enough time to spend an hour at the hilltop and be back in plenty of time before his grandfather rose.

By the light of the taper, he crept towards the fireplace as not to disturb Heini and retrieved a couple of replacement matches from the box on the mantelpiece. After donning his coat and gum boots and closing the farm house door quietly behind him, he blew out the candle stub and put it and the matches in his pocket. Giving his eyes time to adjust to the dark he made opportune use of the outside loo before beginning his ascent of the hill.

As he climbed up the familiar route, at about midway he stopped. Turning, he stared across the night sky and even with the increasing attachment he felt to nature, he had to ponder the mystery of how his grandfather could tell that a storm was on the way because all he could see was what looked like normal clouds to him but he knew you could bet your last halfpenny, Evan would be right and that by morning a storm would arrive.

The dragon under the hill

Although these visits were becoming more commonplace, Jack still got an immense sense of excitement and tingling adrenaline when he approached and crested the hilltop. The sight of the mysterious cairn still held wonder for him and started his heart pumping faster.

Taking a moment to catch his breath and again stare down the valley, that familiar feeling of connection started to build and in solidifying, texture grew upon it. It was becoming stronger but more nuanced as he drew closer in proximity to where the legendary being dwelt.

"Krait! Krait! It's Jack here, I've come alone!" He began yelling before he caught himself and the thought broke through that the connection they had was more non-verbal, more sensing, than verbal. He closed his eyes, concentrated and simply experienced. He felt the wind on his face and moving his hair, connecting and feeling every tiny nerve ending, increasing their sensitivity. Becoming conscious of his body down to the smallest follicle being touched by the breeze, his goosebumps rising, aware of his slowed breathing, aware of his own heartbeat and blood moving through him under the gossamer of his skin.

From that place of peace, he stretched out, becoming mindful of his surroundings, where he was, sounds around him and the smells conjured by the muscle of the air.

Lastly, he concentrated on the familiar feeling of the connection and what it stirred within him, he reached, allowed it to grow and solidify, like nearing footsteps, until he heard something. It was like being caught while falling.

"I am here."

Although familiar, the voice still retained the same stilted alien sound since Jack had first encountered it but he became increasingly in tune with the wave of sentiment the words travelled

209

to him on. On this occasion there was definitely a sense of regard and acceptance.

For a moment the lad revelled in the warmth that met him before collating his thoughts. "I was wondering how you were after last night." He ventured.

The following silence had an edge of confusion to it, which continued as he got his response.

"I am uninjured. I do not recall why you should think I sustained damage."

Not being of a stage himself where he could easily verbalise his feelings, Jack found it hard to muster an alternative way of asking after the being's emotional wellbeing. He thought hard and did the best he could.

"I didn't...didn't mean your body." He tried to explain, "we talked about some things that were really sad. I think I would feel unhappy for a long time after, if it was me."

"Ah, 'feelings' once more. I comprehend your enquiry now," Krait replied. "Time dilutes the violence of the emotion...and clouds the images to dullness, as it does with all things. Grief, loss and abiding injustice will always accompany me to whatever degree. But my hatred for man, that hardly decreased over the years because of the fuel of vengeance I continually fed it. Now, that hate, has changed."

"It has?" Encouraged Jack.

"It was once...a blinding, searing fury", the entity continued, "but now...now it is a cooling ember, removed from the flames."

"I am glad", said Jack, feeling this was good news for his own sake if nothing else. This seemed to be the end for that specific topic of conversation, so Jack moved on to the matter that was still troubling him.

"We were expecting men to come to investigate the hilltop today. I don't know why they didn't come but they will surely be here tomorrow." This worried Jack immensely. He was already on pins wondering what his grandparents would be like after the Reverend Thomas had revealed everything to them. Each time he ran the scenario through his head it ended in sadness and the breaking of the relationships with them he had come to cherish and value immensely over the last weeks. The other new relationships that meant an incredible amount to him also seemed in jeopardy, the thought of outsiders (connected to the military) possibly discovering the creature, did not even bare consideration.

The calm response came as before, "let them come."

It was hard for Jack to discern if the creature's seemingly glib replies when this issue was raised, were due to the fact that there genuinely was no worry there about the situation or failure to fully understand the gravity of what may happen. Or possibly due to Jack not having communicated the possible consequences seriously enough. Forgetting the emotional bond momentarily, he tried to plead his case more.

"But they have skilled men who will come down into where you live." He appealed.

"Have no fear", said the voice reassuringly but sensing the troubled mind in the lad an invitation was sent fourth, "see for yourself."

This invite at once surprised and elated the youngster and it took him a moment to rally himself.

"Yes," came the excited response, "where are you and how do I get to you?"

"Look beyond the cairn to the tallest tree that breaks through the wall of stone. Beneath the tree grows a large bush with thorns, go behind that bush and at the foot of the wall you will find access. Enter there and then I will guide you." Instructed the voice clearly.

Trying to hold the specifics of these instructions in his head, without losing the smallest of details, Jack looked around him. The largest of the trees did stand out, although stunted by its environment and would be considered small by most standards. It was gnarled and twisted into ugly contortions by many years of battling the strong wind and the vengeful weather the hilltop was usually shrouded in. Its sinewy branches held minimal leaves and some boughs almost touched the ground. The moss-covered trunk and part of the roots had merged with an ancient pitted grey stone wall over the last hundreds of years. The wall had not been touched by human hands in a long, long time and was no more than collected rubble. An overgrown shamble of stone, in most places no more than a foot high but here, the natural and the man made had supported each other and become strong together against the callous elements. Without restrictions, the bramble bush had run wild in the shelter of the tree and was at least as tall as Jack and twice as wide as it was tall. It was dense and thick with intimidating thorns that grabbed, mauled and snared Jack's clothing and scratched his skin as he navigated behind it.

As foretold, at the base of the wall hidden from normal view, was an oval shaped, barrel sized hole, plenty big enough for the slender boy to transverse. Its dirt edges had been worn smooth and hard by years of abrasion. He peered down into the depths. It was impossible for the lad to get any sense of depth or of what lay below. Bravely, he pitched himself feet first down the hole, sliding down at an acute angle. It seemed quite a distance until his feet finally met solid footfall, much to Jack's relief.

Steadying himself in the gloom, he took a deep breath and was hit with the damp smell of stale air. Taking the candle stub

The dragon under the hill

and the spare matches he had gleaned earlier out of his pockets, after a few failed attempts, he managed to successfully strike a match on the rough side of the candle holder and then light the stub. Automatically, he shielded his eyes from the light, as they were accustomed to the dim light of the night. The light had a comforting and warming effect in this strange place. Jack was especially pleased to note that his descent had been no more than six feet and there were many exposed roots and jutting rocks which would offer secure foot holds when it came time to climb out.

He looked around him. The surrounding rock for the most part was of a creamy colour and clearly porous. The tunnel he found himself in narrowed to his left but opened up to his right. On closer inspection he could see where the rock to the right had been made shiny and smooth by wear and guessed that was the direction to go.

Jack was unceasingly glad of his small light as the floor was uneven and many obstacles protruded from either side or above. He crept slowly and hadn't travelled too far when he came to an abrupt turn and from there into a space that left him astounded.

He found himself taken from the cramped confines of a small tunnel into an impressively large dome shaped amphitheatre. He walked to the middle, where he guessed was now directly underneath the cairn itself and slowly turned around. From the central spot where he stood, dozens of tunnel entrances of various sizes pinwheeled outwards. Some were only large enough for a rabbit, others you could drive a car through, all leaking from the middle like bicycle spokes. Jack was in awe.

He began to understand the creature's confidence now, you could explore these caves for decades and not enter the same one twice. It would be a nightmare to get lost here, especially without light.

The dragon under the hill

"Come", Krait's voice refocused the lad's mind and sensing the direction the call came from he entered one of the many cave openings. This he followed until it forked, where without hesitation he turned to his left. After negotiating a few more twists and diversions he came to a nondescript opening where he climbed up into a spacious bulbous chamber. It smelled like his grandmother's herb garden, mixed with dried grass but behind that, a seeping musk and the sweet smell of decay. In one rounded conclave there was mass of flattened vegetation, small leaved branches, fern leaves, reeds and grass. Like a large solid, flat nest the lower level was made up old dried flora while nearer the top the fresher of the leaves.

"Lower your light please." The voice was near and tangible now but Jack could not physically see who he was conversing with. He found a small shelf-like cubby hole where he placed the candle which much reduced the glare but still allowed the boy enough light to see.

"Where are you?" Tired of straining his eyes around the chamber Jack blurted out more aggressively then intended.

"Here", the voice said plainly.

As the word filled Jack's mind, the point in the stone wall exactly where he had been staring at so hard, started to writhe and unfold. As if coming to life, the stone morphed and took shape. The shape became more defined, the colour slowly changed becoming a darker yellow then into golden hues, soon he could make out the creature's shape.

Then it became real, the creature's head turned towards him and those huge immutable eyes faced and grasped him, holding him with curiosity and ethereal mystery. "Now do you understand? These caverns are copious and some stretch far and very deep. Should they stumble on where I am, I will not be seen." Relayed the inhabitant of the lair.

214

The dragon under the hill

Jack was awe struck and all his anxiety regarding the investigation of the cairn left him. In fact, Jack felt so secure, like he'd been grafted into the common mind he shared with Krait, it was a thermal spring that warmed and enveloped him until all there was left was the desire to stay exactly in this place, in this time, in the company he was in.

"One second I couldn't see you, the next you appeared. How did you do that?" Jack gabbled in astonishment. Sitting on the stone floor, leaning his back against the smooth wall the youth listened.

"A Naga's scales are an extension of the mind. As we command - they move. How we position them can either reflect, absorb or mirror the light. If we so wish, we can cast no shadow in sun or have no silhouette at night; we can be undetectable to the eye or be a blinding light. These things once we used for the hunt and courtship display, I have used it to stay hidden from mankind all these years." Explained the creature.

"Incredible." Gasped the young boy, "so, what colour are you?"

"In truth," Krait opened up, "a Naga has no colour of his own." There was a pause, it was clear it had been eons since he had spoken of these things, it was taking some time and no little effort to find the right way to explain it to the boy. "Our teeth are shaped to securely hold and tear, not to mash and chew. To help break down and digest some of what we eat we must ingest rocks and stones. These are held in our...craw and stomach, pummelling what we have eaten into smaller pieces. It is from the properties of the stone we gain our outward colouration."

Jack took some time to absorb this intriguing information, such a foreign existence. "So, you are the colour of this stone?" He asked.

"That is correct. It is now my natural colour." Came the affirming response.

The dragon under the hill

"And if you were to eat coal you would turn black?" Proffered Jack.

"Over time but we would not, given other options, as coal is too brittle for the task."

Krait lowered his eyes as something he said sparked thoughts of old memories that he had not considered for very many years.

"When I was but a hatchling, it was a way of telling where other Naga were from. Those of our own nest were mostly white, shades of yellow to orange. From the north were those of purple and fiery reds and from the south deep greens and blues. Each taking on the hues of the minerals that surrounded them. I recall gatherings that crowded the sky even blocking out the very sun. The heavens being full of winged kindred all vying for thermals, each sharing their song, their voice. Some of the ancient ones as big as the mountains themselves."

Due to their reinforced link, Jack began see all as described like painting forming before him the colours and forms held and dissipated, moved and refocused, he revelled in the imagery, a thought struck Jack and before he could stop it was quickly and directly expressed.

"If you are very old, how come you are not very big, not the size I thought dragon to be."

Krait did not baulk or react to the directness of the question as the boy feared but instead considered it and his answer carefully before patiently explaining.

"From the first moment we emerge, we were encouraged to eat and grow abundantly. Space and food were plentiful and being unhindered we will grow to gargantuan proportions over many, many years. These are different times, it is not good to be large or conspicuous, we do not need to be seen or found. We can, if needed, suppress our growth to suit our surroundings. I was young and small when my gathering was ravaged and I began to

The dragon under the hill

live in fear. I have stayed this way since I have dwelled in these catacombs. The age of giants is over."

Absorbing every word, in his mind's eye the young man could see the epic scenes forming and the exquisite giant beasts that were being described to him. Great tears and riffs against the azure sky, they tumbled and spun, glided and dove. Like a thousand blown leaves being broadcast abroad, they never touched, collided or swerved. It was the most free and wondrous thing Jack had seen.

As he spent more time with his host and their bond strengthened, communication became clearer and even memories were beginning, however clumsily, to be shared. The lines in the sand between them being erased. "It must have been some sight to see. Dragons of all sorts of colours and sizes, flying overhead, everywhere you looked." Mused Jack.

"It was."

The air grew heavy with melancholic weight. The emanating sadness was palpable and floated like fog. Jack felt he owed it to his companion to share this moment and these feelings with him and just sat in silent solidarity.

After a while a question occurred to Jack. "What's it like to fly? I imagine it's marvellous".

"To fly? To fly is to be truly free." The answer shot back, the change onto this subject seemed to lift the creature's spirits before a more carefully considered response. "It is the joy of freedom and liberation from restrictions that bind, including the tether to the ground but it is also to be a part of the very air itself. To rise on thermal updrafts effortlessly and allow yourself to be carried where ever the airflow takes you or to dive from a great height hurling at speed towards the rushing ground, waiting until the last possible moment before spreading your wings and swooping low over the land, is to really be alive, even more so in the hunt. Yes, it is marvellous."

The dragon under the hill

The small boy in Jack was tugging at him mentally, pestering him to ask for Krait to take him up there to feel what he described but the burgeoning young man in Jack recognised this for the immature folly it was and like asking for piggyback rides, belonged to another time.

"And, what of Lily?" Krait asked.

This time there was less of the awkwardness and cowering embarrassment attached to the subject and Jack felt able to speak more coherently than ever.

"Oh yes, I forgot to mention," Jack replied. "After what you said before, I kept reminding myself to be brave. Anyway, I was walking with my friend the Reverend, visiting different folk and we went to the farm where she lives.

Lovely it was to see here again but at first it was all a bit awkward, a bit cold. Then the Reverend said Lily should show me around her farm. She started to warm when she was talking about her chicks and ducklings, all fluffy and noisy they were. I was brave, like you said, asking about things and asking about her. In the end we were chatting away very nicely, thanks to you.

But the best bit, when it came time to leave, I tried extra hard to be brave and asked her could I write her when I go back home. Duw, there's happy I was when she said 'yes' and she wrote her address down and promised to write me back."

"That is good." Said Krait.

"I was nearly skipping as we walked home," the lad continued, "there's happy I was."

"I am...glad."

The chamber was surprisingly warm and beyond their conversation, incredibly quiet. Jack let out a prodigious yawn and with sleepiness in his voice asked, "How come you haven't gone to look for others of your kind over the years?"

The dragon under the hill

As he waited for an answer, Jack closed his eyes and rested his head on the wall behind, feeling utter peace and security.

"Fear." Admitted Krait eventually, with a tinge of shame.

"In the beginning, it was all about survival. It was all that drove me, all I could consider. Staying hidden. Staying alive." The voice said quietly and idly, as if he was narrating thoughts out loud without the self-consciousness or awkwardness of knowing someone was listening. "My compulsion was trying to find something of a home and long-term safety. It was not long before the ghosts of the past brought loneliness and aching with them. As time passed I became crippled with pain and anger, hobbled, I limped from one century to another. Each day I was less...less of them, less of me. I thought many times about searching for others but fear always stopped me. Fear of what I might find. That I might find I am truly the last of my kind."

Like warmed oil, the creature's desire to be inhibited in sharing with the boy was becoming less and less viscous. Jack's innocence and simple thought processes bred trust and stirred within the dragon the need to be heard, for companionship and community that had laid dormant for too long. The boy inspired in him the kinship he remembered feeling for hatchlings, the desire to protect and watch over. As the lad eagerly listened more and more remnants from the past became safe to think on and feel again. Doors long locked in his psyche were tentatively opened and peered into. There was the old familiar pain he knew well but there was long forgotten joys and buried pieces of himself.

"Sometimes," Krait ventured slowly, "sometimes...I think I hear something, feel something, right at the very edge of my senses, just out of reach of my perception. Although...", the mood again becoming more conspiratorial and cathartic as the being spoke, "I cannot tell if what I sense is another of my kind, calling in the distance or if the impression I have, are just echoes from the past."

"Echoes?" Repeated Jack, lazily.

The dragon under the hill

"The connection we Naga share," Krait corrected himself, "used to share, is...was... so strong, so tangible that even after the connection is broken the essence remains fading slowly, like scent on the wind. When one of our group was taken from us their..." there was a pause as the best word was searched for, something that could not properly or fully be translated or communicated verbally, "what you would call 'soul' remains and it is easy for us to conjure them into being again in our hearts. Like ripples in a pond, if there is now 'hive' mind, if there are no Naga then, as time goes by the ripples wain and weaken and the essence, the soul becomes diluted, until it is just an echo.

Again, like ripples in a pond", explained the being, "the shared 'hive' mind we have, the ability to communicate, decreases the further we are from each other, becoming harder and harder to hear."

This time as much a personal musing, he concluded his sentiment. "So, these things I have heard, do I desire them to be another of my kind so much that I am conjuring remnants of the past, is my longing not to be the last causing me to fool myself or are there really others out there calling. Reaching out as best they can from whatever sanctuary they have hidden away in, all these years, as I have here. Waiting, as I am here. Too frightened of what they may or may not find, as I am here."

As this cacophony of questions and contending feelings conflicted in the dragon's mind, his small guest had clarity and simplicity of thought.

"You should look." Jack half yawned and half spoke.

This carried much weight with the dragon and he unravelled it like a knot in his mind. He thought about the small and simply way thee boy had responded to his advice and had been brave in situation not easy for him. As he conjured obstacles and excuses but they vanished as quickly. The creature turned to his companion after finally fashioning a response.

Jack was already soundly and serenely fast asleep.

The dragon under the hill

Chapter 20

A storm did come.

How it raged. In violence, blind arrogance and scorn it screamed its merciless bombardment. Full of venom and vigour it pounded and churned, furiously thrashing against every object it met, flogging the land, howling through the whole valley.

The sun was yet to rise but it had little effect when it did. The dark clouds that were heaped and hoarded over the valley would prevent any bright or joyous rays from lighting the land. The vile squalling wind was thunderous and awful in its power, the hard-falling rain driven and spun in all directions. Its banshee-like sounds flamed as it rushed through the trees and flora, like the crash of wild waves on rocky crags or the forlorn howl of a wounded beast. It was terrible and humbling, to be feared and observed from tranquil safely, only to be faced by the bravest or most foolish.

Woken by the battling tempest outside, still shrouded in darkness, Evan lay in the coddling warmth of his bed. He stared into the blackness and listened to the pelting rain pitting the windows and the savage fury of the wind as it tried to rip the little farmhouse from its very foundations and hurl it into the sea. He took comfort that even the mightiest of gales may dislodge a few shingles or rip some felt lining but the little limpet-like cottage had not stood there for lifetimes without being utterly rock solid.

"Cynefin" he whispered to himself, which translated would mean 'habitat' or 'familiar' but in actuality, has so much more sentiment and inflection. Being more justly described as that relationship with the place of your birth and of your upbringing, the environment in which you live and to which you are naturally acclimatised, belong and love. Home.

Feeling the ache in his back that signalled he'd been laying too long in one position on the lumpy old bed they could not afford to replace, Evan knew whatever the time actually was, he

The dragon under the hill

could lay there no longer and stealthily slipped from under the blankets attempting not to disturb the bliss of his sleeping wife. He padded downstairs in the gloom, where he lit two lamps in turn. He greeted his dog who had been stirred by his actions and sat in his usual chair. The old clock showed it to be some time before they usually rose and he didn't want to disturb his wife by preparing the fire or making tea, so he wrapped the coloured quilted blanket that adorned the back of the chair around himself against the cold. Picked up his leather-bound Bible, located his bookmark and continued reading from where he left off the previous night. The forceful blustering sounds of the typhoon outside occasionally threatening to break his concentration.

Later, Maggie was awoken by the familiar sounds of her husband building and starting the fire. The large fireplace caused the smallest sound to echo and travel up the chimney, making it louder and seem nearer. He always got up before her and liked to have the fire already warming the house by the time she joined him. She loved him for this simple act of kindness he had silently committed every single day of their marriage.

The usual early morning preparations complete, Maggie checked the clock and as it was around the time she called her grandson to start his day, not receiving any response or sounds of movement. It was not unusual for him not to react to her calls and she would often have to physically stir the boy from his slumber. What was unusual, was that on entering Jack's room, she shockingly discovered it and his bed were empty. This initially caused utter bewilderment which grew to concern, as it quickly became clear he was nowhere in the cottage.

There saw his boots and coat were gone, as they would be if he had used the outside toilet but as Evan had not seen him pass in the long time he'd been up, they began to worry.

Quickly, Evan dressed for the adversarial weather and opened the door ready to go out and search for the lad, almost tripping over something at his feet. When he looked down he found the missing youth curled up fetally, placidly asleep on the

The dragon under the hill

doorstep. Sheltered from the blasted horrors of the storm by the deep door recess and overhanging eaves.

"Here he is Mags", Evan said with baffled amusement, "I've found him."

Incredulous at his discovery, Maggie came over to see for herself, "well I never..."

"Jack. Jack my boy," Evan roused the lad, gently shaking him by the shoulder.

Two blurry, disoriented eyes slit open and peered up at him.

"What on earth are you doing sleeping here son?" his grandfather asked gently.

Jack looked all around him like someone lost in unfamiliar surroundings. It took him several confused moments to comprehend where he was. He felt very stiff as his grandfather helped him to his feet.

"Er...I...I don't know." His mind a complete fog that he could not clear, he struggled to make any connection to his memory. He allowed himself to by led to the kitchen table and hot cup of tea placed into his ice-cold hands, warming them quickly.

Maggie caringly rubbed life into his shoulders with a concerned look on her face, while Evan giggled quietly to himself, shaking his head.

"I've nodded off myself many-a-time but never outside in the middle of a storm on my way back from the lav. That takes some doing, chwarae teg to you lad." He jested. Being Welsh for 'fair play', chwarae teg can either be used as exclamation to curb bad behaviours or as a comment of respect.

"I just don't understand John", Maggie injected, "couldn't you open the door? Did you try knocking?"

The dragon under the hill

"I don't know Nana", claimed the boy, "I just can't remember."

He repeated himself, slightly more alarmed, "I can't remember how I got there, at all."

"Never mind now" she added, "get warm and get some of that hot tea in you. Let's hope you haven't caught a chill," she gave her husband a concerned glance, "you travel back home next week and what will your mother say if we send you back full of coughs and sneezes?"

Jack was still attempting to jump start his clouded memory and murmured out loud, "I remember waking up really needing a wee, getting up to use the toilet but nothing after that..." his voice faded

"Don't mind me asking lad, if it is just a wee you wanted, why didn't you use the jerry instead?" Evan asked.

"The what?" Questioned a still disoriented Jack.

"The jerry, the po, chamber pot," expanded his grandfather. On seeing no flicker of comprehension in the boy's eyes he explained further, "a large porcelain pot with a handle kept under the bed. So, in the middle of the night it saves you trampling outside, you use it and clean it out the next day. There's one under the end of your bed."

Jack stared at his grandfather gobsmacked, how could he have gone so long without this important piece of information, "you mean all this time...?" Jack exclaimed not able to finish the sentence, sparking cackling laughter from his amused grandfather.

It certainly wasn't a day when they expected visitors but before the full story of the day was told, their little abode would have more visitors than ever before.

The dragon under the hill

Jack was placed in front of the fire with his cup of tea cupped in both hands to warm him through, while his grandmother fussed about him. His grandfather began wrapping himself up again to face the monster that was pounding and bellowing outside. The mechanics of running a farm did not stop for the weather. On top of his normal coat he slid into an old oil-skin and yellow sou'wester hat that was the last resort in such occasions. Opening the door to the cracking sky, he looked out and prepared to leave, staring into the belly of the beast. Heini trotted across and took her usual place by the side of her master. Except on this occasion when Evan bravely adventured outside, the old dog just watched him. If ever a dog's expression communicated anything it was now and it was communicating 'There's no way I'm going out there!'

Evan smiled and said, "I don't blame you ol' girl." Before closing the door behind himself.

Despite his obvious desire not to venture out in this weather, things still needed to be done and checks needed to be made. Evan stoically went about his business without complaint, doing what was necessary. A quiet hero.

Pushing his full body weight against the wind's force and holding tightly on to his hat he firstly checked the farmhouse and its roof, keeping a special eye out for anything that might have become detached. He then checked the out buildings and contents of the barn, making sure the sleeping pigs had sufficient food and bedding, before trudging up the hill in a weaving bobbing fashion, like an expert boxer, as he was blown about and buffeted by the gale. Climbing the hill to check on the welfare of his animals, paying a continual price as the rain sandblasted his face, stinging and making it difficult to see. The experienced old farmer took it all in his stride with simple acceptance and enduring determination.

Evan had rarely been so relieved to re-enter the sanctuary of his little farm house, now all was done and be embraced by the light and warmth. Dripping and sodden, a reflection of the horrors outdoors. The table was set for breakfast and Jack was looking

225

The dragon under the hill

alert and a much healthier colour as he waited to tuck into his morning meal.

About to say grace, the trio were jolted when unbelievably there was a knock at the door. It was too uniform to be something hitting it, blown by the wind but surely no-one would be out in this storm, let alone calling on them. The threesome flashed confused glances at each other before Evan got up and opened the front door.

Standing there bending under the eaves for protection, was the familiar face of the young surveyor Eric and another man of similar height but a slighter frame. Thin but sinewy, he had the steely look of someone built of twisted wire and had the largest Adam's apple Evan had ever seen.

"What on earth are you doing here boyo?" Exclaimed a surprised Evan, "come in out of this weather."

"We won't if you don't mind," responded the already wet Eric politely, rocking as he tried holding himself steady against the imposing gale, "we only wanted to call to say 'hello' before carrying on with our investigations and introduce you to Colonel Jeremy Sharpe here." The introduced man nodded, smiled and shook Evan by the hand with an incredibly strong grip. Eric continued. "Not only is he one of the country's best potholers but he is the Ministry's foremost geologist and will confirm what we suspect about the porous rock make-up of your hill."

With his eyebrows raised Evan exclaimed "You chaps are not thinking of going up that hill in this atrocious weather are you, surely not? Have some sense."

Jerry spoke for the first time, "up it and under it Mr James. Providing I find a decent entry point, it shouldn't take long to determine the composition of the rock formation and strata throughout the scarp."

"You don't want to go meddling up there," Evan cautioned, "it's incredibly dangerous, even in broad daylight."

226

The dragon under the hill

"You needn't worry Mr James, I will take every precaution and shall be perfectly safe," Jerry continued. "I can assure you I have done this sort of thing many hundreds of times and we have the latest equipment." Gesturing behind him to the two vehicles parked there. The nearest, the red Austin 7, was moving about, rocked by the gale's force, like child's crib. The heavy rain melodically hitting the bonnet and roof, sounding like a rolling timber drum. Evan noted it contained the unmistakable figure of the insipid, reviled Mr Deacon scowling inside. Behind that, a British Racing green short wheelbase WHT Bedford van. Out of which Ollie and the two young soldiers were striving to unload boxes, poorly fighting against the wind and rain.

"You must be mad." Evan pleaded with them, "can't you go up another day? The storm will be gone by this time tomorrow," he predicted. "Come in by here, tea is up and breakfast is ready." The invite was echoed by his wife.

"Ah, I'm afraid not," countered Eric, "you see, we've just got the Colonel's services for today only, as he is incredibly in demand, he needs to be somewhere else tomoorw. Besides, once he has confirmed what Ollie and I suspect, then we can report the land as being useless for the Ministry's needs, which I'm sure you'd be happy to hear."

"You are not wrong there, young fella" said Evan before giving in, "well you sound determined so I'm not going to stand in your way, just promise you'll be careful and you'll come straight back here for a warm and some tea afterwards."

They promised and left, leaving Evan to pronounce, "the world's gone mad." Before returning to the breakfast table.

With breakfast finished, they were chatting around the table over more tea regarding the ugly storm and Mr Deacon's group, only to be surprisingly interrupted by the door flying open and a soaked and utterly dishevelled figure stumble in. The proverbial 'drowned rat' flicked and dripped water everywhere, especially when shaking his shaggy hair in a dog like fashion.

"Duw, duw, what a fiend of a storm, there's a wonder I didn't blow away. I'm soaked to the skin." Said a bedraggled Reverend Thomas, who had already caused a sizable pool to form at his feet from the water dripping from his clothes and peeling off his sodden coat.

"Not really the weather for a nice little saunter, Rhodri bach." Evan said, returning to sipping his tea.

"O, you are drenched to the skin mun. You'll catch your death wandering about in this kind of storm," Maggie said in a mothering fashion, "you sit by the fire and get dry."

Rhodri obeyed and gratefully received the fresh towel offered.

"I fully intended to come and visit yesterday," he began while drying his hair, "but I was called away. Sorry to tell you all that Old Nana Price passed away yesterday. Very peaceful like."

"Oh never," reacted Maggie.

"Aw, there's sad." Piped in Jack, who had enjoyed meeting the feisty centenarian.

"One hundred and four is a fair old innings though," commented Evan.

"How are the family taking it? Elsie and the boys?" added Maggie.

"Fine really, it wasn't exactly like they didn't know it was coming. I had to have a quiet word with Albany and Royston, their first experience see," The Reverend said from under the towel. "Funeral is next Tuesday, at the chapel for 2 o'clock and then down to the farm for the wake. You know Old Nana Price, she already had it all planned out long since, hymns and all." He continued, now in his bare feet with his socks drying on the mantlepiece.

The dragon under the hill

"The whole of the valley will be there for that one, I would imagine." Commented Maggie idly.

"Well if only half her relatives turn up, the place will be full Mags." Responded Rhodri, steam now drifting from his socks.

The old friends shared some light-hearted chatter and reminisced about the deceased matriarch and the funny fact that to them, she had always been an old woman.

As he always did, the Reverend Thomas expertly read the room and waited for the optimum moment to steer the conversation his way. Although, this specific topic did concern him and he wanted to prepare the ground as best he could first. As if to show the significance and possible unpalatability of the topic and seeking to lessen the impact, he spoke the first sentence in Welsh.

"Listen," he began seriously, "there is another subject I wanted to talk to you both about and to be honest Evan my old friend you aren't going to like it much."

"No?" Quizzed Evan, both his and his wife's faces looked concerned as Evan got up and sat in his chair opposite his friend.

"You see," Rhodri confessed, switching back to English for Jack's benefit. "Jack and I have been keeping something from you…"

"Oh, we know all about little Lily Hagerty." Maggie interrupted.

"No, no, I'm not talking about that," quashed the Reverend, "we all know those two are going to be wed someday, goes without saying. I knew that from the moment I put them together."

This flippant remark about his entire future delivered in such a matter-of-fact manner, startled and surprised Jack, he wanted desperately to object but words failed him and the conversation moved on.

The dragon under the hill

The Reverend looked intently at his old friends, pointed a finger and said, "now I want your promise on two things. One, you won't get angry with the boy and two, you will let me finish what I have to say before saying anything, don't interrupt, despite what you hear." Both Evan and Maggie who were now both incredibly intrigued and worried, agreed.

"Get on with it, spit it out Rhodri bach, the suspense is killing me mun." Said Evan.

Satisfied, the clergyman began his story.

He began by daring to remind Evan about what he shared with him all those years ago in the makeshift school-yard, what he thought he had seen on the hilltop as a young child. An obviously cross Evan tried to interject but Rhodri raised his hand with authority and carried on. He narrated how Jack had seen something similar while outside one night on that first occasion, his breaking of his grandfather's rules and subsequent nightly investigation of the cairn. He described Cymro's attack on the boy and his rescue by a then unknown entity and its slaughter of the hell-hound, describing what the lad had seen when he eventually witnessed the creature in all its wonder. He expertly expressed Jack's remorse about breaking one of the farm's fundamental rules with a nightly deception to attempt to interact with his saviour and eventual success. Then, how he and Jack had discussed the being and had decided to keep it secret and not tell Evan at first. Up to this point there was a sense that those listening were ready to write the whole tale off as the vivid imaginings of a sleep deprived boy going through puberty, until Rhodri made them think again.

He talked in vivid detail about the night he accompanied the boy to the hilltop and had an incredible encounter. How, right up close and without a shadow of doubt or possibility of there being a mistake, he saw the dragon. He described in minuscule detail everything about it, from its size and shape, fearfulness and speed, from the colour of the centre of its eyes to the smell on its breath; the way the creature had moved and the discourse they had. He expressed his initial terror and fear for their lives and how

230

he had stepped between the beast and the boy and how his concern was misguided. He had a little more difficulty describing the way the being communicated, so Jack, who had been silent up until now, jumped in and described the telepathy and empathy as best he could.

His memory finally restored to him, Jack took over the story telling duties and added last night's encounter to the account. In magical terms he mirrored all that he had been told the previous night. Each word adding colour to his story, adding definition the tale and cultivating the belief of those listening. But with all this clarity and added information the lad still couldn't relay how he got from Krait's chamber to the farmhouse doorstep. The boy ended with a contrite, "I'm ever so sorry I broke your rule granddad."

When the chroniclers were spent and the tale was told everyone stared at Evan waiting for his reaction. Would he explode in anger at their intentional deception? Would he rail in abject disbelief or dismiss the whole thing as an ill-judged joke? Would he stalk away in pain and disappointment?

He stared at the fire in silence.

The wood on the fire spat and crackled, the old clock ticked on and the wailing wind blew outside as they waited for what seemed like eras for a response.

Finally, Evan looked up, "I see," he said slowly climbing out of his chair, then he added, "you two had better get your coats then."

The dragon under the hill

Though a very familiar journey, it had never been so difficult for Jack to ascend the hill. His fight against the wind was energy sapping and he was relieved to finally crest the top. His light weight made each step a concerted effort, not having the physical strength of the adults with him and it took less than a minute for the driven rain to render his coat useless so the blustering incisors could bite unimpeded.

On the way, despite his mind being so awash with thoughts and feelings that raked back years he hardly noticed the storm, Evan had said little about the earlier revelation. Only to explain to the Reverend about the group exploring the very terrain that had been central to their story as the creature's abode and they'd better get up there. The Reverend for his part was amazed the surveying group had carried on with the job in these conditions and said so numerous times on the climb, coupled with complaining that he hated the rain and his 'blooming socks had only just got dry'. Jack had explained that they need not worry about his companion being discovered but Evan overruled his grandson, stating they should go anyway, just in case.

When the trio approached the cairn, they saw five forlorn looking weather-beaten figures trying to hold themselves against the warring wind and bulleting rain, all gathered around a section of the cairn. Ollie was loyally holding on to one end of a rope with Eric making sure it was secure behind him. The two young soldiers were huddled together near the rest of the equipment, dearly wishing they were somewhere else, dreaming of their warm, dry, packed barracks in Brecon. Arms folded tightly, Mr Deacon glowered at the cairn, a general air of distain about him. All five of them were staring at a small crevice that had the rope passed through it. The opening looked too small for even someone of Jack's build to squeeze through, let alone a fully-grown man.

When Mr Deacon spotted the group and recognised Evan, he was visibly displeased and scowled, like an angry cat,

The dragon under the hill

unable to hide his hatred. He hissed as they group approached, "what is 'that man' doing here?" Then nearly hiding behind the two bewildered uniformed lads added, "I have soldiers to protect me."

The Reverend Thomas held up his hand in conciliatorily fashion and answered for Evan, "Now, now Mr Deacon," he soothed, "Mr James is not here to interfere with you personally or the surveying. This is his land don't forget and he has a right to be here for the result."

This, Mr Deacon had to concede, was reasonable but he still harboured plenty of bile for his perceived nemesis. "Very well, see to it 'he' stays where he is and does not interfere."

It was a herculean effort on Evan's part not only to stop himself picking up and throwing the vile little man down the hill but to completely bite his tongue. Although he knew it to be childish, Jack however, could not restrain himself and mimed having a gun and shooting Mr Deacon again, much to his victim's distaste.

Ollie shouted loudly against the wind, "Hello there, this is some weather eh? The Colonel went down about twenty minutes ago. He stopped taking rope and I'm sure will be out pretty soon." His voice had much less conviction on the last sentence, more hope than certainty.

It made for a ridiculous scene, as all of those present on the hilltop, in the middle of a dirty torrential storm, stood still getting wetter and wetter, staring at a small hole, doing nothing but waiting. While doing their utmost to roll with the punches and shunts they were receiving in this most exposed area. Although one of the group was smiling to himself as he could clearly sense something else, a presence, his friend was home.

The normally jovial and sturdy Reverend Thomas was finding the whole experience thoroughly miserable and his mood was as dark as the sullen sky. Soaked through for the second time in as many hours, he felt cold and increasingly grumpy and mustered a mealy, "I didn't even get to finish my tea."

The dragon under the hill

Then, from the much-observed crevice a large yellow torch appeared, which Ollie quickly retrieved and passed to Eric. It was soon followed by a man's hand, which after finding a secure hand-hold pulled, then like a grotesque birth, a helmeted head appeared before a grown man slithered out impossibly, through the small hole. Standing to his feet, the group were still amazed how a man of Jerry's dimensions had crept though so small a gap. He switched off the small electric lamp attached to his yellow helmet, handing it off and sitting on the cairn, removed his harness while Eric and Ollie reeled in the rope. He took a satiating long drink from his water bottle and a few deep breaths before making his historical pronouncement.

"Well I never…it's definitely dolomite," taking another long drink, "the whole thing as far as I explored", to most of the group surrounding him, this information meant little and they needed further information.

"It is absolutely incredible down there, I've never seen anything like it. I wish I had more time. I'd love to come back. Absolutely incredible." He extolled.

Mr Deacon lost what little patience he had and spat out, "never mind all that man, what is the verdict? Is the land suitable or not?"

Every eye shot towards the Colonel and involuntarily Evan found himself holding his breath.

"Suitable! Oh, certainly not!" came the emphatic, half-laughed reply, "It's like swiss cheese down there. It's a warren of tunnels and holes, some so near the surface that the support is paper thin. Under where we are standing is a massive chamber about 30 feet wide and I didn't even scratch the service. You could spend a lifetime exploring down there. No, I wouldn't let a mouse walk on this hill top never mind anything military."

"No! No!" screamed Mr Deacon in disbelief, "there must be some mistake, check again you hackneyed idiot!" yelling directly at the tall potholer.

234

The dragon under the hill

A little surprised at Mr Deacon's over reaction, still attending to his equipment the potholer shook his head, "Nope, no mistake."

This elicited another outrageous display from the small petty man, feeling it all slip away. "Listen you lanky hack! I am on a mission here from the Ministry and this farm is central to that mission. Now I suggest you get your gear back on, get back down that job and do your bloody job!"

"There is no chance of error", responded Jerry very calmly and more reasonably than deserved, while slowly getting to his feet and facing Mr Deacon directly, looking directly at him "and I shall be reporting my findings in person directly to my very good friend Duffy, we roomed together at Eton you know." He said in a matter of fact, for-your-information manner. "Oh, you might know him better as the Secretary of State for War, Alfred Duff Cooper." A large smile growing on his face, turning his adversaries' ashen.

Eric walked up to Evan and stretched out his hand, "It's over Mr James. That's the final word, your farm is safe."

Despite the terrible maelstrom, there followed a great scene of celebration. Handshakes and embraces were shared as finally the threat against the farm and therefore the valley, was over. The relief and joy on Evan's face was infectious. Jack joined in, also overjoyed that the inspection hadn't gleaned even a hint of his hidden friend.

One figure stood apart from the rest, one figure did not join in the celebrations, his tipping point irrevocably reached. Taking hold of his hair and pulling on it tightly, Mr Deacon's visage changed, his expression frightening to behold as he mumbled to himself "No, no, it's not right, I won't have it, I won't". He started to shake, some possession flushed his face red as he began to shout "No! No! it's not right."

The months of stress and strain had precariously built up, the acrimony he faced daily, the threats, the pressure to perform, his continued fury at the debacle of the soldiers he'd been allotted, combined with this final slap in the face were all too much of the man's already fragile state of mind and he snapped.

Suddenly his expression deadened, his eyes glazed as the last drops of his reason dissipated and he screamed loudly. Before any of the others could react, he lunged at the nearest soldier ripping his bayonet out of its holster. He flew at Jack grabbing him from the back and gripping him in a tight neck hold with the lethal blade held menacingly close to the boy's face.

The protesting group made a movement towards the madman and his hostage but he backed away yelling.

"Don't any of you come any closer or I'll slice the smirk off this brat's face. Back off!" There was fury and pure insanity in his eyes, the group were in no doubt he was not making idle threats. Not making fun of me now are you boy? Pretend to shoot me now, I dare you"

Jack could feel the man's course stubble against his face, small the whiskey on his breath and feel the sharp, cold edge of the blade against his face.

The Reverend Thomas raised his hands in as non-threatening a manner as he could and stepped forward saying, "now let's be calm Mr D..."

"Back off, I said!" He interrupted hysterically, "I warn you." Breathing heavily and staring manically he drew the blade deliberately across the trapped boy's cheek. Producing a fine line of blood at first but it soon flowed freely. Jack yelped as he felt the slicing pain and warm blood drip down his now crying face. Mr Deacon seemed pleased with his handiwork, "Now look what you made me do."

"Stop it please" begged Evan, "leave the boy alone and we'll give whatever you want."

The bedevilled Mr Deacon relished having this power over his enemy, the look on Evan's face was like sweet molasses to him and he revelled in its warmth.

236

The dragon under the hill

"Beg."

"What?" questioned Evan.

"I said beg," said Mr Deacon darkly, "on your knees".

Without reluctance the old farmer, suddenly looking every year of his age, knelt down in the sopping mud and looked up, "I'm begging you, let my grandson go. Please don't hurt him."

In response, Mr Deacon laughed a spiteful, bitter, hollow laugh, his sense and humanity long gone.

"Now you are in your rightful place. All this time you've thought yourself better than me, laughed at me behind me back, threatened me, poisoned people against me. Not so full of yourself now, are you?" With a shark like smile, he continued, "if only the rest of your precious village could see you now, in the dirt where you belong."

"You are right, please don't hurt the boy," pleaded the farmer, "I'm sorry for my disrespect. Let him go!"

"Good", sneered the cruel man intoxicated with his new-found power, with devilish intent in his half grin, "that's an acceptable start. Now, you two clowns," pointing the bayonet at the horrified Ollie and Eric "are going to write a new report saying how well the negotiations are going and how useful this land is." They both nodded, wide eyed.

"And you," waving the blade at the Colonel, "you stuck up, privileged dote. You are going to tell your 'friend' the Minister, that this land is fine and that I should be promoted."

"Of course, right away." Jerry said.

"And..." as he thought about his next request something inspired Jack. His hand eased into his pocket and due to practice, in a single one-handed movement he pulled out his penknife and opened it. Like a striking snake, he lashed out with the blade slashing his assailant across the back of his hand, cutting deeply. The psychotic kidnapper yelled in surprise and pain, cupping his

The dragon under the hill

injured hand. His neck-hold momentarily released, Jack broke free and escaped from his captive putting his hand up, pressing to his hurting face.

In deranged fury Mr Deacon leaped after the boy, bayonet raised and yelled murderously, "I'll get y…"

There resounded an ear-splitting noise that even dwarfed the thunderous storm. Something akin to lightening flashed across the edge of their vision and ripped Mr Deacon out of mid-air, forcing him hard into the water-logged ground, stripping his breath from his body.

After the initial shock, the group steadied themselves trying to make sense of what had happened but could barely believe their eyes. There before them, pinning the unhinged ministry man to the ground was a terrific creature the size of a car, straight out of the mists of myth. A living and breathing dragon.

It was a breath-taking and terrifying sight, the creature was frightening in its beauty and shining in its dreadfulness. Bat-like wings spread wide and intimidating and whip tail thrashing forcefully, it was lithe with movement and potent with power. Wholly awesome - a blinding lightning bolt from Zeus, an eruption from Vesuvius, a crashing meteor in capacity and potential destruction. Inspiring fear, haunting sleepless nights and promising death. It burst from primordial legend and detonated in their here and now.

Colonel Sharpe backed away so fast he fell helplessly backwards over the rocks. Ollie and Eric stood motionless, mouths open enough to catch the persistent rain. While the two young staring novice soldiers simultaneously, involuntarily and copiously, wet themselves.

A dazed and greatly shaken Mr Deacon looked up at his attacker and looked into the gateway to Hades. An alien angular face, gaping mouth full of dagger-blade teeth and bright yellow burning eyes, moved snake-like inches from his face. Feeling the hot breath on his skin, a nightmare incarnate, the embodiment of

The dragon under the hill

prehistoric fear had him. He tried to scream but fear had tightened his throat and he made no sound. In response the creature let out a screech of shivering vehemence that cut through the atmospheric cacophony and bit into the very skulls of those present. They crumpled panting, prostrated by its power, trying to shield themselves by covering their ears but only when it stopped did they find relief.

The soldier's drilling and training kicked in and they raised their rifles, aiming at the dragon. Their movement alerted the being, who turned to face them and was about to let out another mind puncturing screech. Spotting the danger, the Reverend quickly moved in-between the soldiers and their target. He put a hand on the muzzle of each gun and gently pushed them down, thinking thoughts of peace he looked at the shell-slocked uniformed youths and slowly nodding said, "It's alright, it's alright".

Appeased, the dragon turned his attention back to his quarry, raised a hook filled claw to deliver the killing blow.

"Don't Krait! Krait don't kill him!" Jack's appeal caused the beast to freeze in mid movement, turn his head and wait as the boy quickly approached him.

Knowing that the creature was listening but also picking up on his true emotions, Jack continued.

"Thank you. You saved my life again but don't hurt him." He pleaded.

"He hurt you. He would kill you, there is only murder in his heart. Men like this are not good." Krait's words transmitted to the boy.

"No, he is not good," empathised Jack, showing maturity beyond his age, "but it is not right to kill him."

Krait took his eyes off Jack and pierced the prostrate man with them, "He is broken...cracked in his mind." Echoing his reasoning behind the execution of the devil dog, Cymro.

239

The dragon under the hill

"Yes, he is" agreed the boy moving closer, mere inches away, "but of you kill him here and now, more men like him will come and they'll never stop hunting you, ever. They will hound you until they destroy you." Jack started to cry. "Please."

In a movement so fast that it had already occurred before the eyes of those watching could register, deadly scalpel-claws unerringly swiped down.

Jack gasped in horror. Unbidden, his eyes flicked to the dragon's prostrate victim, terrified at what he might see. What he did see was the whimpering Mr Deacon, still alive but now sporting a cut across his cheek, mirroring the one he'd dispensed to Jack

"You wish him to live?" There was a pause, "Then he will live." Responded Krait, although he did not release the man.

"Thank you, my friend." Sniffed the youth.

"He will face justice", interjected the Reverend, whose past experience with Krait had touched him sufficiently enough that he could follow both sides of the conversation, "he will never harm anyone again, I promise you."

Krait released his grip and immediately the abject man scrambled to his feet and tried to bolt away. as he turned to run he swivelled straight into a powerful haymaker of a right hook from Evan, delivered with a farmer's strength and Mr Deacon fell dead-weight unconscious, skidding to the ground.

Jack and the dragon shared a silent moment or connection where so much sentiment was communicated but for his own sense of closure Jack needed to verbalise his thoughts and feelings.

"You should have stayed hidden, stayed safe." Said the boy.

"You were in danger." Was the clear explanation. "I felt your pain."

The dragon under the hill

With tears filling his eyes, Jack uttered words he knew to be the truth but did not want to say. "But the cost...You know...You can't stay here anymore, I don't know if we can keep your presence a secret after tonight...you have to go. You have to go... now."

Krait lent his head forward and touched his forehead to the boy's forehead in a gentle act of affection. "Child, all will be well. I know you are right. It is time. Time to leave behind the shackles of the past, step out from fear and begin my search. To discover if any more of my kind are out there. It is time to chase echoes".

The weeping boy raised his hand, gently touching the being's neck. Tenderly feeling the glass-smooth scales against his palm, beneath he could feel powerful muscles moving and veins pulsing blood. The two unlikely friends held their beautiful bond tight to themselves, in a moment Jack had never felt as known or accepted and Krait savoured the exquisite reminder of relationships lost.

"I would speak to the 'Good Man'," uttered Krait, breaking the emotive hold and beckoning over the clergyman.

The Reverend Thomas stepped forward as if summoned by a monarch. Staring the ethereal creature directly in the eyes, able to hear the communicated words. "You will look after the child?" Krait questioned, his head tilted. Although it was as much command as question but so much more intent, infecting the preacher like a virus, coursing through his body seeking truth.

Rhodri gestured towards his lifelong friend who was standing nearby, "This is the lad's grandfather," as if on cue Evan took a step forward.

Krait spoke in recognition, "Ah, the guardian of the land, him I know and have known. I have watched him and those before him." There was a pause before he added, "I would have him know, that since man has claimed this hill, I have never harmed the creatures they care for."

241

The dragon under the hill

Rhodri reiterated this statement to Evan who nodded his understanding to the dragon. With his hand on Evan's shoulder the Reverend continued, "we will guide Jack on his path to becoming the man he should be. A 'good man'."

"So be it." Concluded the wraith before one final look at the sobbing boy.

Jack's heart physically ached as he prepared for the first great loss of his life, when he would lose that beautiful taste of being part of a shared consciousness, that precious connection was about to be ripped away. Piling tears mingled with rain and blood running down his cheek, "I'll miss you." He managed in weak broken notes.

The dragon turned away from the lad, took a few short leaps to the top of the cairn and unfurled his mighty wings, giving them a few exploratory flaps to shake of the water.

"And I you."

Were Krait's parting words, as with a single muscular thrust of its wings and with implausible speed the dragon soared into the air and disappeared into the darkness of the storm clouds. Watched by those mesmerised on the ground, who stood entranced, staring up long after the creature had gone, rain soaked and drained.

The little farmhouse had never been so full. Like some debris blown in by the storm they had cascaded in. A jumble of faces, noises and water-logged clothing, Maggie had unpacked each one like untangling knotted wool.

The now catatonic Mr Deacon sat at the kitchen table wrapped in a blanket, his wounds bandaged, staring straight ahead gently rocking back and forth. He was flanked by both bedraggled soldiers who were currently demolishing a pile of welsh cakes with their tea, neither of them wearing trousers, having given in to Maggie's insistence to wash and dry them, after

The dragon under the hill

she had heard about their 'accident'. The Colonel and the two surveyors were the other side of the table drinking tea, generally concentrating on drying out, body and mind.

Evan sat in his usual chair with the Reverend Thomas in the chair opposite, his socks drying on the mantle for a second time that day. Jack, now changed into his dry pyjamas and dressing gown, sat with Heini on the rug in front of the fire. On closer inspection the cut on his face was not deep and had already stopped bleeding, it was unlikely it would leave a noticeable scar.

Maggie had wanted to rip the hair from Mr Deacon's head when she first saw her grandson's face and they had blurted out their story to her. She had to be physically held back but although enraged and despite being distraught, she settled down when she saw the state he was in, a shell of a man. Wounds were tended to, towels and blankets distributed, wet clothes changed or set to dry and tea and sustenance given, all expertly provided by the ready-for-anything farmer's wife.

And then, silence.

A long weary, necessary silence. Every man wrestling with his own thoughts and questions. A silence full of reflection, confusion, disbelief, wonder and inertia.

Getting up from his chair and leaning his hands on the mantle, the Reverend Rhodri Thomas collected his thoughts and formed the plan. Turning to the group, he broke the mute spell.

"Well," every head turned and looked towards the preacher, "that was certainly not how I expected my day to pan out." His ready smile putting the room at ease.

"Now then," raising his finger, in full orator mode he preached the word to this oddest of congregations, "it is up the us in this room and us alone, to determine what happens from here. We decide what happened tonight. Before we leave this room, we agree together the story we will tell and we will take that story to our graves." He announced, to murmurs of agreement from those present.

243

The dragon under the hill

"It's obvious to say we can't go around spouting stories about dragons, now can we?" He reasoned, the word ignited Mr Deacon into action, who looked around madly calling.

"Dragon, teeth and claws...it breathed on me..." the rest of the sentence was incoherent, mumbled ever quieter.

Thumbing in the direction of the still gibbering heap of a man, Jerry asked "and what about him?"

"Him?" Answered the Reverend, "yes, that poor man needs help but also needs to pay for what he has done..." he left that point and his response to it hanging in the air and started laying out his plan with authority.

"Here is what we are going to do." All were attentive and absorbing every word needily. "We will recount the events of today to the finest detail, exactly how it happened...with the one exception, leaving out the creature from the story in its entirety.

You lads go up the hill in this awful storm, we join you to get the result. Jerry pops down the cairn and brings his verdict back with him, On his announcement, Mr Deacon lost his mind and did attack the lad, Jack in self-defence used his penknife to free himself and Evan did deck the madman" he turned to his old friend, unable to suppress an appreciative smile, "with one of the sweetest right hooks I've seen since Jack Petersen floored Dick Power in '31. The end, so to speak."

Jack, still sitting on the floor at his feet, nodded, then recreated the punch and the sound of a body hitting the floor.

"Once their trousers dry out, the two soldiers will escort Mr Deacon to Twm," for the benefit of Jerry he added, "also known as out local enforcer of the law, Constable Jones and tell their story. Mr Deacon will no doubt be arrested immediately and a call for assistance put out to the police in Beulah. You then can contact your commanding officer and report back to your barracks" They nodded energetically in unison their agreement.

The dragon under the hill

"Colonel Sharpe, you will drop them off on your journey to your next stop off and will submit your report exactly as you would have and back up their story when asked." Jerry raised his thumb.

"Ollie and Eric, go back to your lodgings, pack up all Mr Deacon's belongings and take them to Constable Jones, make a statement and then leave in the morning. Submit your report to the Ministry, exactly as you planned." The surveyors lifted their teacups in assent.

"We'll wait until Twm comes to us for our side of things." He paused, stared at the dishevelled husk of a man that used to be the firebrand Mr Deacon and sadly shook his head. "As for this sad creature, I do hope and pray that he gets the psychological help he needs and gets better but let's face it, in the state he is in now, no one will believe a word he says."

He let his concept sink in a little before questioning the room for a final accord, "now, let's be sure, are we all agreed?"

The dragon under the hill

Chapter 22

The temperature continued to rise as the early morning haze gave way to a bright and cheering sun. The little village never looked so peaceful or picturesque as it did now, the limed white buildings beautifully framed by the deep green hillsides surrounding. The variegated blue sky was dotted with light clouds, like moored white ships anchored at bay. The air was sparkling pure and the ever-flowing river continued to bubble its journey under the old bridge.

It was five days later and the little village was sleepy and tranquil, the day after the bustle and almighty stir of Old Nana Price's massive funeral that had turned the hamlet to a cacophony of swarming voices, dressed in black.

The summer was not quite over for Jack but sadly his visit was. He stood with his little suitcase next to him and perched on top a brown paper bag bursting with food and treats for the long trip, waiting for the bus to arrive and begin his journey home. His grandfather's hand was lovingly resting on his shoulder, the boy keenly aware of the strength and loving warmth it transmitted. As ever, Heini sat at her master's side.

Jack had already said a long and tearful goodbye to his grandmother at the farmhouse and promised profusely that he would write. Maggie, for her part was surprised, as was her husband, how emotional she became. Jack was now definitely one of a very select handful of people who saw the other side of her and she proved it by, instead of handing Jack the packed lunch she'd prepared for his journey, she handed the boy a single apple, allowing them all to share a final gleeful joke together.

The cut healing on his cheek that was now hardly visible, being the only outward difference in Jack but inwardly, it was still a much-changed boy from the one that disembarked on that very spot a few short months ago, that stood there now. Like some ancient cultures' rite of passage, he had come through a life

246

The dragon under the hill

changing experience and out the other side. Not yet a man, he had certainly left childhood behind. He had matured and grown, blossomed and strengthened, he had spread his spirit across the land and the mountain had entered his soul. More confident and assertive, more empathetic and kinder, more aware and conscious. He had lived a whole life in this short period and bought wisdom from all he met, some of it born from a thousand years of anguish finally being laid to rest. He had experienced the first heady scent of love and still felt it's lingering embrace, had his first encounter with death, had looked into the eyes of a madman, had beaten his fears, planted seeds of character and morals that would soon thrive and above all, he'd met the man he would learn to become.

Now he was feeling conflicted. He longed to see his parents and brothers, he had never in his life spent so much time away from them. He had so much to tell his friends and looked forward to kick-abouts and rounders in familiar surroundings but part of him knew he had outgrown them and those innocent joys. He would have to find his own place in his family again, he would find it hard to fit into old habits and behaviours and new friendships would need to be forged, this time on his own terms. It would take time for him to be understood again, the way he was here. He was certainly ready to go home but in another way, he was leaving home. He hated the thought of not waking up to meet his grandparents downstairs. Knew he would miss the farm and old Heini and knew he would never find another friend like the Reverend Thomas. Part of him wished the silly old bus would never come.

Jack and Evan, in an effort to postpone their final good bye, idly discussed the previous day.

"Duw, that was the biggest funeral I've ever seen grampa," mentioned Jack, "the chapel was full to bursting and loads outside."

"Aye lad" agreed Evan, "probably the biggest our little village has seen. Big family the Prices see they came from all over."

The dragon under the hill

"That one boy had no shoes on," remembered Jack, his voice questioning at the oddity of the sight.

"That'll be Albany, that'll be. Lovely lad but he's a wild one. Do what they will, they can't get him wear shoes, he's always been the same." Evan informed, causing the youngster to giggle.

"Did you manage to see little Lily Hagerty and say your goodbyes?" Said Evan, ferreting for information he knew Maggie would ask him for later.

"I did." Responded Jack curtly and that ended the conversation abruptly.

From behind the quietly waiting pair, a familiar voice rung out with its usual melody and warmth.

"Now you weren't going to leave without saying goodbye, now were you son?" Questioned the Reverend Thomas.

On hearing his voice, the lad spun on his heels looked up into his friend's smiling face and embraced the preacher.

Recent revelations and events had done nothing to diminish the relationship between the two dear old friends and when he turned Evan teased, "O Rhodri bach, a bit early for you to be out of bed isn't it?"

"O there's cheeky" he responded, feigning hurt feelings, "now is that any way to speak to your spiritual leader?"

"The only leading you do is straight to the kitchen table to eat my wife's cooking." Exclaimed Evan.

"Oo, what a terrible thing to say," winced the preacher, "now, what are we having for dinner?" Causing them all to laugh.

"At least we'll be able to have some crumble, after the 'midnight crumble thief' by here goes home." Spurring more laughter and a sheepish grin from Jack

248

The dragon under the hill

"Can I borrow 'Scarface' here, for one final little walk together?" He requested.

"Aye, have him and..."

"I know, I know" interrupted Rhodri, "take the dog with us." Arm around the boy he called out, "come on then, you woof." Heini, after a nod from her owner, padded behind them.

"There's sad I am to be going." Said Jack mournfully.

"Sorry to see you go we are too lad. Don't forget to say hello to your mother and father for me eh? And you've got my address and little Lily's address nice and safe, now haven't you?" Asked the Reverend, who received a nod of agreement, before moving on to the subject at hand.

"Now you've certainly had some adventures in your time here, that's for sure but you know that you must never tell anyone about what when on, however much you might really, really want to. Even your family" He cautioned.

"I know" said Jack blandly, "we all promised."

"Fair enough", commented the clergyman. "By the way, I have something for you."

Reaching into his coat pocket the Reverend produced a small, black brand-new Bible. Giving it to the astonished lad, he commented, "Don't worry son, it's not in Welsh. I thought you could carry this with you wherever life leads you, you'll always have a reminder of us with you then."

Jack opened it up and in the inside cover was written in careful decorative writing, 'To Jack, God is making you into a great man. Keep the good Lord at the centre of your life and you will do great things. Your friend, Reverend Rhodri Thomas.'

Jack was touched and humbled, lost for words. None were necessary.

The dragon under the hill

They reached the riverbank and watched the water flow and trouble in silence, enjoying each other's company until the rumbling bus came into sight.

The dragon under the hill

It was a cool overcast January morning and the village square had never been so populated or chaotic.

In response to the horrors of the wartime blitz, Operation Pied Piper strove to evacuate as many children as possible to safer areas in Britain and abroad. A couple of dozen of those three million evacuees, stood in the square - frightened, hungry and bewildered. Finding themselves in a vastly different place, almost foreign, miles from home and their families.

With their names and details pinned to their chest, like little parcels, they all carried their small suitcases or just cardboard boxes tied with string clasped tightly to them, not a few tears fell. After alighting from the bus, they queued up as orderly as they could. At the head of the queue was the billeting officer who, armed with a clip-board, recorded their information and connected them with the volunteers to look after. Even the Reverend Thomas had signed up to 'do his duty' and was leading 'his' little lad towards the chapel.

Although a few years older, much less effervescent and needing help to make the high leap on and off the old cart, faithful Heini was still shadowing her master as they stood waiting to be called over.

"The James family, Bryn Y Ddraig farm?" the billeting officer called loudly.

"Here", called Evan identifying himself, "I'm Evan James."

"Ah good. Mr James, these are your two," he said, like he was handing out something as insignificant as apples, rather than little children. He looked down at what he had just written on his clip-board and without looking up, pointed at them with his pencil.

"This is 9 year old Michael Spender and his little 4 year old sister Sally from South East London." And that was it, that was their summation, their life and their story in one brief, coldly clinical little statement.

Evan looked down to see a very sad looking blonde boy with dark rings around his piteous eyes. He was dressed smartly in a grey blazer and grey short trousers, a white shirt covered with a tank-top with a diamond pattern on the front and a man's tie in a large knot, that must be his father's. Holding tightly on to his hand was a small girl. Her blonde pigtails held with two white bows. Her little woollen coat covered her short floral dress with its clean white collar and she sported white knee-high socks and black buckled shoes. Her blue eyes were red raw from sobbing, finding the long journey more than she could take. Their matching luggage in their other hand.

Evan, sensing their discomfort and feeling of alienation, crouched down and smiling, spoke softly, "Hello little ones, Michael and Sally, is it?" which received nothing more than a robotic nod. "Nice to meet you both, I'm Mr James but you can call me Evan." Playing his trump card, he added, "and this is Heini." Stroking his dog. Although the small girl's face did show some reaction, Evan did not receive the breaking of the ice effect he had expected, normally children would make a fuss of the dog and they'd feel more relaxed.

Trying to keep his voice light he continued, "Right then, there's nothing to be scared of, we'll take care of you until it's time for you to go back home, I'm sure it won't be long. Follow me and you can meet my horse."

His ward's expressions did lift when they met the horse but Evan knew there was a lot more work to do to earn their trust and start building a relationship, who knows what these little ones had been through, seen or experienced.

Helping Heini onto the back of the cart, he quickly swung Sally onto the seat before offering help to the boy.

"I can manage" he said coolly and climbed up next to his sister.

252

The dragon under the hill

"I hope you both are hungry," he began as he guided Merlin in a tight turn, "Maggie, my wife, has put on a lovely spread for you back at the farmhouse."

Again, the only response was a cool one from the boy, "Our mother packed us a lunch."

As the horse clopped through the journey, Evan tried everything he could think of to engage the children and get more than one syllable answers from them. He asked them about their journey, where they were from, their family and any hobbies and interests; he talked about their surroundings, pointing out the different farms, the flora making up the hedgerow, the animals and birds they could see or may see; he talked about the farm, his sheep and horses and waiting there was Heini's working sheep-dog replacement - one of her pups, called Hopran, which was Welsh for 'hopper' as he loved to leap everywhere. Evan even told them all about his grandson Jack who had a great summer staying with them years back and it changed his life. Nothing seemed to break through to his passive companions.

Nearly at his wit's end, Evan had an idea and thought to himself, 'it's just a story, who are these little ones going to tell?' Having convinced himself to go ahead, he started.

"Michael? Sally? Our farm is called Bryn Y Ddraig which in English means Dragon Hill. Can you guess why it's called that?" Looking across at both children who simply shook their heads.

"No?", he continued, "well the hill at the top is peppered with caves and we used to have a dragon living there."

Sally looked at him with surprise and burst out, "what, a real dragon?"

"Oh yes, a real dragon." Confirmed the farmer.

"You're lying," insisted Michael, "there's no such thing as real dragons."

253

The dragon under the hill

"I used to think that at one time lad but then something happened that changed everything." He paused to build some intrigue, "would you like me to tell you all about it?"

Sally's face lit up and she squeaked, "Oh yes, I would."

"Michael?"

"I'm not interested I fairy stories, I'm too old." Came the haughty response.

Evans smiled, "O lad, one thing this story is not and that's a fairy tale."

"Please Michael, I should so like to hear it", pleaded Sally.

"I suppose so. If Sally really wants to hear" Answered the boy, trying to conceal his obvious interest. Evan finally had them.

"Well then…It's starts with the legend of the cairn…"

The dragon under the hill

Epilogue

All those who could speak as to the veracity of any of the tale my grandfather told me that day are long gone, as now is the dear man himself.

Do I believe that he met a dragon as a child? Well, I know he did spend the summer with his grandparents. I know he eventually courted and married Lily Hagerty and she became Lily James, my grandmother. I know for all his stories he shared throughout his lifetime, he still took many more to his grave. I know among his belongings was found a very old, worn and well-thumbed Bible, with a hand-written inscription in the front now too faded to read.

In the end, whether it was one of his pranks spun out too far, the exaggerations of an old man with an enraptured audience or to him the dragon represented something. A dynamic metaphor, symbolising the things of his childhood leaving as he was becoming a man. Which ever isn't important to me. What is important, was the time we spent together and the love shared. The essence is that there was something significant he wanted to communicate through its telling, to me and me alone.

Do I believe that he met a dragon as a child? I believe it doesn't matter in the end, a great story is worth telling.

Although, later something was discovered in that old worn Bible with broken binding and pages falling out all over. It was a small, yellowing cutting from a newspaper. The cutting had no headline and omitted any section that had a printed date or any clue to the publication but judging by its colour it had been stored there for years, if not decades.

Of its short three paragraphs, the first listed the name and age of a salesman on holiday with his family in North Wales who reported a strange sighting to the local police. The next paragraph described how his enjoyable coastal walk had taken a disturbing

The dragon under the hill

turn, as losing track of time and losing the light, he got lost and had to try to make his way back to the campsite in the dark.

The final paragraph was a direct quote from his statement which read,

'I thought I'd climb up to the highest point to see if I could recognise anything. You know lights, roads, anything to get my bearings. Nearing the top, something moved catching my eye. Whatever it was, it was big, ghostly in appearance, long with sharp edges, somewhat angular and then instantly, without a sound, was gone.'

It wrapped up by saying he had taken flight and managed to find his family some time later, reporting the sighting early the next day.

This sparse report had a single word written in black ink in the margin, in what was unmistakably my grandfather's shaky cursive.

'Krait?"

THE END

The dragon under the hill

17556879R00150

Printed in Great Britain
by Amazon